MY LIFE WITH BLONDIE

Jiří Klobouk

Translated from the Czech
by Helena and John Baker

Červená Barva Press
Somerville, Massachusetts

Červená Barva Press
P.O. Box 440357
W. Somerville, MA 02144-3222

www.cervenabarvapress.com

Bookstore: www.thelostbookshelf.com

Cover Design: Jiří Klobouk and William J. Kelle

ISBN: 978-0-9883713-6-1

Library of Congress Control Number: 2013940146

TO DIANE

MY LIFE WITH BLONDIE

1

Blondie is coming to town today. I have been walking around for a whole week as if in a dream. She is my darling! I can't take my eyes off her—subconsciously, at least. In June, she probably first wanted to hop off to the Côte d'Azur. She desperately needed a change of scenery, in order to gather new strength. With all due pomp and circumstance, the Saturday tabloid prints the news that she is staying with Brigitte Bardot at her villa. Damn liars! Nothing makes my blood boil more than these sensation-seekers flying their stories like kites that fall to earth almost before becoming airborne. The fact, is, Blondie and Brigitte don't like each other very much. When they bump into each other in Cannes, at the Café Juliette (or some other watering hole), they only exchange a few words. That's about it.

How do I know this, you ask? You won't find anyone in the whole world who knows Blondie more intimately than the author of these lines—Harley Davidson. Yes. It's really quite unbelievable. By a stroke of fate, my name is the same as that of the famous motorcycle.

Then out of the blue and in the worst twist of fate, I found out that Blondie will be staying in the very same hotel from which I resigned a few days ago. That's because I'd just had another awful row with Melvin. Never have I met a bigger prima donna. I swear it. His job is to repair the dripping taps. And sometimes he changes a lightbulb. Nothing too *technically* complicated—tasks that any fool could not manage with his left hand tied behind his back. But in the Royal Arms, when something goes wrong, we are obliged to call our privileged maintenance man. We are required to *beg* Melvin, virtually on bent knees, to repair the defect. And he behaves as if he had just bought the hotel for six and a half million.

In reality this dump is on the brink of collapse. It belongs to McCarthy—the whole place, including the worn-out carpet in his inhospitable office. He probably inherited it from those poor-immigrant ancestors of his, who went looking for gold in the Yukon. Obviously they didn't find any. Melvin always addresses McCarthy jovially as *Boss*. I deliberately emphasize the capital B. He also goes to cry on his shoulder. So much so that I called him a series of highly appropriate names during our last confrontation: Hercules, hulk, clumsy fool and so on. They fit him like a glove. He's a giant, with a small head and a pea-brain within. That goes without saying. Instead of waiting for my dismissal, I slam the toilet door (opposite the boss's office) and— goodbye Royal Arms.

At home Amanda greeted me with open arms. The entire weekend, I stayed in bed. For Sunday lunch she served roast beef slices with mushrooms, accompanied by Uncle Ben's wild rice. In short—a festive meal. Amanda knows what to do when my nerves have cracked.

But after the news that Blondie is coming to town, I hurried in to see McCarthy. I asked him to take me back. He let me talk for an hour and a half (without even inviting me to sit down), before he was finally convinced that I really was a reformed character. He also made me promise never to slam the toilet door again. Then I had to apologize publicly to Melvin. And furthermore, I had to accept a cut in my already lousy wages. I make even less than Melvin does—some four hundred dollars a week. After tax deductions, unemployment contributions, and the installments for my Ford Escort, I have some two hundred and fifty dollars left to live on. It'll be worse now. The fact is, if I didn't have Amanda, I would have ended up in the line outside the soup kitchen long ago. No wonder McCarthy eventually waved his hand benevolently. A beggar outside Macy's in New York makes this ludicrous sum in just a couple of days. At most I can only afford to go to the movies once a month. There were times when I used to snuggle down in the front row and didn't move until they threw me out.

Blondie has eighteen full-length films to her credit. I saw each one of them at least twenty-six times. I keep a precise logbook full of details—what she was wearing, etcetera. I know all her lines by heart, to the word and to the letter. I could probably recite them backwards.

Of course, the arrival of Blondie is so important it is even upstaging the landing of Apollo 11 on the Moon. Under typical circumstances, all the cleaning at the Royal Arms is done by our chambermaid Ella. I of course need this to change. The whole thing requires a rather sophisticated strategy. I already took the first steps in this direction yesterday. I had it all planned out: I will bribe Ella with a five-dollar bill. Then I will send her to see McCarthy in his office where she will perform the dance of Saint Vitus. She will play the role of a person suddenly struck by a gastric upset so well that she will almost throw up all over him. Donald McCarthy will swallow the bait along with the hook. As if by chance I will find myself outside the slightly ajar door at the precise moment that Ella faints. I will offer McCarthy my excellent services. I will be reponsible for the complete cleaning of all twelve rooms. And that's on top of all the responsibilities I normally have in the hotel in my capacity as receptionist. The Boss will simply stare at me in disbelief. What else can he do? And he will accept my offer. He has (at least he thinks he has) concrete proof that I am taking on, slowly but surely, the appearance of a good little dog obediently wagging the stump of his amputated tail.

Well, on the day of Blondie's arrival I rush around so much that I am almost bent over double, like a Mexican crop picker. Not only do I do Ella's work, but at six I change over to take over reception for Jacques Bélanger. He is quite a nice chap. By the time he has turned up for work, he is already desperately keen to be back on the other side of the river in his beloved Quebec.

Thank God the flop-house I'm in charge of is only four stories. If it ever came to it, I could count all the guests on the fingers of one hand. The least work of all is in Room 204. Three days ago a married couple all the way from Berlin, Vermont moved in. They are on their honeymoon. When I knock carefully on the door in the morning, they send me to hell. I don't blame them!

2

Two days ago, on Tuesday, I selected four of the Royal Arms'
very best towels for Blondie. I took them home so that
Amanda can wash them properly.

Amanda and I have been living in sin for some six
years now. I haven't met a nicer person. I could talk about
her morning, noon and night. And even that would not be
enough. When, for example, she discovered how I talk about
Blondie all the time—even in my sleep—she didn't get
annoyed with me. She simply bought herself a set of earplugs.

Or, for instance, take the other day, when I
announced that Blondie is finally coming. I was not at all
surprised by what I saw in those two deep wells of wisdom
that are her eyes—joy. Yes, tears of sheer joy rolled down
Amanda's cheeks. And this was only because my long-held
dream looked like it was becoming rapturous reality. She was
happy just to be able to live this moment with me.

"Congratulations," she said. "How come it's so
sudden?"

"That's simple," I replied. "It came down from
heaven like a miracle. First of all Colin calls from Kitty
Junction. Jacques Bélanger answers the phone. Colin books a
room in the Royal Arms for Thursday. Jacques asks in whose
name. To which Colin replies that it is for... Blondie. Can you
imagine! She is going to perform in the bar downstairs. I
doubt that those two cronies realize who it is they are *actually*
talking about. Had I been there at the time, I would have
taken care of it *personally*. But I couldn't have been there. You
know... because of Melvin. And then by chance I catch sight
of the newspapers... and there it is, black on white. Blondie at
Kitty Junction! I nearly pass out. Immediately I call Colin. I
explain why I am not at the Royal Arms anymore. He's not
really surprised. As a matter of fact he agrees with me that
Melvin is one sandwich short of a picnic. And then the
merry-go-round begins. I hurry to reason with McCarthy.
And as soon as he mercifully beckons with his little finger, I

dial the number. I pray I will catch Blondie in Las Vegas. Hurray! Luck is on my side. The phone rings in Vegas. I say, 'Royal Arms here. Harley Davidson.' I ask for Blondie. Some man tells me Blondie is having a massage. Damn slipped disc. The man's name is Harry. Yes, Harry James. Just like that famous trumpet player. I kind of confirm Blondie's reservation. And he says he will pass the message on to Blondie. I can rely on him. Jesus Christ. Would you believe it, Amanda?"

"It's like a fairy tale," she said.

"Absolutely. You know that I've been waiting for this miracle for the last thirty-three years."

"Christ managed to get himself born and dead in that time."

"You're absolutely right."

Amanda circled around me slowly, as if to engrave my every detail in her memory one last time. "I understand how you feel, Harley," she said.

"I feel like a marathon runner," I answered. "Half a mile before the finish, you see."

"Which Olympics do you have in mind?"

"Aah," I sighed deeply. "This one takes place in ancient Greece. I've been running for four days and four nights. And in such terrible heat. My legs are giving way beneath me. I can hear the crowd in the Colosseum thundering. Thank God Blondie's waiting there for me. Otherwise I would have collapsed outside the gate, ready for the vultures."

"Is she waiting there for you?" Amanda said in wonder.

"Of course. Just a short distance from the finishing line. I virtually arrive like a messenger of love. As soon as I catch my breath we go off to Egypt."

Amanda rolled her eyes ceilingward as if strenuously searching for something up there. "Egypt?" she asked. "What for?"

"I promised my Angel I would build a pyramid in the Egyptian desert as an expression of my undying love. It will be made of the brilliant white ashlars of Carrara marble. And right at the top of our pyramid, on the summit, a neon light bearing Blondie's wonderful name will be flickering for all the world to see."

I don't expect that living with me is very easy for Amanda. But my own life is none too easy either. She must realize that. Apart from those difficult beginnings in Europe (mainly in Austria and Germany), I have in my curriculum vitae two failed marriages. As a result, however, I can boast of having fathered two daughters who have turned out much better than I did. Furthermore, I fought for Blondie in Vietnam. I was lucky to get out alive. Ever since my return, I have been trying to pen my eye-witness account of that matter. It is something between a long letter and a short novel. Jacques Bélanger calls it—*la nouvelle vérité vietnamienne*.

Amanda, of course, is only thirty-six. Her whole life is ahead of her. Mine, on the contrary, is almost behind me. Recently I turned fifty. It's a rather awful thought. No wonder I'm emotionally exhausted. It's all that eternal waiting for a *miracle* to occur. I'm a tramp with a restless mind. A dreamer. An occasional man of letters and a sometime drummer.

Yes, I am a big band drummer. In all, I am simply a man (in all his smallness and greatness, wretchedness and magnificence, childishness and emotional impulsiveness), a man fully devoted in body and spirit to his historic love for that unrivalled human being—Blondie. In other words, I'm head over heels in love with her.

I'm a fool. That's it. Completely crazy. That's because Blondie is my everything. Whilst she, on the other hand, *probably* doesn't even suspect in the slightest that any Harley Davidson *actually exists*. And that's about the current state of affairs, in a nutshell form, of course. Or—it might even be suggested—in an inexcusably simplified one.

As I say, I have been living some six years at
Amanda's, on the second floor of a certain brick-red building.
The house next door is built of gray bricks. Our apartment
has two bedrooms. When we sit on the balcony, we have a
view of a park. The washing machine is in the kitchen, due to
no space anywhere else.

Now Amanda has been standing next to it for over a
quarter of an hour. She's turning the four towels from hand
to hand—the ones I brought from the Royal Arms to be
washed especially for Blondie.

"Listen, Harley," she says. "Before I put them in, do
you think I should embroider them with the initials B.B.B.?"

"B.B.B.?" I repeat uncomprehendingly.

"You know... Blondie! Blondie! Blondie! What do you
think?"

She stirs my heart, as usual, with her empathy. She
looks after me like no one else. And she is always smiling. But
behind her smile, I can tell there is hidden sorrow. I know
there is, one hundred percent. I can read her mind like a
book. I would like to console her with a few words, such as:
"Don't take it so tragically, Amanda." Or, "Don't worry. Out
of sight, out of mind." By this I mean myself. But this would
not change anything at the moment. Blondie is simply on the
horizon—*in the backwoods*. Nothing can be done about it. It's
an unshakeable reality.

It dawns on me that instead of words, I should hug
Amanda. I should dance around the kitchen with her, then
carry her off to the bedroom. We would fall into bed. She can
have a good time with me. One more time she can bite into
me. I will not protest. Why? I will close my eyes. I'll imagine
I'm some place else. She can feel free to tear me to pieces
while I'm still here. It won't be long before I go. Take me!
For God's sake, do it, no matter what happens. Do what you
want with me. In the whirl of a drum solo. Boom boom
boom. Ta-raa ta-raa. Help yourself. Because *this* is the last
time between us. Yes. The last time. Goodbye, Amanda. Be

very happy. Thanks for everything. It's like that, my girl. In life as in music. *Andante, allegro, prestissimo... fine.*

Yes, I am completely exhausted emotionally from the unstoppable stream from my own subconscious. Of course, what follows is a ridiculous farce. Pathetic! If anyone saw it, they would fall apart laughing. The only thing I manage is to reach out helplessly towards Amanda. I stumble forward like a child just learning to walk. My ears are all red, perhaps with exertion. Or with shame. I don't know. Quite simply I behave like an incapacitated, senile idiot. Really! I would like to walk through the wall (or fly through the window), but I only crash into an empty bird cage. It is suspended from the ceiling between the window and Amanda. Why is it empty? That would be a long story.

Oh well. I'll tell it briefly. On top of all this Blondie excitement, we lost our canary. He simply vanished. He is of a brownish-yellow colour and his name is Tiger. Amanda and I are both absolutely devastated. He has not been seen in his cage since Sunday last. Usually we let him fly around freely, through the open door and onto the balcony. Until now, he never failed to come back. But not this time.

We couldn't sleep for several nights. Especially Amanda. (To be truthful, though, she often snoozed on the balcony). For three days we have been calling out into the tree-tops – "Tiger, Tiger, Tiger don't mess around, come back. You fool!" But perhaps a cat has already eaten him. We don't know. We put an advertisement in the papers. So far no success.

Well, the ad did generate some sort of a response. We get weird phone calls from loony terrestrials. They are interested in everything except in the fate of our canary. They enthusiastically take advantage of this opportunity (our telephone number and our misfortune), in order to solve their own personal problems. They simply have to confess their own wretched anguish. The most frequent reason for said wretched anguish is the lamentable state of the international political scene (especially in the Middle East, Eastern Europe, etc.), followed by fuel and cigarette prices. And don't forget those ever-longer hospital waiting lists. Especially the ones for transplants of life-important organs! Someone needs a healthier heart. Another has to have new kidneys. And they are all afraid that they will not live to get what they need. Amanda and I feel sorry for them. We explain that we would like to help, but we can't.

Oh well. The unexpected arrival of Blondie, slowly, unfortunately, but surely, pushes the canary into the background. Thank Goodness. A man only has one set of nerves. Otherwise we would be on the phone forever, talking about things we would not normally discuss with strangers for anything in the world. On the other hand, Amanda and I can now spend the whole day talking about Blondie, and generally without the slightest problem. That is because the difference between this and the Middle East or liver transplants is that we are able to fall asleep and wake up again with Blondie. That's how things are. I never hide anything from Amanda. She can see my cards anytime she pleases. And she definitely cannot complain about not having sufficient information. I bombard her with it day in and day out. She hears about any insignificance whatsoever (of course assuming that there is such a thing as *insignificance* as far as Blondie is concerned), including the details of Blondie's visits to the dentist—Doctor Oscar W. Morgan, who has his office in Beverly Hills.

On the other hand, Amanda sometimes comes out with items of news that are so riveting, I can't understand how they ever escaped my attention. For example, there was a re-run on television three years ago of that unforgettable Blondie film "The Last Day of Dick Hammersmith," and she noticed out of the blue (in the scene where Blondie and Dick are on the ski-lift and Dick's left ski falls off), that Blondie has a small, but nevertheless rather unsightly, wart behind her right ear. This obviously took my breath away. I have already seen the film in a wide-screen cinema numerous times. But of course the ugly (though rather small) wart is an absolute novelty for me. The only possible explanation ensues herewith. A bright woman (who looks at things with reserve and from a dispassionate point of view), has a more refined observational talent than a man who is blinded by ardent emotion.

At last! Amanda throws the towels into the washing machine. She adds the detergent and turns the water on. Then she sits down on one of the three folding armchairs on the balcony. I only bought the third one last Monday. For the time being I am leaving it folded up so as not to provoke Amanda too much.

Surrounded by the ramparts of the neighbouring trees, she pretends that she has fallen asleep. But I can imagine that from the moment she found out that Blondie was on her way, sleep is quite out of the question for her. I understand. She needs to work a lot of things out in her head, such as what's going to happen now and so on. I feel sorry about the burden she has to bear on her slender shoulders. There are lots of unknowns. For example, how are we going to go on living here? I could stay with Blondie at the Royal Arms for a short time. Fair enough. But for a *short time only*. And this is exactly one of the most precarious of my problems. When I was—so to speak down—in the dumps, it was Amanda who offered me a roof over my head. I only hope that she will realize that my current situation is even more *desperate*.

Everything depends on Melvin. That is to say, I could really stay with Blondie at the Royal Arms for the whole week (and thus we would not bother Amanda), if I had a guarantee that the clumsy hulk would leave us alone. He is rather unpredictable. All he has to do is find out when he turns up for work on Friday morning that instead of minding the reception area I am actually wallowing in room 403 with Blondie—and all hell will break loose. He will rush upstairs with a light bulb or something. But, finding the door locked, he will begin knocking, first with his hooked index finger.

When nothing happens, he will bang on the door with his fist. First with one. Then with both of them.

Blondie will obviously be so upset that she will start screaming at him. It will have something to do with us getting the hell out of here. But she shouldn't do that. She doesn't know about Melvin, about how easily provoked he is. He'll start kicking the door. It goes without saying that McCarthy will do nothing except dial 911 for an ambulance. It is equipped with two 400-pound giants (even bigger than Melvin himself) in white overalls and with a straightjacket. So our Hercules will end up where he always predicted I would end up. And that's not such a bad thought.

3

I consider it only sensible (if not provident) to prepare
Amanda for every possible alternative. First and foremost,
should the inevitable happen (if, for example, Melvin is carted
off to the funny farm), Blondie would simply have to step
over the threshold of this abode. That's a) so that we could
continue to breathe in peace. And b), to work out what we
must do later. Otherwise it will hit Amanda like a bolt from
the blue. And that's most undesirable. Unnecessary confusion
will break out. A game of dominoes with a far-from-
predictable outcome would begin—a game during which the
dominoes would collapse, one after the other—crash bang—
in uncontrollable chaos. And this is something I wish to
avoid at all costs. Otherwise a series of routine habits would
quite simply be ripped out by their roots, after all these years
of uninterrupted growth. I also want to avoid having a
whole lot of less noticeable matters (such as the intensity of
Erocascade, Blondie's special perfume) strike at these roots
with incredible velocity. All the fun (especially for Amanda)
would end then.

Once Robert Greenwall very aptly remarked, in his
excellent paper "The Existent as Agent," that if two steel
balls collide on a table without a cloth (as opposed to the two
moth balls which roll towards each other on the carpet
beneath the table), the elements unfold in a space surrounded
by several walls (such as that of Amanda's apartment) with a
velocity expressed only by six digits ending with nine zeros.
Such a supersonic sequence of events is likely to have
catastrophic consequences, comparable only to a
thermonuclear reaction. The fact is that Greenwall's theory
can best be appreciated by people in my situation. One must
leave nothing to chance. The number of possibilities is
endless.

I will describe just one possible scenario. As soon as
the morning sunlight tickles Blondie under her nose, she
stretches until her bones crack. And then she hurries, in my

dressing gown, out onto the balcony. There she makes herself comfortable in one of those three armchairs. She lights up a cigarette. Before she even crosses her left leg over her right she calls out to me, "Harley, honey! What kind of a peculiar tree is that?"

"Which one?"

"The one with the impossibly long sticks, hon!"

"Oh, that one! Well that's a catalpa... angel," I answer.

Amanda (she slept on the living room sofa for the first night) is naturally very interested in our conversation. In the blink of an eye she storms across the kitchen in one of her most transparent negligées. It seems as if she already has everything worked out. In particular, she has calculated on the fingers of one hand that nature is one hundred percent on her side. One only has to remember the fact that both Harley and Blondie turned fifty this year. This makes Amanda fourteen years our junior. Or even twenty-eight years, if you multiply the age difference by two. No wonder she hops around joyfully on one foot. And then she heads for the bathroom. She leaves the door open. She is especially keen for us to listen to ten minutes of her regular morning toilette, including that never-ending gargling of hers.

Then, having found out that Blondie exhales the smoke from her cigarette with her lips pouted in the shape of an O, she doesn't waste another second. With her index finger she flicks a single white stick out of Blondie's cigarette pack, without asking her permission. Then she rips out the filter tip and lights up with Blondie's lighter. And immediately she stinks the place out with even denser clouds of smoke, with her lips pursed to form three letters. I state these in alphabetical order—x, y and z.

Due to the fact that she has never before held a lit-up cigarette in her hand, she breaks into a terrible cough. I live through a few moments when I'm scared she might not survive this dreadful personal trauma. Blondie, on the other hand, acts as if Amanda doesn't even exist. Or, if she does, it is only in the sense that the steam escaping from a boiling kettle exists, or perhaps an invisible ghost from beyond the grave.

And all this after my having gone to such great lengths to explain. You see, I will have talked to Blondie from behind the steering wheel of my Escort as we drive from the Royal Arms. I will have explained just who exactly is this Amanda, and that my relationship with her is not until death us do part. It's more or less a liaison based on a mutual understanding that we should simply get along well, so as to make life easier for both of us—without any unnecessary complications like, say, going to the altar. And I will swear to Blondie that without her (Blondie, of course), I could not and cannot truly talk about living—for without her I am merely existing from one day to the next.

Now I am attempting to open a can of G-19 juice. Blondie asked for it a short while ago. It goes without saying that I have a supply sufficient for several months. The cans roll from one end of the apartment to the other. They even spill out of the closets. But what I cannot find right now is a can opener. We always have about a half a dozen of them. In my mind I suspect Amanda has hidden them away somewhere. G-19 is in fact Blondie's favorite drink. And these *trivialities* are in Amanda's log book.

Blondie refers poetically to this nectar as "the garden in a glass." A rather exaggerated term, I think, especially when first I have to force the contents out of their can. Of course, Blondie's relationship with the gifts of nature is generally well known, ever since her first tomato-juice commercial. I can still see her from the days of black-and-white television as if it were today. Blondie in her bikini jumping about on the beach, with the Golden Gate Bridge of San Francisco in the background. And in the forefront an inflated balloon bears a slogan: "Ramino tastes a treat— it's Blondie's favorite!"

"Catalpa!" Blondie bursts out laughing. She shakes her head charmingly. It's a rather delayed reaction, but understandably so. She is in a different environment, after all. Who would not be disoriented?

Amanda, in the second chair, rests her feet on the third one, up to this point unoccupied. She frowns a little. As a matter of fact our catalpa is her favorite among all the trees in the whole park, in just the way G-19 is a drink Blondie could not bear to be without for one whole day. "What's so funny about that?" she interrupts her own silence.

"Funny?" Blondie reacts. "If there is anything that is *extremely* comical, then it's your feet on Harley's chair, Miss!"

"With ice?" I ask through the open door. I have just managed, with the help of a hammer and a screwdriver, to bore two holes into the lid of the can.

"Well, that depends, hon," Blondie declares with that ringing voice of hers. "If you've just taken that *fantasy* out of the refrigerator, then it's fit for immediate consumption. But if you've let it stand in the hot summer air on the kitchen table—in order that we could make love, you incorrigible rascal—then I have no option but to ask you to drop at least three ice cubes into the elixir."

"Very well," I answer.

"And you can bring me a large pot of tea," orders Amanda.

"The kettle is on," I shout. I start running around like a headless chicken. And before anyone can react, like a waiter in a five-star restaurant I hurry on to the balcony with a tin tray rattling with glasses, cups, saucers, tea spoons and the lid of a china tea-pot.

So, one pot of tea for Amanda, one G-19 for Blondie and another one for me. If I were to take tea with Amanda, Blondie might be offended. She most certainly would be offended. On the other hand, Amanda can sensibly evaluate my situation. To be frank, Blondie's so-called *garden in a glass* is nothing but abysmal slops—with ice or without. But due to the pleasure with which she is sipping it (she is winking at me roguishly), I have no difficulty in succumbing to her evil charms.

No one says anything for a long time. Suddenly Amanda (up till this point she is sunk in the corner of her armchair with a cup of tea in one hand) lifts up her head, looks into the crown of the catalpa tree and calls out: "Tiger, Tiger, Tiger!"

Blondie nearly drops her glass. She looks at Amanda in amazement. She is probably expecting an explanation but will not get one. So she looks up at me for an answer. Her expression asks something to the effect that Amanda could well be as mad as a proverbial March hare. Or, if she is in fact normal, does it mean that we have built a zoo in the catalpa tree? Or perhaps some kind of a Noah's ark?

I look as if it didn't concern me at all. In no case should I mention the canary. It's like talking about the weather, like what would we do if suddenly there was a downpour. "And the water rose and rose—until there was a flood." Only in Noah's time, it had been chucking down for forty days and forty nights. Today the beautiful sun is actually shining. Unlike Noah and his worries (about how, for example, he is going to stuff all the giraffes, elephants and squirrels together into the ark), I am sitting on the balcony between two women. I squint my eyes and behold Blondie's platinum hair shining like diamonds in the sunlight. And I cannot believe that it is me who is guarding this dazzling treasure.

If Amanda is in the mood to explain anything to Blondie (for example who Tiger is), I certainly have no intention of getting involved. No way. I would assume the role of some traffic cop waving his arms in the middle of a crowded intersection, imparting wisdom on how to drive a car to someone who sits behind the wheel day in day out. Strictly speaking, Amanda has been navigating our Escort for several years without so as much as a scratch. Unfortunately, one cannot say that about Blondie. She's had several nasty crashes. Mostly in a red Corvette. For example, there was that time in California, when she drove into a palm tree, on her way to Burbank. Poor little girl. She was in a hurry not to be late for the recording of the Danny Donnovan show. And all for nothing—D.D. did not even include her in the program.

It was Raúl Ibanesios's fault (who else's could it be?). His own spot was extended by a good twenty minutes.

Raúl Ibanesios is, by the strangest coincidence, Amanda's favorite singer. She owns a copy of every one of his records. I remember the occasion as if it was yesterday. I was watching television with Amanda, waiting for that jerk to get off the screen and make room for Blondie. But that dandy, against all my expectations, began to sing "Only You And No One Else" as an encore. A real soppy number. Amanda was over the moon. And what's more, he then persuaded Danny to sing a duet with him. Oh well!

As I was saying, I'm not used to teaching people the Highway Code or to forcing my own interpretation of the rules on them. It goes without saying that the only exception is Melvin. People like him require—as it were—constant attention. In my opinion, they should never be allowed to drive any motorized vehicle. Melvin, of course, insists that it's me who should be banned from driving. Apparently I approach a sharp corner like a Kamikaze pilot. And thus I threaten *(inter alia)* world peace. According to him, I have no civic responsibility. I should wake up to the fact before it's too late. He would gladly help me. It's completely ridiculous. It doesn't matter to him that he's not doing the work he is paid to do in the Royal Arms properly.

For example, take today. I've had to ask him *five times in total* to repair that loose blind in room 403. That's Blondie's room, by the way. It will be precisely there where, in a short while (a couple of hours is like a drop in the ocean compared to eternity), she will be hanging her perfumed clothes on those wire coat hangers.

4

On Wednesday after work I go to Bayshore Mall. I want to buy something special for Blondie. It should be something rather demonic, like a magic bar of soap. As soon as she lathers herself with it, she will call out as if enlightened by the Holy Spirit itself, "This must be the work of someone whose name is Harley Davidson! How come I was never even aware of his existence? Where is this wonderful person *right now?*"

Naturally I would be right behind the bathroom door. I would reach out longingly with my arms, at the same time praying to the Good Lord that some comet (like that one in Bethlehem) would announce the great news to Blondie.

I am going straight into one of these specialized shops. They all have fancy names like Soap Cherry Barn or The Smell Right Factory. I sniff all the possible and impossible products. I ask the tarted-up sales girls some technical questions. They don't know very much. As a matter fact, they are far more interested in which category of customer I belong to. They ask very carefully if it is a present for my wife—or if I am a bachelor or a widower—and exactly who is the lucky lady?

When I state that I am choosing a rare soap for Blondie, they are not in the least surprised. I am obviously talking about the Blondie from the cartoon strip, whose husband is that imbecile Dagwood Bumstead. This harmless idiot spends his entire life as a couch potato, stuffing himself with multi-layered sandwiches. And when the time comes for him to go to work, he has to run so fast he wreaks havoc all around. Usually it's the postman who has to pay for all this. Just at this very moment he's coming to the door carrying a bag full of bills from Blondie's latest shopping sprees.

I lean on the counter so as to impart to the sales girls (in a suggestive voice) the type of present I need to dazzle *my own* Blondie. First, this soapy substance should come in the shape of some mythological figure. Eros, for example, retracting the string of his bow. I would arrange it in such a way (I explain) that as soon as my Darling gets into the bath, Eros will fire the arrow (hitting her right on her pretty little bottom), and because the arrow is made of soap, Blondie's silky skin will be covered with fluffy soap bubbles. Then these bubbles, the size of peaches, will begin to burst and evaporate. And whilst they are bursting and deflating, Blondie will hear in her ears a delicious melody—Harley's compelling chimes of love.

No wonder the girls are living through every moment of this with me—they don't utter a sound. Some even shed a few joyful tears. And in order to express myself not only in words, I stand right in the middle of the shop with my legs apart and, raising my voice an octave, I begin to sing in front of my stunned audience: *"La la la, in the storm, in the desert, in the heat or on an iceberg... la la la, the lovesick knight looks into the far distant azure... la la la, look, from the skies the princess descends as if in a dream... la la la, my love, my vision, this is the end of my days of crazy longing!"*

The girls are applauding enthusiastically. "Bravo, bravo!" exclaims the one with braces on her teeth. "I can truly recommend this reliable product for Blondie." And she thrusts something even smaller than my thumb nail into my hand.

"How much?" I ask.

"Thirty-eight dollars." she replies.

"Are you joking?" I get upset.

"Okay, okay," she tries to pacify me. "I hope that Miss Blondie doesn't find out how stingy you are."

"On the contrary," I wave my arms. "I'm not interested in any *crap* for less than a hundred dollars. Understand?"

Finally I end up with an eight-by-six-inch box. Inside there is body oil, talcum powder and a soap bar in the shape of an extremely podgy Grumpy—one of the seven famous dwarfs from the Snow White fairy tale. It costs exactly one hundred and twelve dollars forty two cents.

On the way home I buy a bouquet of thirty-three roses—one for each year of my waiting for Blondie. I will hide them in her hotel room closet tomorrow. As soon as my Angel finishes her shower, I will go down on my knees in front of her. What will follow may be easy to imagine.

I hurry home to Amanda. She will certainly be most interested in what happened. But she's not home yet. I call Steinbergs. Amanda works there as a cashier. Apparently she's on her way. At last, around 10 p.m., I hear the door.

"Look," I say, and open the box. "Only one hundred and twelve dollars."

"Really?" she shakes her head. "In the drugstore round the corner this only costs fourteen fifty."

As usual, when I get terribly excited, I start to stutter. "F-f-fat G-grum-py? Just like t-t-this one?" I ask.

"Even more obese," she replies and disappears into the bedroom. She returns with a vase. She counts off the six freshest roses. "Six roses for six years of our life together," she says. "Have you something against that, Harley?"

Shortly afterwards, she falls asleep the moment her head touches the pillow. I can't understand it. It is our last night together. She hasn't even kissed me good night. Of course I would be better off staying awake. These Vietnamese nightmares are not very good for my health or my psychological equilibrium. It begins as usual. I am sitting on the green grass in the middle of a group of tear-stained GIs. It's just before Christmas. Home is far away. We are completely surrounded by enemy jungle. My eyes are clinging to the image of Blondie. She is floating over a stage wearing a blue sweater, red shoes and a white mini-skirt, with Pat Bell on one side and a couple of comedians on the other. From my visual angle they look like Dick Van Dyke and Mary Tyler Moore.

My Angel is humming the last verse of "Rudolph the Red Nose Reindeer." Around her head beautiful butterflies flit to and fro. They settle in her hair and look like little bows. And then it begins. Out of the blue, a trap door opens underneath Blondie, as if planned by the sort of kidnappers who stop at nothing. Before I realize it, my Darling disappears, microphone and all, into the red hell of an impenetrable jungle. I want to go after her. But my legs feel as if they are tied together. I fall face down into the mud. I am suffocating. I scream with fear. Amanda is shaking me wildly. It's only 3 a.m. My pyjamas are soaked with sweat. I go to get another pair. I grope around a bit. Then I hit my head on the bird cage. I can't understand what I am doing in the kitchen. Finally I'm so pooped that I fall asleep on the toilet seat.

5

At 9 a.m. after I've done Ella's chambermaid work, Jacques Bélanger, who is behind the reception counter immersed in a crossword puzzle, greets me. He has such a heavy French accent, it takes some time before I can actually work out what he is asking: "The name of the street in Mexico City where Trotsky was hiding before he was assassinated...? In the middle is a 'g'."

I sigh with relief. Jacques has no time to notice that I'm clutching a large brown paper shopping bag. It contains the Grumpy soap, a bouquet of red roses for Blondie and the banana Amanda gave me for the journey to work. She said good-bye to me with the admonition that I should think of her when the time came to throw the banana skin into the garbage can. My inventive partner often uses symbolism of the sort not even a Zen monk could possibly understand.

I fall into one of the two scruffy chairs in our mini-vestibule. We meet in here whenever McCarthy has something *extraordinarily* important to tell us. I say, "I don't know, I don't wish to know, and even if I knew, I would not tell."

"So you wouldn't tell Jacques even if you knew, Harley?"

"I'm not interested in Trotsky out of principle."

"But when I know, *Mon Dieu*, I say, *non?*" he begs.

My silence is like the grave's. I don't know the name of that particular Mexican street in any case. But I pretend that if I really wanted to, I could recall it just like that. Jacques sinks his teeth into the golden-framed eraser on the end of his exquisitely sharpened pencil. He mumbles something under his breath. Doubtless it has something to do with Anglos having no idea what good manners are.

But I'm only teasing him, of course. If there is just one *normal* person here whom I get on with, then it's this good Quebecois soul. During our sessions with Melvin, he is always on my side. That's the first thing. And secondly, there's no need to explain anything in explicit detail to someone of his intellectual calibre. He's as clever as Voltaire. He knows exactly where I came from. And, in principle, he even knows where I'm going.

I—as opposed to Melvin, who quite simply avoided the war by the mere expedient of getting into his battered Volkswagen in New Jersey and crossing the Canadian border a few hours later—have two and a half years of skirmishing north of Saigon behind me. I say it just like that, as if it were nothing much. But, in reality, I came pretty damn close to death in Quang Nam-Da Nang province once. Jacques understands that. And now he apparently assumes that I am almost on my last legs mainly because of *some*—Blondie. He is however tactful enough to consider it to be my own private affair. He once told me in strictest confidence that in a dream he had made love in a bathtub full of Champagne with Madame Bovary. If Melvin were ever to hear such a thing, he would tell Jacques in no uncertain terms that by dreaming about sexual intercourse with some shameless female he's only trying to hide his latent homosexuality.

Oh well. Anyway, Jacques has abundant knowledge, based on his studies of the world, especially French history. He has read lots of books, from Diderot all the way to Sartre. About a month ago, he found time to explain to me the true significance of the French Bastille for the Quebecois. As a result, some of the things happening here are now much easier to understand.

Of course, as far as Melvin is concerned, just attempting to ask him what is, by and large, the most rudimentary question—like who assassinated Abraham Lincoln and why is more than enough to make him puff up like a rooster on a pile of manure. Or if I ask would he kindly *outline* (since he is an American by birth) what he personally thinks the reason for the North-South Civil War was, he immediately starts to put me down. Only I, myself, Harley Davidson, know how many innocent children, women and men I have killed. That's a). And as for b) he—himself—has a clear conscience. Never mind the fact that all wars are immoral—like the hunting season in the state of Connecticut.

At this moment Jacques takes the pencil out of his mouth. It makes a smacking noise, like a cork being extracted from a bottle. He swears, "*Sacrebleu!* A sort of blue color... the third letter from the left is a 'd'."

"Indigo," I say.

"Harley! You're a genius!" he exclaims enthusiastically.

It is very flattering, and I swell out like a peacock, but nothing lasts forever. As soon as my gaze falls on Melvin's tatty tool box, I shrivel up. For your information, in the box there are six screwdrivers, a hammer, a quarter sheet of sandpaper, a chisel, a wood saw, a soldering iron, a wrench, a switch, a small plane and three different types of pliers. Then there are some lengths of wire, some string, a few screws, nails and a couple of water taps. Nothing out of the ordinary. The only item worth noting is that enormous screwdriver. Its rubber handle is designed so that it can't slip out of one's hand. It's for when Melvin has to use all his strength.

This whole junkbox resembles a coffin. Melvin has a habit of *sitting it down* in one of the chairs, as if the thing had buttocks and arms and could speak. It looks as if it used to be painted red, before its owner covered it with stickers. They proclaim peace in sixteen languages. I will give one example: "Be active - or else you will be radioactive." That's in German.

Why am I talking about this? It really is time for me to get out of here. A lighted cigar in the ashtray confirms that Melvin is not far away, visiting non-smoker McCarthy's office. It would be all I needed for him to find me here. I mean, he would start pumping me as to the contents of the brown bag and so on. I doubt whether I could get away with just showing him the banana from Amanda.

So I'm not waiting for any more of Jacques' questions. I take the elevator to the fourth floor. On my way I enquire about the health of Matt Jackson in 402. His guide dog answers for him. They both arrived in town for some sort of gardening conference. In all Benny barks six times. I gather from that that neither of then could possibly feel any better.

Quickly I slip into Blondie's room next door. One can say that my Angel will have quite a decent view from here. Definitely the best one in all the Royal Arms. When dawn breaks, she will be able to see a little of the greenery in the park opposite, through the gap between the high-rise apartment blocks. Maybe even the children's swing, if anyone should happen to be swinging there at the time. I've also arranged a pair of deckchairs and quilts on the flat roof, just in case Blondie would like to breathe the fresh air under a blanket of night sky. We shall see. It all depends on the circumstances, and mainly on her mood. I will certainly not omit from my romantic plans the obligatory bottle of Champagne—Blondie's favorite, Ernest & Julio Gallo, from the sunny vineyards of California.

In no time I'm ferreting around, from one end of 403 to the other. I want to make sure that everything is spic and span. And I don't intend to leave the minutest detail to chance. I must spray the walls, ceiling and carpets with the scent of pine forest. I carry on inexorably in this way. In the bathroom I stay on my knees on the pale pink bath-mat for at least half an hour, inspecting the floor. Some time ago, you see, Melvin upset a tin of grease on this very spot. Then, before I even have time to polish it with a paper towel, I find I have to breathe all over the cracked mirror. The pillow, on which Blondie will this very night spread her platinum hair (bob-cut, á la Cleopatra, the classic hair-style of today), will have to be fluffed up to make it seem like a work of art.

I will leave nothing to chance. In the drawer where the Bible is kept I put a book of my own poems. I published it at my own expense in nearby Cornwall. I discovered through an advertisement a guy who can print this type of thing literally while you wait. The book has thirty-three pages—one poem for each year of tormenting separation.

One typically has to be born a poet. However, in my case this is not so. If it weren't for Blondie (as my shining inspiration), I doubt I'd even manage to come up with one decent verse. For example, on page 27, I begin lyrically by simply stating that I am waiting for Blondie's twenty-seventh year. It's now January and I tremble with anticipation at what February might bring. Usually I end these laments with a note about how staring into the dim distance and waiting is giving me a splitting headache. But I won't give up. I only hope that this year is the last year of this *crazy* longing—my love—it won't be long, period. Evidently, nothing ever happens. So I turn the page and carry on longing on another blank sheet of paper. I admit with true self-criticism that these lines are first-rate babble. Pathetic figments—but straight from the heart.

What can I say? Nothing, except that I will give this collection of poems the title BLONDIE. It's obvious why. BLONDIE by Harley Davidson. It has a gray sleeve, with a greenish tinge. It's a hint on my part of the color of my sweet leopardess's eyes. A river runs across the middle of the cover with the rising sun beyond. There is a bench on a river bank. And on the bench are two people—Blondie and me holding hands. And she is resting her head on my trembling shoulder.

I will have the required number of copies printed—one hundred and fifty in all. That will be enough to cover our overheads. We shall give some away and keep the rest. I will send a few copies to Amanda by post and a few to my daughters. If Blondie expresses a desire to adopt them, we'll have to try, for six months to start with. Afterwards we shall see. All this suddenly makes me feel melancholy.

And that's not all. Tomorrow, when I depart (probably around ten o'clock) with my beloved in a golden carriage drawn by two snow-white palomino horses (after which I will have nothing more to do with this damn establishment ever again), I will give a copy of the publication to Jacques Bélanger as a parting gift. He deserves it. And if he insists, I will scribble a dedication: *To Jacques, who sits on top of the world, where he rightly belongs - Harley Barley*. So that it rhymes.

And then I must date it, so that everyone remembers this day forever. Of course Melvin could have a heart attack from a parting gift like this. That is perhaps not such a bad idea. I would bet he has never in his life read anything written by any of his famous fellow countrymen—Walt Whitman, for instance. Not to mention 20th century examples like Jarrell and Kinnell. My God! I've just realised that I should also *sell* a copy to McCarthy. After all, he did take me back again, thereby enabling me to meet Blondie.

As I go on talking to myself like this, I nearly forget the most important thing—a welcome letter for Blondie! I slap my forehead and swear at myself. Immediately I sit down at the desk behind the television set, which is covered with writing utensils. I set to work at the speed of lightning. Even before I know what I want to say, I have four densely written pages in front of me. Mostly I repeat again and again that we (Blondie and I) have been anticipating this moment all our lives. And that we have finally lived to see it come true. A bright future awaits, spread out before us like the Atlantic Ocean. But immediately I cross it all out. One ocean (even one as vast as that) quite simply cannot express the grandiosity of our plans.

In truth I should write a full thirty-three pages (I'm just beginning to think seriously about starting on the fifth), but I'll say the rest to Blondie in person. Finally, I just manage to squeeze 'Your Loving Harley' into the bottom right-hand corner. Then I kiss the letter, fold it and insert it between the first two pages of the book.

6

Suddenly it's quarter past ten. I rush downstairs to change over with Jacques Bélanger in reception. And, incidentally, as I do so, I remind him that across the road at Maria's Corner Variety they stock his favorite fruit yogurt. His mouth starts watering straight away. You see, I don't need any witnesses. Not even him, although he's quite decent—for a queer.

As soon as he is out of sight, I call Las Vegas airport. I ask to be put through to Trans World Airlines. The very moment I hear their pleasant Hallo, I ask if their Boeing 737, flight number 815, is airborne yet. And I am immediately moved to tears. That silver bird, they inform me, ascended into the azure sky like a feather— at exactly 10:06.

Then I ask if Blondie is sitting in the third row by the window, near the starboard wing. The voice goes dead silent. They do not answer such questions. This is in accordance with the international convention on passenger air transport drawn up in 1921 in The Hague. Come what may, they will say no more—not even in reply to such trivial inquiries as what is the airplane's precise wingspan, the number of flight hours the captain has had, or whether there are sufficient reserves of fuel on board, etcetera. Only that the aircraft in question lands (after one short stopover in Denver and a longer one in Chicago) in the place I am calling from at 6:40 p.m.

I try to catch my breath. Even without the help of a calculator, I can work out that I have a mere seven hours and fifty minutes in which to get myself psychologically together.

I reach for the newspapers. But Jacques' crossword interests me about as much as the weather in Greenland. I keep turning the pages in order to find a reference to the arrival of my Darling. But it's all to no avail. Except for the announcement (drowned in the flood of other advertisements), that Blondie will give a *solo* performance in Kitty Junction at such and such a time, there is not a damn thing! The ticket costs $6.25.

I had anticipated finding a strategically placed article (preferably on the front page and in bold type), explaining to the venerable readership that seeing Blondie is first and foremost a unique *artistic* experience. Alas. The merest mention of anything remotely connected with *art* will do far more to discourage people than to lure them in. Just like that last time, when Ornette Coleman, the jazz star—*anumero uno*—performed here. And the hall, with a two-and-a-half-thousand capacity was almost as empty as a park in a rainstorm. Amanda and I were in the second row. Behind us were a handful of other enthusiasts. Even Amanda would no doubt have preferred Raúl Ibanesios—that awful troubadour of hers, as everyone knows.

What more can I say? Only that if anyone thinks that Blondie is no longer the *Phantom* of the opera, they should not forget all she has given the world—if nothing else, her very existence. In my opinion, she has given the world at least as much as Marilyn Monroe would have given had she not committed suicide. But, anyway, why am I getting agitated? The less fuss there is around my sweet little Blondie's arrival, the better. It will guarantee that I will have her all to myself.

Quite frankly, in spite of this fact, I worry my head silly. Blondie is now (*floating*) in the air. In a few hours the car door will slam outside the hotel. I can already see it: My God! The taxi is here. I don't even know on which side of the entrance to stand. The left or the right? My knees are turning to jelly. Maybe I should faint. And even if I don't, I am still left speechless, incapable of saying a single word. Then, I stutter terribly. So terribly that when Blondie asks me what day it is, I can't even manage to blurt out "Thursday".

I try to calm myself down. Basically, it's like this. I should not get uptight. And in order not to get uptight, I will have to fortify myself. And that means only one thing—I must not merely wait for this nerve-racking experience to begin and then jump in head first. I will simply imagine that Blondie is already behind the door. And I'm up to my neck in it. And I'll stay that way until my nerves are as strong as steel.

Then nothing will bother me anymore. And then, when Blondie *really* does appear at the door I shall be thoroughly prepared for it. I shall pick up her suitcase as if it were a matchbox. And in the elevator that takes us up to her room, I will tell her all kinds of stories. That's it. Sheer sensation. One doesn't say —"difficult training, easy battle" for nothing. Yes. Life's like that. Like in 1944. On the day called D-Day. It'll be as if I'm preparing for the landing on the Normandy beaches. And, so, I have to rehearse, so that everything will go like clockwork. In the worst case, I shall use some tricks I learned in Vietnam. Why not?

I am not waiting for anything anymore. I begin my preparations with gusto. First I hear the taxi arrive. Then an unexpected gust of wind rips the newspaper out of my hand as our glazed swing-door suddenly flies open. I lean across from the reception counter. My heart misses a beat. Literally. Yes, instead of Jacques Bélanger carrying a fruit yogurt, I catch sight of—Blondie. She is looking around the entrance lobby like a mermaid washed ashore on the coast of Newfoundland.

Everything she has with her is inside a small suitcase made of crocodile skin. Before I can recover, she begins to approach me. With muted steps—just like she did in her first film "The Boundless Prairie." She played a seven-year-old orphan girl adopted by an Indian family. At this very moment it looks as if I am the Paleface and she the Indian Chief. Let's see what will come of it.

I don't have to wait long. The moment she bumps into one of the bulky armchairs in our mini-vestibule, she stops dead in her tracks. Then she wets her little finger with her lips. She lifts it into the air as if she is trying to determine from which direction the wind blows. Alas, only she knows what she is up to. I even expect her to say something like *"Icha-sa-mula-naka."* But instead she purses her lips and breathes out, "Good evening."

This truly stirs me beyond belief. I thank God that this is not a real invasion. This is some kind of a dress rehearsal for something that has yet to happen. When it does my feelings will really explode. Otherwise it would be a disgrace. For example, I can only manage a few steps forward, but even these make me grip the reception counter so as not to topple over. What's more (and as I anticipated), I am speechless. I open my mouth - and nothing. Like a fish out of water. Finally I stutter, "Bbb...lon...die." And then, "G-good ev-v-ening."

Suddenly Blondie's eyes nearly pop out. She exclaims, "Listen, were you skiing in Aspen when I was shooting The Last Day of Dick Hammersmith there?"

"N-n-no, I was n-not. B-b-but I saw you in that film s-s-seventeen times in all."

"Really? You are not by any chance...?"

"Y-yes. Ha...Harley...Davidson."

She repeats, "Harley Davidson?" And then, "Oh yes. I get it now."

I should have known that. She squints her eyes, which immediately gives me chills. I know from which direction the wind blows. It's the same look she gave that crazy Dick Hammersmith. I'm not exaggerating. Almost the whole of that pastiche is about the two of them spending sixteen years in the same lunatic asylum. Dick was a patient and Blondie was his consulting analyst. Blondie (within her role) obviously does everything to help Dick return to normal life. And thus both of them find themselves in the State of Colorado. Blondie is trying (as a last resort) the so-called shock treatment of a free fall on Dick. The hardest job for her is to get Dick to make a ski jump. On the way to this neckbreaking jump she accompanies him with these already classic words, "Oh for God's sake! Jump, Dick, so that I can see what it will do for you!"

But Dick begins beating about the bush. He claims, for example, that his first and last jump was something he did the night before in the hotel, by accidentally touching (whilst waxing his skiis) the burning-hot iron. Moreover, he claims (so as to make the plot more complicated and therefore more dramatic) that the first snow of the entire season fell that same night—all one and a half inches of it. And that, according to his judgment, is not enough. It would be like jumping into a children's paddling pool from a 30-foot springboard.

Now, from her interrogating look, I realize that although Blondie made this film years ago, she is still living her role as a psychiatrist. She obviously can't get it inside her pretty head that, although Dick Hammersmith was a hopeless case, he had a normal name—Dick Hammersmith. Whereas (although I look normal) I introduce myself as a famous motorbike.

But then, luckily, she casts her gaze over the room. When she realizes that I cannot possibly be Dick, because this dive certainly isn't the Aspen Hilton, she asks, "Are you the owner of this establishement, Harley?"

I clear my throat. "Melvin thinks he is the owner. But that would be a long story."

"Melvin?"

"He changes the lightbulbs here, amongst other things."

Again Blondie squints at me. "I see," she replies. "I will do all I can, Harley."

I almost burst into tears. The harder I try, the more it looks as if this scene is happening on the screen. Oh well. I shall have to work hard on this. In Normandy nothing was one hundred percent certain either, let alone Vietnam. There, the Commies kidnaped Blondie in front of my very nose and dragged her into the jungle. No, I shall play it differently—with reserved dignity. Like a hotel employee, in fact. With thorough and absolute correctness. I will point my trembling hand in the direction of the reception desk. "Would you like to check in, *Miss*?"

Three gracious steps. And it looks to me like a three-mile-long fashion parade. Blue shoes (she wore red ones in Vietnam) gently patter across the dirty-brown carpet. (On this exact spot, Melvin dropped his lit Havana cigar, and before he had the decency to pick it up, it burned an ugly hole in the material.) Gazelle legs in fashionable nylon stockings, studded with embroidered butterflies, disappearing under the hem of a black skirt interwoven with silver threads. It's worth noting that in Vietnam her skirt was even shorter and was white as snow.

I peep over my Darling's shoulder. My teeth are chattering feverishly. With dusty blades, the fan up by the ceiling lazily cuts through air now heavily laden with Erocascade perfume. And at the same time it lifts up all the necessary paperwork. I wait for Blondie to fill it in and immortalize it with her signature.

"Are you here alone?" she asks without looking at me.

I wipe the sweat from my brow. I could say that Melvin is lurking somewhere around the corner. And that Jacques has just popped over the road to fetch a yogurt. And that McCarthy is probably in his office planning another trip to Brazil. But in the end I simplify the answer to a minimal, "All alone, Blondie."

My sweetest shakes her ballpoint pen as if it were a dead mouse. "I'm also terribly alone. In every way. Do you understand, Harley?"

As if I didn't! I have an accurate logbook—a good 33 years on the subject already. I've traced her every step. I know when she visited a hairdresser *alone*. And so on. But instead of ceremoniously explaining that from this moment on she won't ever again have to complain about loneliness, I just shuffle about helplessly. Finally I manage to blurt out, "On the r-r-roof there are two deckchairs for us and a bottle of Ch-champagne."

"Thank you very much," she replies. "Perhaps another time. It's been a long day for me. Surely it has for you too, Harley."

Basically a negative response. But when uttering the word *Harley* she gently tickles me under the chin with the end of her ballpoint pen. It's not a very significant gesture. But, since I'm drowning, I will grab it like a straw. Blondie is clearly *suggesting* that I should not be so coy and that I would be better off plucking up some courage. She really would like to know what is hidden behind my facade of an obliging hotel employee.

Nothing will stop me now. "Everything is ready for your long stay, Blondie."

"One night will pass quickly, don't you think?"

"The night I have in mind...doesn't know daybreak."

"Ah...really?"

"Trust me," I whisper conspiratorially. "This night of mine is something you have never lived through, even during the day."

Blondie leans her head backwards, as if she was hovering somewhere in the clouds. As she returns my pen, she gently scratches the palm of my hand with her nail. "You're a rather interesting person, Harley. Can you show me to my room now? Please."

"I'm at your service." On the way to the elevator I offer her my arm. Without hesitation she takes it. "I hope that you had a good rest on the French Riviera?" I ask.

"Don't talk about it," she sighs. "I stayed with Brigitte Bardot. Can you imagine?"

Of course I can. The Saturday tabloid didn't lie (for once), but as one could easily have anticipated, it was sheer hell. As soon as Brigitte saw Blondie's crocodile-skin suitcase, she blew her top. Wasn't she ashamed, gallivanting around the world with something that once belonged to a living creature?

While Blondie is telling me all this (next time, she says, she would rather sleep under a bridge), the elevator keeps throwing us about from side to side. I imagine that the Royal Arms is the Empire State Building, and that we get stuck without power on—where else?—the thirty-third floor in total darkness. Although my beloved would quickly find a lighter, she would as if *by chance* drop it on the floor. That's a sort of trick, old as mankind itself. Once there was a time when ladies of noble birth (as if by chance) used to drop their silk handkerchiefs onto the floor. And the result is basically the same. It's a matter of how best to catch the suitor's attention.

Before I realize it, I find myself crawling on my knees. Instead of a lighter I come across Blondie's ankles. I start kissing them. But what in the devil's name happens next? Just as I drag my hot lips up towards her no less lovely knees (these preparations for the Normandy landing are probably even more interesting than the Normandy landing itself will be), the elevator jerks to a halt. The light comes on. There is a black hole of a corridor in front of me. Blondie is nowhere to be seen. I call out in all directions. Not even Benny from 402 bothers to bark.

But behind my back Jacques Bélanger smacks his lips. "Can you imagine, Harley? They didn't have the two-percent yogurt with kiwi again. Only this full-fat strawberry one."

7

The very first time I see my chosen one is as a seventeen-
year-old in a street in Vienna. I don't even know what I'm
doing in Austria, or from which direction the wind has blown
me in. I am probably wandering across Europe in the hope
that I might encounter my parents. To this day I haven't the
slightest idea what they look like, or if they survived the war.
If I have Jewish blood in me (my features would suggest such
an eventuality), it's a pointless effort. My parents would have
gotten rid of me while escaping from the Nazis so as to save
my life. They themselves would have ended up in the gas
chamber. It may be true, but on the other hand it may not.
Most Jews had this misfortune. And many Poles as well. On
the other hand, the Swiss came out of it unscathed. They
were simply lucky. Only a fool would rob a bank of the
money he had previously deposited there.

Anyway, I was born the day I saw Blondie. I'm
strolling around Rotenturmstrasse in the sweltering summer
heat. At a newspaper kiosk I see her face smiling at me from
the cover of a magazine. I freeze in my tracks. It's a beautiful
full-page photograph. The screaming headlines herald her
name: BLONDIE—with six exclamation marks. Thanks to
Providence, this magazine is displayed at the end of the front
row. Had the magazine been displayed in the second row
(covered by the first), I would have never set eyes on Blondie.
When I think about it even today, I get goosebumps on my
skin. How incredible it sometimes is that our whole life can
depend on some mere chance moment.

For instance, that kiosk could have been closed due
to the vendor's illness. Or Hans, as this particular one-eyed,
one-armed and one-legged war veteran is named, could have
fallen asleep in his wheelchair as a result of consuming a vast
amount of alcohol. And, as sometimes happens, a lighted
cigarette could have fallen out of his mouth. And the
wretched soul would have burnt to death alongside Blondie
before the fire brigade even had time to unroll their hoses.

The possibilities of what might have happened—but thank God—didn't are endless.

As soon as I recover from my initial daze, I ask Hans, "For goodness sake, who is this amazing creature?" And I point a trembling finger at Blondie.

One-eyed Hans leans out of his window. He says, "How should I know? I only have one eye."

I shake my head in disbelief. "If I were selling magazines, I would know everything, Sir. You still have a brain, don't you!"

"Listen, young man," he replies, "Either buy something or move on. Once you only have half a brain you only have half the answers, understand?"

Discussing anything with him is a horror story. Really. In the end he grabs the last copy in his steel claws (he has them screwed onto the stump of his only arm, the left one) and waves it before my eyes as if it were an old rag. I get really scared. What if a passer-by throws the necessary few shillings onto Hans's plate (decorated as it is with painted cuckoo birds) first? And before I could get over it, that *someone* would jump onto a tram with Blondie, and—goodbye. I would never see you—Blondie—again!

Luckily I am the only customer on Rotenturmstrasse. I swiftly plunk down the last of my money in front of Hans (about three times the actual price), and with Blondie clutched to my chest, I hurriedly disappear round the first corner. As soon as I look into her ravishing face, every bell on all the spires of each of Vienna's churches and cathedrals begins to toll. I say to myself that Blondie is named exactly as she looks. Her hair is as light as a ray of sunshine. She is just like that Goldilocks from the fairy tale. I am dazzled by such beauty. Never before have I been completelycrazy over someone. Well and truly, that same Saturday afternoon I decide to love Blondie and only Blondie from then on. Nothing will ever separate us. And not only that. As soon as I meet her, I will marry her. And we will remain together until death do us part. Amen.

Not far away there is a small park. Completely intoxicated, I sit down on a bench. Blondie's slightly open mouth looks as if it is whispering my name: *Harley!* I let slip as an echo: *Blondie!* A man passes by. He is curious to know whether I'm alright. He comes to the conclusion that I am suffering from an epileptic fit. And that apparently is a serious illness. You see, I am pressing Blondie to my lips. I wriggle and sigh. I ask him if he speaks English. Because I need to know what is written about Blondie in that American magazine. He replies that he doesn't speak English and, even if he did, he has far more important matters to attend to.

I'm not going to be put off. I start begging the passers by to show compassion. I promise them the moon. Soon I have more than enough prospective "customers." All the tramps, beggars and local vagabonds surround me. Most of them insist that they have learned English in royal or diplomatic circles. It goes to show that this is only their "idée fixe." Despite staring at the article in question for at least half an hour, they haven't a clue among them as to what is written in it. If only they would simply shut up. But to top it all, they never stop talking nonsense about Blondie.

One ragamuffin even insists, "That's the famous figure-skater!"

This rather surprises me. "How can you tell?" I try to find out.

"How can I!" he gets upset. "It's all here in black on white."

I send him to hell. As he leaves I shout after him, "You can tell those fairy-tales to your grandmother—if you have one! If Blondie was a figure-skater, they would not be writing about her in the August issue but in the December one. She would be wearing mittens and a woollen scarf. And her skates would be draped over her shoulder. Don't you think so, my good man?"

He does not. Putting his hands into pockets filled with holes he departs for God knows where. On page fourteen my theory is cleary confirmed by a small black and white photograph. In it Blondie stands on a stage in front of a microphone—without skates! Anyway, if she were a skater, she would be gliding on the rink upside down, having just completed a perfect double Axel.

In any case, one glance at Blondie (doubtless at the beginning of her career) moves me to tears. I guess she must be roughly six and half years old in that picture. The organizers had even forgotten to lower the microphone. It's about a head higher than her. Poor little girl, she is trying as hard as possible to reach it on tiptoe. But it's not enough. So much effort only causes her to stick her tongue out in a rather charming fashion. She is wearing a checked skirt and her braided hair is draped over her shoulder. Even at that age she looked like a child prodigy.

Some drunk is staggering his way round the bench. He is offering me Blondie's address in exchange for a beer. For two he would even give me her telephone number. I thank him very much. He was probably digging in the garbage bins and came across something written on the label of a cheap bottle of vino—something he now offers to anyone interested in having a pen pal in far-off America for money.

In the end I manage to enlist the aid of a white-haired old lady who had shuffled into the park with her collection of knitting needles. She had just started knitting the sleeve of a Norwegian sweater. Her name is Gertrude Steinbach. As soon as she looks into my smitten eyes, it triggers her own memories. Apparently she lived in America for seventy-eight years. Only recently did she return to Austria in order to die. I guess she is about ninety-two.

And she has one last wish. She refuses to die until she can be sure that someone buries her here, in Vienna, in the cemetery, next to her husband. Two days after her wedding she left him and went over the ocean with some opera singer. This baritone, during those endless immigration procedures on Ellis Island, lost his voice because of all the stress. Terrified he would be sent back to Europe without Gertrude, he jumped into the sea and swam across to Manhattan. There he opened a wholesale fishmongers' store. These were difficult beginnings. She could not stand the stench of fish; she nearly went out of her mind. And all this time she was still thinking about her first husband. So she returned to Austria in her old age and somehow put her affairs in order.

It's all very interesting, but I'm dying to find out something about Blondie. I'm worried in case the old lady decides to breathe her last behind all those knitting needles. Not only would it be my responsibility to bury her—but she would carry *the secret* of Blondie to her grave!

And, as if to spite me, instead of beginning to translate from the magazine, she says, "I wouldn't like to die in America, because no-one there knows what happens to them."

"Is that so," I shake my head in disbelief.

"Oh yes. They often mix up the coffins and the cadavers there."

"Really?" I pretend I'm interested.

"Or they deliver your ashes to the relatives—even when you've specifically written in your will, and underlined the fact three times with a red pen, that your ashes should on no account be delivered to them."

"And what does one do with them then?" I enquire graciously.

"The best thing is for complete strangers to scatter them into the ocean. But there is one snag."

"My God, what's that?"

"Instead of scattering you over the Pacific, they could do it over the Atlantic—or vice versa." The old lady takes a long pause, leans over to me and whispers in my ear, "Remember, Harley, it's the fault of the Chinese."

I ask why the Chinese, but old Mrs. Steinbach puts her finger on her shrivelled-up lips, as if she has already told me all she could—and that no one else, apart from us two, must find out.

Otherwise we might be struck by disaster.

I'm going crazy trying to get something about Blondie out of Gertrude, but she won't stop repeating that the worst place for dead bodies is New York City. When her neighbour died in the hospital, her remains got lost in the elevator somewhere between the twenty-sixth and twenty-fourth floor. Only after seven weeks did they find her (tied to the stretcher) on the roof next to the air conditioning. Someone had cut off her left toe. This was all the responsibility of one particular religious sect with headquarters in Shanghai.

At the precise moment that the old lady leans towards my ear, no doubt to whisper (just in case) the address of the cemetery where that beloved husband of hers lies at rest, I scream so loudly that she jumps with fright, "My God, and what about Blondie?"

"Is she dead? Well, she has nothing to look forward to, my boy."

"No she's not dead. She's alive! Look! She is breathing!" and I wave the magazine in front of her eyes.

She moves her glasses towards the tip of her nose. "A very nice girl. Aren't you lucky."

The sun is reaching the horizon. The old lady finishes knitting the sleeve and starts the other one. Only then do I learn that Blondie is by God's grace a talented singer, actor and dancer. Something like Ginger Rogers. She has many interests, such as riding a bicycle and stamp collecting. When she was three years old she wanted to be a lion tamer.

All her glory began two years earlier in the State of California when she won a television competion for the best Christmas carol in the category for girls under fifteen years of age. This song, aptly named Ho Ho Ho, was not only composed, sung and played on the piano by the girl herself, but she also danced it to her own choreography. I ask Mrs. Steinbach how it could be possible for someone to both play the piano and dance at the same time. Apparently, they have nothing to say about that. In any case, Bing Crosby and Fred Astaire congratulated Blondie. From Hollywood to Paris offers have started raining down on her. One even came from as far away as Transylvania.

I don't know when or how I can thank the old lady. In the morning I wake up in the park on the very same bench. The magazine is stuck behind my shirt. But I do remember one thing. As I am falling asleep, the old woman, from time to time, wipes her nose on the unfinished sleeve. Then she says in an emotional voice, "You are right, Harley. She's a charming girl. And you know what? When you speak to her, give her Gertrude Steinbach's fondest regards."

8

McCarthy's so-called Brazilian jungle, "The Little Royal Arms Amazon" (as he proudly calls it), is situated on the top floor of our cozy little hotel. In my opinion, it is heaven reaching towards lunacy. Some years back the boss spent his vacation in Rio de Janeiro. He came back a changed man. I remember the occasion as if it was yesterday. Before even unpacking his suitcases he insisted on having some twenty-five wheelbarrows of the best-quality gardening soil delivered to the fourth floor. Two short men took three long hours to empty it all into a three-foot-high barrier thrown together from cedar-wood planks. The moment they were ready, McCarthy called an important meeting in the mini-vestibule. A fan revolved above our heads, perhaps to stop us from sweating during such an important ceremony.

First, the boss ceremoniously handed Melvin a pair of size-fourteen rubber boots. Then he gave him a cardboard box full of canvas bags containing the seeds of tropical plants that he'd handpicked in Brazil. Clearly, by this gesture he was officially bestowing upon Melvin the role of hotel gardener. Apart from his normal maintenance duties he was now in command of the jungle. In practice it means that when the seeds he has sown germinate, they will need watering. Well, plenty comes to he who waits. In this case, for he who doesn't water, all will dry.

Anyway, McCarthy spent most of the first week hanging around the edges of his newly born Amazon jungle. With tears in his eyes he watched as the clumsy bald idiot splattered around in the mud or fought with his spade. He dug holes into which he inserted the seeds, to the accompaniment of great sighs. Two by two they went in. He talked to them as if they were his children.

Our chambermaid Ella complained the most, of course. All the way down at the reception desk I could hear her swearing. Melvin had to go to the room, which now belongs to Blondie, to fetch water. And everywhere Ella looked, she saw the footprints left by the giant. They undoubtedly reminded her of the ones belonging to that famous Snowman who appears from time to time in the Himalayas.

I made no attempt to hide my negative feelings. I've been rather skeptical from the very beginning. This monstrosity takes up half the corridor. In that dark recess opposite room 403, the only light is provided by a 60-watt bulb. And what's more, the difference between the climatic conditions prevalent in the Amazon and in this town are, at the very least, as great as the difference between the Earth and the Moon. And in my opinion, Melvin is not exactly the ideal candidate for an efficient gardener. He keeps on stumbling over the flower beds like a bull in a china shop. Needless to say, everything he has sown will be well trampled long before the seedlings ever have a chance to send forth their first fragile and succulent little shoots.

Oh well. Several months later, to my utter amazement, a dense green jungle sprouted up. In places it even reached to the ceiling. A colourful medley of red, velvety-black and yellow flowers emerged from healthily robust stalks. My eyes were completely dazzled. Everywhere I went, I shook my head in disbelief.

On top of this, we were also seriously wondering whether McCarthy is slowly but surely going crazy. He had a rubber tree, two grown coconut palms and thirteen plastic flamingos delivered to his little Brazil. And Melvin (now almost an expert-tropicologist), topped it all off by telling us that the only things missing are humming waterfalls, just like Niagara.

The Boss was so enamored of this idea that he immediately locked himself up in his office, without sleep or food for three days. We all walked round on tiptoe, waiting and bursting with expectation. On the fourth day, early in the morning, (all pale and thin) he poked his head around the door. And, to no one's great surprise, he summoned Melvin inside.

The ensuing *pow-wow* lasted for almost six hours. The giant then announced enthusiastically that a huge tank would have to be built on the roof. It would be necessary to bring in a supply of water under pressure. It will subsequently be left to circulate according to the laws of gravity. But once the Boss calculated the expense of this extravanganza (as well as the fact that Ella gave an ultimatum that it will be either her or Niagara), he had to say good-bye to this fascinating vision, doubtless with a heavy heart.

In any case, a crew from CJOH TV came to do a shoot for posterity. A brief item went on air just before midnight at the end of the evening news bulletin. The Boss and Melvin stood between the lianas. You could hardly see the Boss. He has a very short build. Melvin, on the other hand, towered over the nearest palm tree by a foot. He was almost bursting with pride. This was when McCarthy commended him publicly for his well-executed work. As a reward he will give him a cassette of original carnival music, which he himself recorded in Rio. From this moment on, Melvin has his very own entertainment. He elbowed his way through the bushes with a watering can in his hand, whistling South American tunes, a Walkman swinging from his belt. He couldn't sleep, even after the day shift. Sometimes he would even rush in to the hotel, his pajamas under his trousers, to sprinkle the Boss's rare sprigs on Sunday.

I must admit that McCarthy's imitation of the Brazilian jungle sometimes makes my blood boil. For example, take today around noon. I realize that it is high time for some refreshment. I have the banana Amanda gave me upstairs, together with the roses, in Blondie's room. So I make a dash for it, two steps at a time.

Up until now nothing out of the ordinary has occurred. But suddenly it happens, and just when I have no inkling anything is up. I do a double take. In the little Brazil on my left, somewhere between those thirteen flamingoes (the Boss's favourite number and bird), a dry twig suddenly cracks. But it doesn't end there. Almost simultaneously I trip over Melvin's tool box.

The last time anything like this happened to me was some thirty miles north-west of Chu Lai. A terrible coincidence indeed. The moon was hidden behind clouds. Here, for a change, a lightbulb flickers thriftily. An eerie gloom prevails. The thing in the jungle made a cracking sound—and I stabbed it instinctivelywith a bayonet. It farted, sounding like the air expelled from a tire. Here, in the Royal Arms, if Melvin should jump out of the Amazon, the only object I could stab him with would be a ball point pen.

All hell breaks loose. Something jolts me as if I were a mere wisp of a thing. It's giving me a full-Nelson and tries to apply some other wrestling holds. In the end it gets in the way of my feet. As I fall, I manage to grab it. It's hairy. It's wagging its tail. But I only recognize it by its damp muzzle.

Thank God. I'm wrestling for life and death with that stupid pooch Benny. Not that you could call it wrestling. He's already given up voluntarily and is licking my face in friendship. But I'm not out of it yet. Far from it. I manage to get more and more tangled up. Between my teeth I now have the lid from Melvin's tool box. In my desperate fight for survival it turned upside down. The contents have spilled out all over the place. I'm praying that its owner doesn't appear before I chuck all his goddamn gear back where it came from. But this won't happen. Behind the door to 403 I hear a noise, like someone knocking a chair over.

Blondie suddenly screams, "Help!"

Melvin laughs sacrastically, "Ha ha ha!"

Then Blondie shrieks, "Is there anybody there!"

Melvin whinges, "Nobody will hear you here, Baby. Understand?"

And Blondie's howling, "Harley! Harley! Harley!"

Melvin repeats incredulously, "What... Harley? Which Harley?"

I'm not about to waste another moment. With an incredible burst of speed I lurch forward. I hit the door so hard it creaks. Suddenly I have a sinking feeling that the whole hotel is crumbling in on me, brick by brick.

9

Of course, I burst into 403 head first—probably just like Dick Hammersmith did that time in the Aspen Hilton. When Blondie lights up a cigarette in bed shortly after midnight, Dick assumes (in his wildest schizoid fantasy), that she has fallen asleep and that the cigarette has dropped out of her hand and set fire to the pillow on which rests her halo-crowned head.

Lo and behold—I stare into a roomscape enveloped in a cloud of smoke. I set about investigating the cause. Naturally, there's no trace of Blondie. Then I notice Melvin's legs. They are sticking out from that stench-pit beneath the bed like a pair of gigantic tooth picks. Some people, amazing as it may seem, are even able to see through a thick mattress. He guesses straight away who has come in.

"Yabba-Dabba-Doo!" he resounds joyfully. "I'm so glad to see you, Harley."

Of course, I wasn't born yesterday. As usual, he is making a grand show. He likes nothing better than to manipulate events shamelessly. The last time we met was around eleven o'clock in the elevator. And now he's greeting me as if we've just met for the first time in fifteen years at the Donald MacDonald High reunion. There's no point in delaying it. I stagger round the side of the bed, deliberately stumbling over his legs, so as to determine his true mental disposition.

"Can you please be more careful," he almost weeps.

"Are you looking for something under there?" I enquire.

"I'm tightening a bolt."

"What bolt?"

"You know, Harley, the one that holds the bed together. Understand?"

He is starting again with this *understand* business. And he doesn't care that what he says seldom makes any sense. "Isn't the bed holding together?"

He responds with condescending kindness. "Can you imagine how right you are! I was just passing by, by chance. And it almost fell apart."

If I didn't know him, I'd be duped. But he's lying through his teeth. He hit the hay in Blondie's bed. That's the truth. I can just see it now. He fell onto the mattress and now he's lying there snoozing like a beached whale. A four-hundred pound Hercules—one who can't even fit into a normal bed. The spitting image of De Gaulle, as Jacques says. But with a stunted brain.

In any case, this is not the first time Melvin has broken one of the Royal Arms' beds. However, the real tragedy this time is that he's virtually demolished my entire artistic endeavour. As I said previously, I have been working on it all morning. Every minute detail has simply got to be in place. And now this catastrophic devastation. Blondie's bed looks like a bombed city. The pillows are strewn across it and the bedspread all crumpled up. The less said about it the better. The thing I'd like to do most would be to cut off those protruding shinbones with a metal saw. But of course I could scarcely afford to soak everything in here with his blood.

I ask nonchalantly, "When you gonna finish, Melvin?"

"Quite soon, buddy. Why do you ask?"

"I have some work to do here."

"You don't say! Like what?"

"For example, I have to air the room."

"Seriously? Do you really mind if I smoke?"

"Whether I mind or not, the fact is you're holding me up."

While I am standing there, I suddenly have a gorgeous colorful dream (in the middle of my black-and-white day), that the bed has fallen on top of Melvin. First he groans. Then he becomes rigid. Then Jacques and I are pulling him from underneath the debris by his legs. When we yank him out, his eyes are glazed, as if he has definitely been snuffed out. A Cuban cigar stuck between his yellow teeth is releasing clouds of smoke. I spit on the cigar to stop it smouldering.

But alas, at that very moment the giant springs back to life. He starts crawling out, extremely elegantly, as if Blondie's bed was a Rolls-Royce and he, Melvin, had just changed its oil and filter.

He gets onto his feet, but not for long. The bed creaks when he falls onto it. "See? Doesn't give an inch. Isn't it great?"

I don't know why but I am compelled to ask, "Have you ever slept *'á la belle étoile,'* Melvin? You get what I mean, grass, stars, the croaking of frogs?"

My question makes him hurriedly assume a sitting position. "You know, I used be a boy scout once. We slept by the bonfire. Cooked a farmhouse soup in a small pot. Cleaned our teeth with our fingers in the stream. But it's a long time ago, Harley. I worry about other things now. You, for example. Coincidentally, yesterday I went to Steinbergs to buy a couple of tins of sardines, the ones that come in tomato sauce. I could easily have whizzed through the express checkout in two and a half seconds. But, *on purpose*, I went to the queue at Amanda's till and stood there for half an hour. And you know why? To cheer her up. She doesn't deserve this from you. She has bags under her eyes. I bet she cries every night. So, what's going on?"

"We've lost Tiger, Melvin. That's what."

He makes a face as if I've just stood on his ingrown toe-nail. "Look, Harley, I really was expecting some kind of an answer like that. Next time, just don't say anything, will you? My God. You're losing touch with reality. That's your problem. You should never have shot at anyone in Vietnam. Understand? Once you aim and press the trigger... it's the end. I know that from my own father. In 1949 he caught a deer in Connecticut *outside* the hunting season. And you know what happened? A couple of days later he blew his own brains out. Poor Dad. He simply had a guilty conscience. Just like you, my friend. You must recognize the truth. I've suspected it for some time. You're going mad. You should have deserted to Sweden. To hell with having to be in Asia. Now it rebounds on you after all those years. You're playing the hero. Or are you?"

I leave him to it. Let him babble away. At least he won't complain that I deny him his freedom of speech. He is very sensitive on that point—on what hisAmerican constitution guarantees him. And he doesn't even mind that he deserted his patriotic obligations in New Jersey and fled to Canada.

"Jesus Christ. Tiger is our canary, Melv. Let me explain it to you. He escaped from his cage last Sunday, and he still hasn't returned."

He sighs. "It doesn't matter how you explainthis to me, Harley. I *understand* it all perfectly even without the words."

"So what are we talking about?" I enquire.

Melvin puffs smoke towards the ceiling. "About the fact that the family is the basic unit of civilized society. Like parents, like children. You should realize that. An apple never falls far from its tree. Understand? Imagine a hopelessly sold-out concert hall. Can you do that? The audience is dead quiet. And do you know why? Because my two daughters and your two daughters are playing a piece for four hands on the piano. And then suddenly the lights come on. The question is, who do you think the audience is applauding more... my daughters or yours? Well, what do you say?"

The worst thing is that I have to pretend that I am having a conversation with a *perfectly* normal person. I make out that I'm thinking very hard indeed. Melvin swings his wrench in front of my face, as though it was the pendulum of a grandfather clock.

"I think, Melv," I say quickly, "that the audience is applauding *your* daughters much more."

At this he of course jumps up enthusiastically, almost hitting the ceiling. "Your thoughts are quite correct, brother. Because in order for daughters to excel, they need understanding parents around them. And, as you know, your daughters are absolutely lacking this attribute. Because they were born to two different wifes of yours. Jesus, can you explain to me why you haven't married Amanda yet? I'll be your best man. Would you like that? Please say that you would!"

The last time I heard something of the sort was on the radio. It was not so long ago. I was driving my Ford down the expressway. I almost had an accident. It was about some girl called Brenda Wilcox who wanted to marry the younger brother of her fiancé John. Problem was, just six months ago he married her older sister Elizabeth. Such open-ended nonsense. Every word constituted a psychoanalytical absurdity—very similar to this nerve-racking experience with Melvin. How can I explain that I can't possibly ask him to be my best man when, as we speak, my Darling Blondie is floating somewhere above the Mid-West in her Boeing 737. In just a few more hours we will fall into each other's arms.

Out of politeness I ask, "Can you make it anytime, Melvin?"

"Why yes! Don't hesitate. Absolutely! Tomorrow, if you like. Just let me know when you and Amanda agree on a wedding date. OK?"

"Sure."

"Thanks. That's quite a weight off my shoulders, I assure you. It's my great desire to see that your daughters have some kind of parents."

He doesn't seem to take in consideration the fact that Sandor is thirty-one and living with somegirl in Paris. When I enquired last Christmas just what she thought she was doing, she slammed the receiver down before answering.

Ingrid is eight years younger. She manages OK, living in Oconomowoc. That's in Wisconsin. The last time she wrote she said that she was breeding rabbits in a big way. Apparently she even exports them (already frozen) as far away as New Zealand.

At this precise moment Melvin starts whistling and heads for the window. At last he notices the loose blind. I've told him about it at least five times. Once again he whistles and slips out into the corridor. It takes quite some time before he returns. When he does reappear in the doorway he is brandishing the longest screwdriver in his arsenal. He stops right in front of me, and pokes it jokingly into my belly.

"Someone has upset my toolbox outside. Can you guess who?"

"No, I can't," I reply.

"If you can, let me know. OK?"

"OK."

I play ignorant. I don't really want to have to tell him about my fight with that hairy beast—Benny. Melvin's yellowish, owl eyes are staring at me from behind the barricade of his thick eyebrows. He's waiting for me to blink. But he blinks first. Obviously his nerve has gone.

On his way out he grabs a chair. He climbs on it. Regaining his balance, he sets to work with gusto. At the same time he announces, "Can you imagine? A bolt came loose here. Understand? But what is that compared to the fact that Micky and I are celebrating our silver wedding today? It's been a quarter of a century of mutual earthly paradise. What do you say to that, Harley? Doesn't hearing something like this make it seem as though even *your* own dream has come true?"

To be honest, I've never met his Micky in my life. But I know more about her than if I'd spent twelve years in school with her. Not a single day goes by when Melvin doesn't give us some reminder of her, making her out to be like the most godly of all goddesses and the guardian of his family hearth. Apart from her other sensational qualities, Micky also has the ability to cook lasagne in sixteen different ways. Once she even raced with the Golden Arrows bicycle team of Saratoga. She got a bronze medal for her efforts.

I want it to sound as though I think it's an exceptional occurrence. So I say with all due ostentation, "Sincerest congratulations from my heart to both of you, Melvin."

He stops whistling as if shot. Immediately I have to ask myself whether I did not exaggerate with the sincerest bit. Perhaps I should have omitted the words—*from my heart.* Or simply used the expression—*congratulations.*

But, for whatever reason, he steps down from the chair. His stale tobacco breath hits my face like morning dew from a foxglove leaf. "Jesus! If I had known that our silver wedding would put you into such a visible frenzy, I would have kept my mouth shut. Can you forgive me that, please?"

In moments like this I don't really know whether I'm dreaming or not. On the one hand he is begging like a small child. And on the other, he is waving his enormous screwdriver in the air, as if he was about to stab me with it. So I decide not to hang about any longer. I start running as fast as I can and trip into the elevator.

10

It's Jacques Bélanger. He's slapping my face. "Harley! *Mon Dieu!* Are you alright?"

I'm lying on the elevator floor. Luckily I come to before our Francophone begins throwing cold water all over me—or giving me mouth-to-mouth resuscitation. "I've just escaped certain death," I report. "Melvin wanted to murder me on the fourth floor."

Jacques is helping me to my feet. "Nothing new," he replies. "That monster will eventually do away with us all."

Melvin is not terribly fond of Jacques. Whenever he can, he imitates his French accent and from time to time he brings up the mystery of the disappearance from Quebec of the internationally recognized traffic sign STOP. Surely, everyone in his (Jacques', that is) beloved Paris must understand what stop means. One's vehicle becomes immobilized on that particular spot and that's it. But in Quebec, one is forced to consult the dictionary to discover the secret behind the word *arret*. I can almost hear Melvin lamenting, "For Christsake, Jack, it's *absolutely logical*. When it says stop, it means stop. Don't you think? Why complicate such a simple matter?"

I fall into one of that pair of shabby armchairs in our famous mini-vestibule. My head is spinning. Who could have imagined such a thing? I popped into Blondie's hotel room to eat Amanda's banana—and I only just escaped with my life. If Blondie suddenly sailed into the Royal Arms (I close my eyes and imagine such a marvel), I would be quite incapable of greeting her properly. Jacques brings me a glass of Perrier. I accept it with gratitude. "Melvin's got a screw missing in his brain," I state.

"You speak from my heart."

"He went for me with his longest screwdriver."

"He should be locked up in a loony bin."

"He wanted to bury my dead body in the Amazon."

Jacques rustles the newspapers. "You were damned lucky. Other people are not always as fortunate as you."

"What are you talking about?"

"Oh, you know. Not one day passes without some kind of catastrophe. It all started with the Titanic. Then there was that terrible crash in the London Underground. An avalanche in the Swiss Alps—twelve dead. A few people have also jumped off the Eiffel Tower. And, a short while ago, they've said on the radio that another plane has just come down. Imagine that. The third one this month!"

I swallow drily. I want to say something, but not a sound emerges. Finally I manage to stutter, "W-w-what...p-p-plane are you talking about, Jacques?"

"What the hell do I know? Except that everyone's dead. Including the pilot."

My blood curdles. According to my estimation Blondie should have left the Midwest by now. Perhaps she is lying there torn to bits, somewhere in a ripening corn field, approximately four hundred yards from her smouldering crocodile-skin luggage.

With enormous difficulty I get to my feet. I mumble something under my breath about needing to get some fresh air. I know one thing with 100% certainty: If I were to use the phone right in front of Jacques' nose, all hell would break loose.

As if by chance, McCarthy emerges from the office. But when he hears my babbling, he stops in his tracks. At the same time Melvin comes crashing down the stairs. Finally they're all standing behind me, listening to my sobs. I can't stop.

I stumble out across the street and into the nearest telephone booth. It takes me a good five minutes of searching through the directory before I find the telephone number of the airport. The moment they pick up the receiver I scream, "My God, is it true?"

"Hello," they sound unexcited. "What information do you require, please?"

"The plane with Blondie crashed!" I moan.

I hear the thundering sound of jet engines. Obviously I got directly through to the hangars. It would appear the person is suffering from chronic bronchitis. He has a coughing fit. Finally he manages to ask, "The plane with Blondie, you say?"

"Yes, yes, yes," I shriek with horror. "With Blondie! Blondie! Blondie! They've just reported it on the radio!"

"Seriously?" he enquires. "On which wavelength?"

"I've no idea!"

"OK, take it easy. My name is Fred. I will look it up on the computer. One moment, please."

He is terribly kind. And he tries to get involved. Right from the very beginning he lets me know that his name is Fred. Apparently this helps calm the distressed customer. It lets us know that we are a part of one big family. But whenever I call someone regarding something *very* important and he or she announces that they will look it up on the computer, I know in advance that their search will take several hours, or even an entire day. Generally it takes until midnight, at which time they have a short break. And then, refreshed by a cup of coffee, they renew their investigations the following day. And so the days, weeks and months go by. I get bald, my back aches (we have the same problem, Darling, but with the difference that you can have yours massaged in Las Vegas by Harry James, and I have mine seen to occasionally on Sundays by Amanda)—and what's even worse—my eyesight is failing rapidly. Since quite some time ago I have had to wear glasses, not only for reading but also for long distances. Sometimes even that doesn't help. I am constantly bumping into things with my head.

I suffer in this way whilst awaiting their reply. They seem to be endlessly delaying giving their answer. And Blondie plays the principal role in all this. Soon it becomes apparent that no computer knows anything at all about Blondie. I am advised to deliberate on whether or not she *really exists*. When I hear this sort of talk, I obviously lose control of my senses. How can someone doubt, on the basis of what is written on their flickering screen, the existence of the person with whom I go to sleep night after night and wake up each morning? And my polite Fred is now full of these doubts. I bet he spent a long time searching for her on his cute little machine. And should my query be substantiated, I bet you that he would begin questioning whether or not this Blondie really did possess an air ticket, and whether the passenger who took off from Las Vegas this morning seated on the right by the window overlooking the Boeing's wing was her, or some other Blondie seated on the left by the wing of a completely different Boeing. Out of the blue, it looks as though out there in the world there could exist not one, but *two* Blondies!

On top of this some kid (I guess he is about eight) starts circling the telephone booth. To kill the boredom, he keeps kicking it with his running shoe. I open the door and shout at him, "What do you want, you brat!"

"When are you going to get out of there?" he asks. "I need to call my stepmother." He kicks my leg. His shoe feels like metal. I groan with pain.

"Just one little moment," says Fred, the amenable airport employee. "I'm rapidly approaching the conclusion of this puzzling mystery."

"Is there a fire?" I ask the brat.

"There might as well be," he replies.

"There was a plane crash," I explain.

"When it crashes, it stays on the ground," he states learnedly.

I try to bribe him. "Here, take a buck. Buy yourself chewing gum."

He doesn't fall for the bait. "Most of the passengers are mincemeat," he informs me. "The headless pilot hangs from a tree by his leg."

"How do you know that?" My teeth begin to chatter.

"It's just been on TV."

"Don't talk rubbish."

"When I grow up, I will kick you in the head, just for a change," he predicts. "Why all the excitement? You can't escape death, however hard you try. Death is... *something definite!*"

Just when I become interested, the man at the airport with bronchitis starts coughing. It's a good minute before he's through with his fit. "I've got it, Sir," he suddenly announces victoriously.

"Is she alive?" I exclaim.

"Was someone supposed to have died?" He sounds astonished.

"Blondie!"

"Well, that hasn't come up on the computer, Sir," Fred replies politely. "The only thing that fell from the sky during the last twenty-four hours is a small plane three miles south-east of Malecula."

"My God, where the hell is Malecula?"

"Two thousand miles north-west of Australia."

I hang up with relief. The wise kid in the street says, "Remember, man, life is only chance. One minute you're up, and then the next you're down."

Immediately I vacate the booth and he jumps into it. If I had more time, I would like to wait for him and engage in a lengthy debate. I would be interested to know why he has a stepmother. I would be certain to discover a host of incredible details.

But by now I am already waving my arms wildly in the air. I feel like a newborn babe. I'm floating on the pavement on my way to the Royal Arms, like a bird who has just grown a pair of wings. I'm shouting at passers-by, "Blondie is alive! Blondie is alive! Don't you understand this, people?" Sure, most of them do. They immediately cross the road. In other words they are doing everything humanly possible not to restrict my happy flight.

11

Actually I'm kidding myself. The flying is not so hot. If I float, I feel like a wet chicken. In the end I'm glad to make it back to the hotel where I collapse into the armchair like a sack of potatoes. Jacques Bélanger, behind the reception counter, can't believe his eyes. "Have you been knocked down by a car, Harley?"

"Something much worse."

"Or by a fat lady with an umbrella?"

"Oh, some kid kicked me on the shin."

"Why did he do that?"

"The youth of today, Jacques."

"This would never happen to you in our neck of the woods."

"How come?"

"We are more cultivated. Better manners."

I sigh. "It's been a bad day. Everybody wants to hurt me."

"With one exception."

"What's that?"

"Who was it who found you in the elevator?"

"*Merci*... Jacques. And I mean that too."

"Not at all. By the way... McCarthy has gone."

"Good news at last."

"Where shall we send Melvin?"

"Hell would be best."

"You know what?" The Frenchman chokes with laughter. "Why not send him to Hanoi for a couple of beers!"

We both fall about laughing—until my kicked leg starts to twitch. The very thought Melvin, with a jug of beer in the Vietnamese jungle, deliberating on war and peace—is a kind of real surrealistic caviar. Sheer delight. As ever, when Jacques hits the nail on the head, his jokes are beyond compare. I never deny that I'm rather fond of this clown. He could even make a person on the brink of suicide laugh.

Regarding for his remark about the Boss, the latter summoned us up here to the mini-vestibule around 10 a.m. and announced that he was leaving shortly to attend the opening of the Henri Rousseau exhibition in Montreal. The only one among us who hasn't a clue who Henri Rousseau is is Melvin. Jacques is standing next to him and counts up to ten, aloud of course (un, deux, trois, quatre,etc.), so as not to make too hasty a decision whether to laugh or cry. His grimace confirms his inner conflict to the rest of us.

When McCarthy notices the way Melvin's ignorance is affecting Jacques, he carefully (i.e. with words chosen especially so as not to bruise his ego) explains to his personal adviser that Rousseau is a naive painter from the land of the Gallic rooster. He served as a customs officer on the French-Italian border some time around the turn of the century. Only after he retired did he become famous because of his paintings—heaven's above!—mainly depicting images of phantasmagorical jungles. Melvin, the official manager of the Royal Arms Amazon, cannot believe his ears. And so he just blinks and scratches the bald patch beneath his flat cap. He has never painted anything in his life (except the ceiling in his bedroom), but he can always try. He begs the Boss to bring him a catalogue from the exhibition. Well, it seems he would like to be sure that what he has just heard is actually true. He's not going to believe it until he sees it there in black and white.

After the exhibition, McCarthy and his wife are planning to go to a lecture: "Will The World Survive The Year 2013?" by Professor Adam Berkowitz. He should have kept the information to himself. As soon as he hears it, Melvin becomes excited and starts saying that if things continue this way (referring to interpersonal relationships), the world won't even last until 1999. He only calms down when the Boss suggests that this sort of serious discussion should best take place tomorrow morning in his office once he gets back.

They are traveling in their new Oldsmobile. Mrs. Boss will, as usual, drive there and back. This is to enable McCarthy to relish the scenery. As an enthusiastic nature lover (unfortunately with a leaning towards alcoholism), he always has to count the number of birds he sees sitting on the branches of passing trees. So that he can define the various species, he always takes a special handbook and a pair of binoculars with him. But it's no use. However hard he tries, nothing on this flat land can possibly compare with Brazil.

Jacques starts rummaging through the drawer. Next thing, he is waving a tube of antiseptic ointment in front of my eyes. "Could you wait here a few minutes, Harley, so I can give my face some first aid?"

"Sure," I reply. "Feel free."

"Merci beaucoup, mon ami."

As he disappears round the corner heading for the washroom, he salutes stiffly like some clockwork toy in bad need of winding. It's no easy life for the Frenchy. Everyone has problems, but in any case, I would far prefer an occasional kick on the shin to having to suffer from acne rosacea, like Jacques. The Latin makes it sound as if it were some sort of rose bush in full bloom. In fact it's a pretty nasty disease. I cannot recall ever seeing Jacques without those spots on his chin and nose. They itch and sting terribly. Sometimes the infection also inflames his eyes and blocks his nose. Once he showed me an entire page on the subject photocopied from the Lappier Encyclopedia. Usually it affects people between the ages of thirty and fifty. It is, in its own little way, tragicomic—making Jacques look as if he's going through delayed puberty. This is obviously grist to Melvin's mill. He assures Jacques that he is only handicapped like this because he doesn't have regular sexual intercourse. Apparently if he got married, the spots would simply vanish the morning after the wedding night. He points to his own face. Underneath those three days' of stubble he has the skin of a baby. Thanks to Micky—naturally.

A typical Melvin gag, this. Though we always suspected that Jacques had taken to the bottle, because of his red nose, it is now clear that our Frenchman suffers from acne rosacea. In the washroom he smears antibiotic cream all over his face several times a day. Then he has to wait for it to dry. Afterwards he wipes it off with a Kleenex. As far as I am concerned, I would definitely choose ten kicks on the shin to having to endure this unique and never-ending misery.

12

I roll up my left trouser leg. Not a pretty sight. Below the knee is a bruise the size of a tennis ball. It shines with all the colors of the rainbow. At the slightest touch I shriek with pain.

"Oh, by Saint Jerome!" a familiar voice suddenly hums from across the mini-vestibule. "Are you alright?"

Normally I would jump up and begin to get mad. It sounds as if my Angel was just climbing the stairway to heaven. But after that previous experience (where Blondie literally evaporated from the elevator on a trip up to her room), I'm keeping my cool. I mumble to myself, "Harley. You know what's going on. *The real* Blondie is hovering somewhere above the earth in an airplane. This Blondie is *unreal*. That's it. Sent to test me. A personal ordeal. The so-called Blondie of Normandy. Yes. A mere dummy. Remember? With this Blondie you are doing no more than training for the invasion. Is that clear?"

Just for fun (or for my own amusement) I follow my gaze across the carpet towards the source of the honeyed voice. I am unable to make it further than half way to the swing doors. My sight collides with Blondie's ankles poking out from a pair of now yellow shoes. In her hand she is holding a bigger item of luggage than was her crocodile-skin suitcase, one that has two zips. It is made of chequered weatherproof material. She is dressed in a pink suit. She looks really great. The last time she was wearing a black skirt interwoven with silver thread. It was much shorter than the white one worn in Vietnam. A charming straw hat is perched on her head, garnished with an artificial daisy. I'd say she looks even lovelier than she did at 11 a.m. during our dress rehearsal.

Before I can recover from the shock my sweet little Angel is kneeling on the carpet before me. She inspects my wound in big close up, making the observation, "This looks awful."

"Do you think I will lose my leg?" I moan.

"Only over my dead body," she states resolutely.

And she really means it. Immediately she sets to work with gusto. She pulls one zip to the left, the other one to the right. Then she yanks a tin box from her luggage. The lid is marked with a red cross. As soon as she unwraps her medical instruments, she begins administering first aid. To start with, she blows tenderly on the contusion. Then she massages it gently with the velvety tip of her index finger, using a violet ointment. Then with an orange one. And for the lucky third time with a colourless one. This last one makes up for its lack of colour by having the stench of bad eggs. Finally she puts the bandage on. She remarks, "Don't worry about it too much. I too sometimes stumble on the stage. I fall flat on my face and break my nose. Or graze my elbows. Do you understand, my dear...?"

"Ha...Harley. Da...Davidson."

"Of course! Harley Davidson! That time we were together in the elevator. My God, where did you suddenly disappear to?"

"I didn't disappear anywhere. I was there the whole time."

"Oh no. You have to be joking. You left me on the brink of despair."

"It looks like fate has played a nasty trick on us."

"The next time we're not gonna put up with it, are we?"

Blondie again squints, her eyes turned into slits. I am beginning to have serious worries that it might end up like the last time. Everything that I've said or done she considers a mere rehash of what the evidently loopy Dick Hammersmith already said in Aspen. I realize that my immediate task is to convince her once and for all that I am the quite normal and well-endowed by nature (as far as originality is concerned) Harley Davidson. I am well-liked by everyone because they enjoy my company, say, in front of a roaring fire. And if people really like someone, they are quite capable of doing anything in the world for them. Even falling seriously in love with them.

In the surge of my gratitude I manage to stammer out, "B...Blondie. Th...thank you for everything."

"Oh," she waves her hand. "Not at all, my dear." She puts the first-aid box back inside her bag. She zips up both fasteners. "That's it. And now we'll stand on our own two feet, shall we?" She helps me out of the armchair. "That's fine. And now, please, we'll just take one step forward, shall we?" She opens her arms, in case I fall forward. "Excellent. And now another one. This is really tremendous, Harley! Does it still hurt?"

"It's getting better."

"How did you get this injury?"

"Some kid kicked me on the leg."

"My goodness. And why?"

"He wanted to get me out of a telephone booth. I was trying to tell him that I was calling the airport. That it was urgent. Jacques Bélanger had just heard on the radio that a plane had crashed. I was obviously dying from terror. What if something had happened to you!"

Blondie's eyes have filled with tears. Evidently, she must have visualized those thugs kicking me in the street just because I was worried about her. Oh well, if she knew that I've been suffering like this for thirty-three years, her eyes would gush like two thermal geysers. Suddenly we find ourselves standing so close to one another that if either one of us stumbled just a tiny bit, we would fall straight into one another's arms.

"Harley. Would you be at all capable of escorting me to my room?" whispers Blondie.

I screw up my face in pain. "I'll try, with your help."

This has the appropriate effect. She picks up her valise with one hand and supports me with the other. And so we stagger to the elevator. We fall only once during the entire journey.

As soon as the elevator takes off, Blondie says, "I'm

still sick to death."

"Why?"

"Oh, don't ask. I lit up a ciggie on the plane after lunch. And the stewardess descended on me like a bloodhound. I was ordered to put it out immediately. So I told her to get to hell. At the height of forty-thousand feet, as the captain had so kindly announced over the intercom. She also informed that they could make an emergency landing on the nearest highway. From that point I would have to walk. Do I, Blondie, really deserve this? What do you say?"

"If I had been there, I would not stand for any of that."

"What would you have done?"

"First and foremost, they would quite simply have to apologize to you."

At this point we reach the corridor. Blondie does a double take. She points to the jungle. "What is this supposed to mean?"

"Our boss is crazy about Brazil."

"They don't have anything like that even in Las Vegas."

We walk resolutely on. My Angel continues supporting me. To be honest, I cling to her like a wet jacket. I repeat to myself that the intensity of our relationship keeps on increasing with each additional moment.

One thing is certain. As soon as my Angel steps over the threshold of door 403, I shall delay no longer. I will begin immediately. First, I will drop onto my knees. Then I will give her the poems and the bunch of roses. With tears in my eyes I will tell her exactly who Harley Davidson *really* is. As an intro, I will probably tell her about Vienna—how she bewitched me from the cover of that magazine in the kiosk. How I was truly only born at that particular moment. Gertrude Steinbach should see it—if only she was still alive.

Huffing and puffing, we reach the door. But instead of Blondie opening it and triumphantly pushing me inside, she drops her luggage onto the floor. Almost all of it lands on my foot. She props me against the wall. The foreboding premonition that something is terribly wrong is not even disguised by the fact that she is clutching my hands in hers. I can't believe my ears. "Thanks for the escort, Harley."

And that's all. Absolutely all. I am left as if I had just been given a scolding, and stutter, "B...Blondie...if it is p...possible, you s...see, I don't k...know how to say it..."

"I understand, Harley," she smiles back. "I am perfectly willing to carry on with this. But another time. Not now. I can't concentrate on two things at once. Can you understand that? I have an evening performance ahead of me. And I need to rehearse a few pieces. I have to try on a new wig. And so forth. Maybe I will even have a little nap. Five minutes, and I'll be as fit as a fiddle. OK?"

"W...when will it be p...possible to continue?" I ask.

"What about tonight? she replies. "Is it convenient for you?" She kisses me on the forehead. When my knees begin to turn to jelly she enquires, "Harley? Are you capable of making it to the ground floor on your own?"

I nod. There is nothing else I can do. She slips inside the room as quietly as a mouse. The door lock clicks behind her. I put my ear to the door. *Darling. At least I can listen to your surviving in there without me. To the way you breathe.* My heart beats like a rabbit's; one thousand pulses per minute. Maybe one thousand three hundred. I can hear Blondie going to the window. She pulls up the blind, then yawns. No wonder. She must be as tired as a kitten who's been chasing a mouse. She cracks her knuckles. And then silence.

But it only lasts a brief moment. Now she opens her suitcase. One zip left. One right. I can hear footsteps. Or rather a pitter-patter. I know exactly what's going on in there. My Angel trots into the bathroom with a toothbrush in one hand. In a few seconds she will discover my Grumpy soap. But then all of a sudden she shrieks, "My God! What are you doing here?"

"Stop screaming, Miss," Melvin mumbles. "Can't you see? Your tap is dripping."

"Tap? What tap?"

"In every normal bathroom you have at least two. Isn't that so?"

"Are you mad? Get out of here immediately!"

"Take it easy, lady. One wasted drop of water per second equals 795 gallons a month. Can you imagine how much that comes to in a year! What would my boss say if I didn't attend to it?"

"I say get out of here immediately, you bumpkin, or I'll call Harley for help."

"What? Do I hear correctly? Harley? You mean that loveable imbecile of ours? Heaven help me. He's no use, Miss. Ha ha ha!"

Melvin chokes with laughter. I am not about to wait for more. I rattle the door handle violently. Then I kick the door. Blondie screams for help. "Harley! Harley! Harley!"

I retreat to the edge of little Brazil. I stand there, balanced on one leg. And at the very moment I'm ready to dart out like a shot and smash down the door with the full force of my body, Jacques Bélanger taps me on the shoulder. "Before I forget, Harley, Melvin was looking for you. Apparently he needs to speak to you urgently. Well, it's not terribly urgent."

I look at him. His face is caked with the drying remains of that white ointment. He looks like a real clown, or a creature from beyond the grave. "Do you know what he wanted?" I ask.

But instead of answering, he is staring down in the general direction of my legs. *"Sacrebleu,* do you know that your left trouser leg is turned up over your knee?"

As if I didn't. I bend down to demonstrate my enormous bruise. But I can't believe my eyes. It's as if there was nothing left of it.

13

A few months after my introduction to Blondie on a magazine cover, I married Ilona. Hungarian refugees had suddenly flooded the streets of Vienna. I came across my first wife by a wastebin in Schwarzenbergstrasse. She was chewing on a piece of greasy paper and clutching a shabby violin case under her arm.

"What's going on?" I enquired.

Instead of answering me she burst into tears. Her face was dirty. Her hair was strewn with straw and manure, as if she had just emerged from the stables. It was January, but she wore a pair of sandals and no socks, and a torn skirt. Her blouse had no buttons. She held her decollatage with one hand to preserve her modesty.

She looked like a Gypsy. Everything on her was black—her hair, eyes, complexion. It was all the darker for not having been washed for a very long time.

Eventually Ilona spit the lump of paper into the wastebin. She answered in quite good German, "They cut off my father's balls. And my grandfather's. They cut my mother's breasts off, as well as my grandmother's. Then they threaded a line between two lamp posts and hung the whole lot there like so much dirty linen."

"Who are they?" I asked.

"Don't you know what's going on?" She looked quite astonished.

I answered truthfully. "Wherever I go I think only of Blondie."

Instead of being in any way interested in who Blondie might be, she nailed me with her gaze, doubtlessly hoping to discover which side of the ideological fence I'm on. I kept my cool. As Blondie lives in America, she is not in the least interested in what's going on in Hungary. That's why I prefer to mind my own business.

According to what I heard from Ilona, not a single stone was left unturned in Budapest. And all this in the name of restoring a fairer degree of social order. Described in vivid red or non-red colours, first of all the Reds were hanging the Non-Reds. Then the Non-Reds were hanging the Reds including Ilona's parents and grandparents. She would have met the same fate, had she not suddenly realized that she had plenty of time ahead of her before it came to dying. So she grabbed her father's beloved violin (he used to play the Internationale on it with a wild passion) and didn't stop until she arrived in Austria.

It was the middle of winter and Ilona told me all this on the streets of Vienna. I didn't know what to do. If I left, who knew what would happen to her?

She found the solution herself. She wrapped up her account of the dramatic events with the words, "And so I'm going round in circles here, without my senses and without any aim whatsoever. Torn away from my own proletarian roots. I'm reduced to chewing on a greasy piece of capitalist paper so as not to die of hunger. Sometimes I play the violin to remind myself of my father's revolutionary ideals and to keep myself sane. And so I'm asking you straight, will you marry me?"

"How urgent is it?" I asked.

"If we can't manage today, then tomorrow," replied Ilona.

Before I could recover my poise, she threw her arms round my neck like some marriage-crazy girl—to let the whole world see that it's a *fait accompli*.

"Alright, Ilona," I agreed. "I will marry you but I cannot guarantee how long our marriage will last."

"Why Harley, for God's sake?" she asked.

"Because my true intention is to marry Blondie."

"Doesn't matter," she replied. "I'll take it as it comes. Better one bird in the hand than two in the bush, eh?"

Ilona was 23 years old. I was almost eighteen. That explains why after our becoming engaged next to the garbage can, she had the greater overall say in everything that followed. I more or less only existed to fulfil her pious wishes. My first task was to stand on the street corner with an open violin case at my feet and to tell people that we were orphans abandoned by one and all. She pulled out her violin. It looks like that same precious Stradivarius, on which Paganini himself played. She struck up a fiery gypsy tune.

I didn't understand what happened to me. I couldn't keep my eyes off her. When she tilted her head to one side in order to put her very soul into the heart-rending melody, I said to myself: "Now is high time to make the change from innocent youth into full-grown man."

My fiancée finished playing with a brilliant staccato. We counted five schillings in the violin case. Not too bad for a start. The Viennese walked by, dressed in warm overcoats. We were shivering, almost naked. Gesturing towards the spire of the nearby church, Ilona accidentally disturbed a flock of birds. They began to circle above our heads. She suggested we consult a priest about our future together.

The moment I banged the knocker against the heavy church door, Bertolt opened up to us. He looked like God himself. His straw hair was as curly as a sheep's. A pair of golden-rimmed glasses sat on the tip of his red nose. His angelic chubby cheeks were the colour of ripe peaches. Under his chin hung another chin. His meaty lips were covered in grease, as if he had just got up from a table buckling under the weight of the food laden on it.

When my bride-to-be explained why we had come, he blessed us with the sign of the cross. Then his white, soft hands beckoned us to follow him inside. As Ilona and I marched through the windowless corridor to the presbytery kitchen, we held each other round the waist. We breathed in the heavenly smells. Bertolt informed us that we came just in time. Rosa had not yet cleared the table.

At the very instant we sat down, filled with the hunger of wolves, the cook began waiting on us. To start she served something that looked and tasted like pheasant *nach Jägerart*. This was followed by a seafood speciality cooked in wine. It was in the shape of a twelve-pointed star. As for the main course, Rosa referred to it as *der göttliche Leckerbissen*. In fact it's a Wiener Schnitzel cooked until golden. A full bowl of potato salad sat on the table. Ilona had a second helping. After a small pause, a Sacher torte completed the feast. We washed it down with a cup of coffee topped with whipped cream.

A cuckoo clock ticked above our heads. Bertolt, sitting opposite us, did not utter a sound. He was happy to watch as we enjoyed the food. When Ilona swallowed and licked her lips, the man of God swallowed and licked his chops simultaneously. Since we had absolutely no time to say grace before the meal, we prayed out of politeness as soon as we polished everything from the plates.

In the meantime Rosa ran a bath. My future wife got in first. Rosa scrubbed her back. Then it was my turn. I climbed into the fragrance-filled water. I could hear Ilona behind the door begging to be allowed to come in and soap me all over. Rosa reprimanded her, "Plenty comes to he who waits." After the bath we followed her in our bathrobes into a huge room. A heavy chandelier hung from the high ceiling. A blue rug lay on the cracked parquet flooring. By the window Bertolt awaited us in an armchair. Through the window one could clearly see into the snow-covered gardens beyond. The air in the room was saturated with the scent of myrrh.

On a softly cushioned sofa we sat down facing Bertolt. We must have made an interesting sight, with our knees huddled together and showing from under the bathrobes. Even after her bath, Ilona's skin did not look much lighter. It was quite obvious we were made from different dough.

Ilona asked, "How long will it be before you marry us, Holy Father?"

"It's difficult to say," he replied. "Maybe a month, maybe three."

"Three months!" My future bride almost had a heart attack.

Bertolt smiled benevolently. "My impatient little lamb. Don't jump into water before you know how to swim."

Ilona, used to plain speaking from birth, explained indignantly to God's representative, "I know how to swim, Father. And I will teach Harley here tonight. Besides I'm in a hurry. If at any time Harley happens upon Blondie, he'll dump me. And so, you see, I don't expect to have to wait more than a week. Of course, I hope that God in heaven will turn a blind eye to our doings. For it is my intention to start a family with Harley long before you give us your blessings here on earth. What do you think, my good Mr Bertolt?"

"My dear girl. The Lord above is merciful. But, as far as the Vatican is concerned, down here matters are not so simple."

"Dear Christ. And whom do you serve... Bertolt?"

"God is almighty." Bertolt hung his head humbly.

Ilona sighed with visible relief. She jabbed me with her elbow. "You see, Harley. What did I tell you? If you really want something, go after it and don't look either left or right. In the end you will get it."

Meanwhile Rosa brought a carafe of red wine. As soon as Bertolt refreshed his lips, he urged us to confess everything that might be troubling us, without fear of God. If we have sinned, he will forgive us on the spot.

Ilona didn't need to be asked twice. When she recounted her revolutionary experiences, i.e., how they castrated both her father and grandfather, Bertolt started to fidget. Even God can get shaken up, you see. My wife-to-be didn't really believe in Him. However, should the ecclesiatical hierarchy be interested, Jesus was actually the first Marxist. He took from the rich and gave to the poor. That aside, she was glad to have escaped from Hungary. Here in Vienna one could find free, in garbage cans, things that would cost the earth in Budapest shops. Besides, there was no one left there. Here, on the other hand, she found me. And so she fulfilled her life's dream. It had always been her dream to marry someone who could not swim.

With these words my fiancée nudged me with her knee, hinting that it was my turn. And also apparently that I should make it brief.

I felt in top form. I was on my third glass of that red nectar. I believed I should explain why I think I'm a Jew who never knew his parents (without even broaching the subject of how I came to be called Harley Davidson) but I thought it would definitely be too long a story.

And so I began by saying how I was *really* only born last summer immediately after that memorable first meeting with Blondie in Rotenturmstrasse. I make my living by working in hotels, I continued. That's in case Blondie should happen to make a reservation in one of them. I would be the bell boy riding in the elevator with her. The rest is up to people's imagination. And if this doesn't come off, I plan on becoming a professional drummer, in some big American band. Like Artie Shaw's or Glenn Miller's (even though Glenn Miller's now plays without Glenn Miller). And ideally I would be drumming in a band backing Blondie's singing. I can foresee a long tour (let's say nine months, all the way across South America), during which time we would get so well acquainted (and also so used to one another) that on our triumphant return to California (where Blondie currently resides) we would be quite unable to live without each other. One would simply not be able to take a single step outside without the other—we would be tied by a bond of relentless love. So Blondie would sing and I would drum. And we would continue this most wonderful life until death did us part. And death would, I suppose, come one day, one hour and one second to both of us (if for example our touring coach, God forbid, fell into a fjord somewhere in Norway), whereafter they would bury us together in one coffin. I emphasize—*together.*

Somewhere in the middle of my endless eulogy Bertold's eyelids closed. I could hear the contented breathing of his sleep. Ilona obviously had enough of Blondie, which she promptly made clear by passionately biting into the lobe of my right ear. Blondie was probably floating before her eyes like a slice of Hungarian salami. So while the priest snores, she sighed with longing and I cried out in pain. Rosa, watching through the door, concluded that enough is enough.

She led us on tiptoe up to our bedroom on the second floor. Wishing us all the best, she left us there. After all the inhumane strife we had been through, we should sleep the sleep of angels.

There followed a swimming lesson which would even make the stone statue of Saint Boniface learn how to do the breaststroke. When I began to drown (which was quite often), Ilona pulled me out by my hair. When she got tired (which was very rarely), I took the initiative and showed her what I have learned. In the final analysis I reckoned that my inexperience was actually an advantage. More often than not I just followed my intuition for self-preservation. It seemed that my natural instinct to stay alive excited Ilona more than the performance of some great expert who can easily master any given swimming style.

Beyond the windows dusk was falling. We made love in that fragrant bedroom with its soft mattresses, featherdowns and fluffy pillows as if there was no tomorrow.

From time to time the whole room lit up. Bertolt came to the bedside looking for all the world as if he had a halo around his head. "So how are you getting on with your swimming, boys and girls?" he enquired.

And breathlessly Ilona shouted, "Communism is sex!"

"Don't you need a lifebelt?" the man of God looked worried.

"Revolution, electrification, orgasm!" thundered my boisterous Hungarian.

"The Lord Our Shepherd is looking over you, my little lamb," Bertolt reprimanded her.

"God is Lenin," retorted my red animal.

I woke up in the morning to soft piano music drifting up from somewhere on the ground floor. Ilona was sleeping on my left. On my right side Rosa was bending over me. She held a plate of freshly baked apple strudel and a pot of steaming coffee. Before I took my first bite I realized that I was no longer the Harley Davidson I used to be. I had encountered love in a form that had previously remained concealed from me. I saw the dark side of the moon. And I loved Blondie all the more. I knew now what was in store for us.

Bertolt married us at the beginning of April. Almost on his knees he begged us not to leave the presbytery yet. He had apparently become accustomed to our pleasant presence. He insisted that the silence and emptiness in the room upstairs would be unbearable both for him and Rosa. Ilona and I stayed another fortnight. Then we had to go out in to the world. In a small hotel both of us found work in exchange for a room, board and a few schillings of pay.

One evening as we sat down tired at our bare table, Ilona saw fit to announce, "I'm pregnant. It will be a girl."

"How do you know it will be a girl?" I wondered.

"A mother's sixth sense," she said. "We shall call her Sandor."

"But that's a boy's name," I couldn't help saying.

"Correct. Sandor, after my father and my grandfather."

I shook my head. But all to no avail. Ilona's logic was based on an ideology more distant to me than the nearest galaxy.

Eight months later, the day Sandor was born, I sent a telegram to Blondie somewhere in the States informing her how glad I was that it's a girl, even though she would bear the name of a Hungarian boy.

14

So Melvin has been looking for me. He needs to speak to me urgently, though *it's not terribly urgent.* I think the sentence formulation speaks for itself. It clearly testifies to the mentality of its creator. If Melvin had left a normal message with Jacques, such as that he would very much like to discuss something with me—period—without the *it's not terribly urgent* bit, it would have looked, quite logically, that when we run into one another by chance, I should remind him that he had something important to tell me. One could call this a gentleman's agreement requiring no more than a handshake. Enough in itself.

However, the pair of us could never shake hands on anything. It's as simple as that. We never agree on any matter. It seems people usually carry whatever soundness of mindthey have from childhood through into adulthood, at which time their mental and physical personalities take final shape. In my opinion, Hercules simply grew big too quickly. His brain was simply unable to keep pace with his body. To this day it's still trying to catch up. I have my doubts, though, as to whether it will ever make it. The worst of it is that I have to fill my mind with Melvin at a time when I have very different worries. I could leave it till later. Why bother? But deep down I have an inkling that I cannot allow myself such a luxury. If I don't take care of this matter immediately, I could end up having to pay for it later. Later means—when my sweet little Blondie gets ensconced in room 403.

I begin from the top of the building, on the fourth floor. I'm betting I'll find him snoring away in one of the rooms. I try little Brazil. I listen out for the sound of our "great" gardener walking around with his watering can. Not a twiglet cracks.

The last time I ran across Melvin was about an hour ago. That was when he wanted to kill me, if you please. If he wants to talk to me about his tool box, so be it. I'm at his disposal. I will tell him straight that it was I who tripped over it and turned it upside down. The moment I see him, I'll tell him about my wrestle fight with hairy Benny and all that. And how I was convinced it was he—Melvin—who put me in that Nelson. I'll spill the beans in my own interest. I refuse to spend the rest of the day worrying about which corner he's going to jump out from and scream at me like some kind of monster, "Ha! I've got you... Harley!" A typical practical joke á la Melvin. Why doesn't he just go to hell?

The door to Blondie's room is slightly ajar. In the heat of his unsuccessful pursuit, Melvin failed to close it. That much is obvious. I peer inside. All I can see are the pillows scattered over my Darling's bed. No Melvin and no tool box. So I continue searching systematically. Next door, in room 402, the impression I get is much the same. The door is half-way open.

But inside, the situation I behold is somewhat different. Diametrically so, in fact. Matt Jackson is standing by the window with his dog. They are both looking at something outside. Benny's front paws are propped against the window sill. His tail is wagging. He is quite a beast. If I ignore the tail, he looks from behind like a big black bear.

Initially, I wonder what exactly Matt Jackson could be doing at the window. Being blind, he can't see a damn thing. But soon all becomes clear. "Come on, Benny, what the hell are we looking at?" he urges the dog impatiently. He repeats the question several times, tugging at the dog's collar. "Out with it, you idiot!" But then he corrects himself. "Tell me, my dear little big dog with such clever eyes. I'll give you a sausage. Or would you rather a fishstick?"

Incredible debate. Debate! What am I talking about? It's unilateral pressure on the poor animal. Cruelty.

"You're not gonna let me go crazy standing by the window without telling me what's going on out there... Something wonderful no doubt, you nitwit!" Matt is becoming more and more agitated. In the end the dog gets bored. He barks three times. Jackson reacts enthusiastically, "Really? You're not kidding? She is standing on the balcony completely naked, lovely, hale and hearty?" Benny reduces the number of barks to two and a half. He prods his master in the ribs with his muzzle. "I understand, lovely, hale and hearty, but wearing a negligée. But that's not bad either. Which floor, Benny? Hurry, hurry, before our piece of flesh disappears!" The shaggy beast barks five times and pokes Matt in the ribs twice more. "Really? Eleventh? What color is her hair? Well? Good doggie!" Benny licks his hand. "What? Red like a fox? That's wonderful! Exactly my type!" the blind man exults.

From where I am standing by the door, the best view I can get is of their fluffed up backs. I sprint back into Blondie's room. Her windows are facing north-west, just like Jackson's window. I focus my gaze diagonally upwards. I can't believe my eyes. On the eleventh-floor balcony of the condo opposite the Royal Arms, which looks like a shack cowering in its shadow, there really is a plump redhead in a negligée exposed for all the world to admire. And, in a show of not seeming idle, she pretends to be feeding popcorn to the seagulls gliding by.

I hurry back. Matt Jackson is in the middle of enquiring of his faithful friend, "What about her breasts? Big, pointed, irresistible?" Benny barks three times. Then he gently bites into his master's leg. "Ouch... you bastard! You're joking? Seriously? You've measured them twice and each time they were 38B?"

I stare at the pair of them in astonishment. This really is crazy. The dog and his master are trembling with excitement. What's more, Benny dribbles. Suddenly he lets out a hostile growl. That's when he picks up my scent. Immediately Matt asks, "Is there someone who's no business being here, Benny?" After three barks Benny makes a throaty sound, rather like a motorcycle with a perforated exhaust driving off.

The blind man states, "Look, Harley Davidson. Would you please leave us alone? The gardening conference is not until tomorrow morning. Understand? What we do in our leisure time is none of your or anyone else's business."

"How can you tell who you are talking with if you're differently sighted?" I cannot refrain from asking.

"What do I have Benny for?" Matt snaps back. "He can see around corners. As a puppy, he could even see through walls. But now he's too old for such things. What do you say to that, Benny, you incredible old pooch? That when you were a pup, you had eyes up your arsehole. Isn't that so?"

Benny, something of a cross between a great big Newfoundland and a collie, licks his master's hand twice in response. Then he barks one and a half times. Finally he utters an extended growl. Jackson interprets obligingly. "Someone called Melvin was looking for you. But apparently it's not that urgent."

Of course. In a short while everybody and their mother will be talking about how Melvin is looking for me all over. He's even plagued poor Jackson with his problem, picking his brains as to whether or not he's seen me.

On finding out that it's a blind person he was pumping, he'd immediately tried to depict the situation in words. Down to the most trivial detail. For instance, he gave a full explanation of who he, Melvin, is, and what he's doing in the hotel, etc. He divulged *confidentially* to Matt that the person he is looking for carries the same name as that most famous of all motorbikes. He tapped his forehead with his index finger (which caused Benny to react), by which he wished to say that Harley Davidson is by no means as famous as that most famous motorcycle, but rather that he went funny in the head during the goddamn war. Which is quite logical.

He can certainly talk! He has his fixed theory. After all, there are a great number of wretched souls like myself, wandering across North America. Quite frankly, we all have a screw loose. It's as clear as the sun in the sky. No one had explained to us whywe should go out and kill our fellow men. And then he started to involve his own *goodself* in this yarn of his. He said that he's a peace-loving human being. He wouldn't hurt a fly. Even if it was the last fly in the world.

What a load of baloney. I could just as easily explain to Matt that I couldn't possibly have gone mad, because I knew perfectly well what sort of cause I was fighting for. If for nothing else, then at least I was fighting for Blondie—and for everything she means to me. To put it simply, I was fighting for the perfect ideal. For the belief in undying love, which ignites me by its very existence.

But why should I bother? I couldn't care less. And so I thank Matt for the message. I say goodbye to both—master and dog—respectfully, like I would to a V.I.P. I behave extremely diplomatically. I tell Benny to inform his master that I am leaving. This animal doesn't behave like some silly castrated poodle. As it happens, he knows full well that, although Jackson is blind, he can probably hear better than him, an old dog. He therefore doesn't feel it necessary to bark even once.

On the way to the staircase I shout into the jungle, "Melvin, Melvin!" both to make sure he isn't there and for the hell of it. Perhaps he's asleep in there somewhere. My voice would certainly call him back from the dead. I listen, just in case. Wasted effort.

All this is beginning to annoy me. In fact, so angry do I become, that, if I was holding a grenade with its pin removed, I would chuck it right into the heart of the jungle. But I haven't held a grenade in my hand in a donkey's lifetime.

I wouldn't have enough strength to pull out the pin in any case. I feel completely debilitated. It's probably caused by my recent lack of appetite. Even Amanda is telling me to pull myself together, to have at least one little morsel of the elaborate meal she has prepared for me. Otherwise I shall end up as thin as a rake and Blondie will not recognize me.

Well, she's probably right. Except that Blondie could not recognize me whether I was fat or thin in any event. She's never seen me in her life. But be that as it may.

What follows only confirms what a sorry sight I have become. Instead of descending majestically to the floor below like a man, respected by all, proud and sure of himself, I fall flat on my face and down the staircase like a rotten pear. Or a pumpkin. Take your pick. What else can I tell you? As I end up, on all fours, on the third-floor landing, I can hear the sound of someone whistling. I'm on the right track. If there's one person here in this building who's constantly whistling, it's Melvin. The sound is wafting from somewhere around the corner.

I crouch down. Just to be sure. I hold my breath. Somehow I want to categorize what it is I'm hearing—to classify it somewhere in my brain. The analysis of a whistled melody is a most important lead. It tells unfailingly of the mood the whistling person is in.

I can't believe my ears. It's Mozart's *Eine kleine Nachtmusik*. I don't know what to think next. Even if he tried, Melvin lacks the basic prerequisites for being able to interpret real classical music. European culture is as distant to him as the Moon. But he can imitate anything. For example, Gershwin. It's all in order to set a trap for me. My intuition tells me to be extra careful. Don't be surprised by anything. That's the first rule. As I know from my vast reservoir of experience, attack is the best form of defence.

I don't delay for another second. I leap around the corner, heedless of danger, and shout, "Ha! Here you are! What was it you wanted... Melvin!"

15

Mr. Hornsby nearly falls off his chair. He is sitting in the corridor next to the door of his room. A mini transistor radio dangles from around his neck. From it can be heard the strains of *Eine kleine Nachtmusik*. The magical sound of a flute reverberates up and down the corridor. Without a doubt it serves as the background accompaniment for his hygienic endeavor—soaking his feet in a washbowl.

I have really screwed it up. My sudden counterattack turns into a personal fiasco of considerable proportions. In fright Hornsby drops his book into the bowl. A couple of pages are completely soaked in water. I apologize profusely. I wave the book in the air to dry it. I'm trying to repair the damage I've caused.

I know Hornsby from Jacques' tales. Together they've shared some incoherent, lengthy discussions, evidently of a philosophical nature. As I can see for myself, this diminutive man is an avid reader. And, according to Jacques, an indefatigable walker. He checked into the Royal Arms three days ago. In that time he's managed to explore every single brick building in every corner of this city, from east to west and north to south. He charts his way by the sun. If ever it's hidden behind clouds, he uses a compass. He has contempt for anything on wheels. Even bicycles. Cars, planes and trains are for wimps. According to him the only way to see North America is on foot. And, so far, he has already marched half-a-dozen times around the Earth. Now he's doing it for the seventh time.

"My God, what are you doing out here?" I wonder.

"Something inside the room smells real bad," he complains. "You can't breathe properly in there."

"What could possibly smell so bad in there?" I reply. "Our chambermaid Ella gives the room a thorough cleaning every day."

He holds his nostrils. "Ugh! Yuck!" he mumbles in disgust.

I feel compelled to investigate. I start going round and round, from the bedroom to the bathroom and back again. Through my nostrils I take deep lungfuls of air. Something really does stink in here. What if that huge propane tank is leaking? They placed it across the road, opposite the hotel. And, just recently, Ella had to kill three mice here with her dust pan. Maybe there was a fourth one, which got away. Maybe it went to hide in Hornsby's bed. Yes, that's it. It died there of either hunger or fright. I lift the pillow and the mystery is solved.

"Your socks are what stink," I announce. I stick a paper bag under his nose. It's full to overflowing. He shoved all his dirty socks in without washing them. And they reek accordingly.

He sniffs them. "That figures," he agrees. "I've no wife, that's why. If I had one, it would be different. My laundry would be ironed. My dinner would be ready on the table. And a little sex from time to time would not go amiss. Do you know anyone?"

I don't quite know what he means. "For one night or permanently?" I try to find out.

"What if I only gave it a try until morning?" he muses. "And then we shall see."

I start to advise him to look in the telephone directory. Under Escort Services he might find what he's looking for. Then I visualize the dames of easy virtue streaming in. What if one of them, as if *by accident*, even enters room 403—just when Blondie and I are holding hands? That would be all I needed—my Angel thinking that some tart is eager for her turn.

"I will think about it," I tell him.

"What about yourself?" He catches me off guard.

Instead of attempting to satisfy his curiosity by telling him about my relationship with Amanda I blurt out: "Blondie is coming today."

"Blondie?" Hornsby repeats the word enthusiastically. "That's wonderful, is it not?"

"She will be here around dinner time," I put it more precisely.

"You don't say," he replies.

Even I myself don't understand why I'm talking about such sacred things with a man I've only known for a few minutes. But I can't help it. Impatience is steaming up in me like inside a pressure cooker. I'm emotionally drained. I feel the need to cry on someone's shoulder. To open the valve, as they say. Amanda is not on hand. Melvin could not even be considered for such an onerous task. Jacques would no doubt interpret it in his own idiosyncratic way. And the Boss is in Montreal. That only leaves Benny. But I doubt if letting him lick my face with his rough tongue would help much.

The simple fact is that Hornsby, at first sight, inspires confidence. One only has to look at him to know he is a nice guy. He is balancing on the edge of a chair with a full rucksack on his back. A red baseball cap sits lopsided on his head. Its surface is completely pierced through with a display of shining badges. A stick, which he obviously uses as a walking aid, hangs on the backrest of the chair like the pendulum of a clock that has stopped ticking. However, his most touching features are those spindly little legs. They stick out from the washbowl like two broken toothpicks. His thighs, which look like a frog's, are lost inside the ample dimensions of his shorts. I'm only guessing, but I reckon those high, lace-up shoes under the chair weigh more than their owner. But what really inspires confidence are Hornsby's blue guileless eyes. They're enough to make anyone want to confide in him, even to go so far as telling him those things he needn't know.

"So you know her?" I ask.

"Look," he replies. "Let's be clear about one thing first. Didn't Blondie commit suicide?"

"That was Marilyn Monroe," I say. "My Blondie continues to breathe like no one else does. In such a way as to make the grass bend. Sometimes even the trees. And whatever she breathes out.... I breathe in. We practically breathe in unison. It's one complete cycle. You understand?"

"I see," Hornsby declares. "I also lived through such a drama some time ago. It was in the days when they didn't speak much in films. Her name was Rosemary Goldstücker. I think Charlie Chaplin himself brought her over from Germany to Hollywood. Her biggest role was in The Swing. Her hair was the colour of tar. Her eyes were like charcoal. My God... she could breathe! Unfortunately she broke her neck. She was young. So very young. She fell off a horse on the coastal path near Morro Bay."

"Where is Morro Bay?" I ask politely.

"Oh. On the Pacific Coast." He begins paddling with his feet in the water. "Is your pretty blonde coming with a friend by any chance?"

"I doubt that very much," I reply courteously. At this moment it crosses my mind that the old man could well be a bit senile.

"Doesn't matter," he replies cheerfully. "We shall see. But one thing is sure. You can't hurry with sex. I need at least four hours to get ready for it. And the same afterwards. Before I can get myself together, the rooster is already crowing beneath the window. And that's when I just happen to find myself on my travels in a barn with the unmarried daughter of some farmer, who, apart from rearing cattle, also keeps chickens. It can't be helped. At my age, the signals going into the brain only move at a snail's pace. Oh my! Once they used to arrive with the speed of lightning. Sex is a real science. That much is pretty obvious. And if the worst comes to the worst, well, maybe I'll run into some *mademoiselle* down in Quebec, which is my next port of call. Or in New Brunswick. From there I shall head slowly south. Through Maine, Cape Cod, Rhode Island, all the way down to Florida. At least I'll get warm there. I think I'll skip Arizona, however. Originally I had planned on going there because of the cacti. But in Mexico they are more plentiful than potatoes. So it all boils down to much the same thing. You know, I've just thought of something. Do you think I will be able to manage in Quebec speaking only English?"

"Sometimes yes, sometimes no." I reply.

"Damn," he swears. "A person can't even make himself understood in North America. Should an opportunity regarding sex present itself, I wouldn't even know how to respond to it in French."

"Don't worry," I try to calm him. "That's an international matter."

"How do you mean?" he asks.

"That you don't need words."

"I see." He nods his head. "I shall mime it with my hands. Excellent idea." He lifts his feet from the washbowl. They look awful. They need at least six bandaids. I offer to bring him some from Jacques at reception. He won't hear of it. Blisters dry best when exposed to the circulation of the air. Suddenly he remembers, "Someone called Melvin just went by carrying a big box. He was looking for Harley. Is that you, by any chance?"

I nod in agreement. "Harley Davidson."

"You're not kidding. Harley Davidson... like that famous motorbike?"

"Fate wanted it that way."

"Beautiful name! I would change mine for yours right now. Arnold Hornsby means nothing to anybody. But hold on. What do you mean by... fate wanted it that way?"

"That would be rather a long story."

"I'm not hurrying anywhere."

"I, on the other hand, don't know whether I'm on my head or my heels."

"Do you own this here?"

"What, this shack?" I pretend to look offended. "What do you take me for? I'm a mere employee here. General lackey. But there are advantages to working in hotels. One of them is that sooner or later the guests will go to bed. And then I have the whole night to myself."

"And what do you do then?"

"Something that Jack London used to do."

"You write horror stories!"

"And sometimes also poems."

Arnold Hornsby nearly falls off his chair for the second time. "How amazing! I read everywhere I go. And when I'm not going anywhere, I read even more. What are you working on at the moment, Harley?"

"It takes place in Vietnam."

"Jesus, my boy! I fought in Korea!"

There are tears in his eyes. He stands up in the washbowl. We embrace each other like a father and his long-lost son, as if we had already buried one another years back yet suddenly met up again. Hornsby is crying on my shoulder and I his. We can't stop. Arnold insists I should call him Arnie. Then he asks me whether I *had to* kill anyone in Vietnam. When I answer that I did have to once, in the jungle, in self-defence, he admits that he, Arnie, also *had to* kill once, in a rice paddy. Also in self-defence. That's why, when he has a choice, he prefers to walk. Apparently as soon as he stops walking, the cadaver begins swimming through the water before him. Face up.

I tell him, "I've one more chapter to write."

"So why aren't you writing it?"

"I can't move from the spot where I am."

"How come?" he wonders.

"Writer's block."

"Where did you get stuck?"

"On the edge of the jungle."

"Seriously? And what are you doing there?"

"I'm pulling my hair out."

"You're kidding. What happened?"

"They kidnapped Blondie and took her in there!"

Hornsby is pacing up and down on the carpet, drying his feet. He wants to know everything from Adam on. Who are *they?* What is Blondie doing in Vietnam? Why did I join the army? And so on.

At length I begin with the first chapter. How Pat Bell, the actor-presenter (renowned mostly for playing corrupted bankers or drug pushers) called Blondie in Italy on Monday (she's making her penultimate movie in Sicily – "My Pony Tony"). Pat went down on bended knee and begged Blondie to join his travelling troupe. Around Christmas she would fly to Saigon to cheer the GIs. Tuesday goes past. Then Wednesday. It's Thursday already. Blondie calls Pat in Salt Lake City (where he is in the middle of making his forty-fourth film) and asks for the details. For instance she is extremely interested in the total length of the program he's putting on, and how much time she would have for changing between the individual scenes. When Pat assures her that she would have at least five minutes, she agrees to take part without further ado.

At this point Arnie Hornsby stops right in front of me. He stares at me incredulously. "Harley, Harley. What are you babbling about for godsake? Is this what you call horror Jack London style? Have you never read the blood-curdling story Jerry From The Islands?"

I admit to Arnie that I haven't. I add that at the very first opportunity I will leaf through it. Just to be sure not to stir him up again, I omit the following nine chapters (Blondie has meanwhile fallen in love with Count Scarletti in Italy—on page sixty eight—and, all gray, he commits suicide by popping a cyanide capsule). I throw him straight in to the main whirl of events that occur after Pat Bell and Blondie and a couple of comedians (they look like Mary Tyler Moore and Dick Van Dyke) land in Saigon in December. That same evening, Blondie, Pat and the already mentioned pair of clowns visit a famous watering hole. They spend an agreeable evening together. No one would suspect that Blondie will never even complete her rendition of "Rudolph the Red Nose Reindeer" the following day on account of the stage collapsing under her. And that is when she disappears.

Arnie discovers that while all the others (including the generals) are running around like headless chickens in panic, I set out on the kidnappers' tracks without delay. I am propelled forward by my love for Blondie. I am also fully aware of the fact that without my Angel there is no life—neither in heaven nor on earth. The crisis deepens about three miles further on. Then I find out (by suddenly turning round) that I'm not quite alone in my pursuit. Someone called Wayne Piscopo from Nebraska is following in my footsteps. It turns out that he is the only son of elderly parents who are relying on him to return home to the farm as soon as he's done his patriotic duty. When I make a cautious enquiry as to what he's after, he replies without any mincing of his words that it's Blondie. And when I ask, with even greater circumspection, why it should be Blondie, he snaps back saying that he's been in love with her ever since he was nine years old. He insists it would be impossible to contemplate any future existence down on that farm in his native Nebraska without her.

His Blondie mania rather complicates matters. When I suggest he should try forgetting all about her, I am informed that he has released the safety catch on his machine gun. That's all I need. But there's nothing I can do. I pray to God, hoping that He will take up my cause. For the time being I must pretend that we are *both in it together.* I remark that it is of the utmost importance for him to maintain his sanity, in case Blondie should think we are both crazy. This is supposed to calm him down. By now we have reached the jungle. We pause for breath. I beckon for Wayne to lead the way. But he motions with his hand that he wants me to go first. So we are standing there bowing to one another. Complete theater. We are simply playing on each other's nerves.

Hornsby shakes his head. "Harley, I beg you. Never go into the jungle. Even if Blondie is standing behind the very first tree. It's all a trap. As soon as you stick your head in there, the Commies will lop it off with a machete. Or else you might fall into a pit with wild beasts at the bottom. You know what? You need a real Vietnamese guide to get through the jungle. A professional who knows it like the back of his hand.

And you are very lucky. By coincidence I know one of them personally. Let me introduce him to you. His name is Hua Kua Pooh."

"Who is he?" I enquire.

"Something like Winnie the Pooh. But in different colors. Remember? A.A. Milne? The famous writer? But this Pooh is also Hua Kua. Well and truly, he is a great friend of the Americans. Born in the jungle. But his father got a job at the Environment Protection Agency in Washington. Believe me, I haven't met a better guide anywhere."

"But how will I find him?" I become interested.

"Quite simple," replies Arnie. "You will hoot into the jungle like a snow owl. Like this." He makes a mouthpiece from the palms of his hands. Then he hoots beautifully, "Too-wit-too-woo. Try it, Harley."

"Too-wit-too-woo." I do my best.

I would have expected that after this owl-hooting, Melvin might appear on the corridor. But no such thing. Nevertheless I thank Hornsby for his advice. I tell him, "You're an incredible old man."

And I set out to descend one flight of stairs. As I make for the staircase, Arnie calls after me, "Let me know how you got on. If needed, I can stay another week. As you know, I'm not hurrying anywhere."

16

I glide along the second-floor corridor. Behind the door to 204 the tireless couple of newlyweds from Berlin, Vermont are continuing with their heavy breathing. No trace of Melvin. I descend to the ground floor by the back staircase. Just as well. Half-way down I can hear the monotonous sound of sawing. Melvin is in the basement. He has a small workshop there for emergency repairs. I find him bent over a vise, in whose jaws is gripped a rusty nail. For a reason known only to Melvin he is endeavouring to file its head off. As usual, his tongue is sticking out as if to assist him in his strenuous activities.

When he sees me he pulls the tongue back into his mouth and says. "Yabba-Dabba-Doo! I thought I would never see you again."

"What's the matter?" I say.

"Don't ask." He walks to a wall covered with tools. There he changes the medium-sized file for the biggest one. Before starting to file with it, he spits on both sides of the tool. "I have very bad news for you."

"What news, Melvin?"

"Terrible, Harley. You won't believe it."

He releases the vise and turns the rusty nail 180 degrees. Then he tightens it again. When he prepares to put the spit-covered file against the half-cut head, I breathe in hard, "Melvin, I... I..."

He doesn't let me finish. "I know, Harley. I know exactly what you want to say. You're a good sport. Really. You want to report that it was you who kicked my toolbox over. You even made up some incredible story and told everyone how something jumped out at you from my little Brazil and grabbed you. Held you in a full Nelson and knocked you to the ground. Some crap like that. So thanks for your kindness, brother. I don't really deserve it. Honestly, I will never forget such a thing. Perhaps God will reward you somehow for your deed. The truth, unfortunately, can't be cheated. It's black and white. Either yeah—or nay. Nothing in between. Zilch. As big as Philadelphia. Geddit?"

"But it really was me, Melvin," I insist. "It happened exactly like you said. Boom, bang. Including that full Nelson."

Melvin puts an even greater effort into his filing. He releases the grip and removes the nail. He blows the filings away. Finally he looks at his great masterpiece with eyes narrowed in the light from the bulb dangling on a slim wire from the ceiling. "It could not have been you, buddy. As I know you, you would never do anything as bad as that."

"I swear I would. Do you want to bet?"

Melvin evaluates the result of his work with a satisfied whistle. "No you wouldn't, Harley. You would never rob me of fifteen dollars."

I open my eyes wide. "Someone has stolen your money?"

"Correct. I was the victim of a treacherous robbery. Underneath a little box filled with screws there was one five- and one ten-dollar bill folded four times. My toolbox upset. Money gone. I'm such a naive idealist. The moment I knock off at six o'clock I was planning to stop off at a supermarket to buy Micky something beautiful for our silver-wedding anniversary. And now I can buy her not a sweet damn thing. In the whole world you won't find a more unhappy person than me. And what's more, it'll be the ruin of my idyllic marriage. We were living together like two doves. Yes, yes, Harley. Divorce looms over my head. Speaking man to man, I'm in absolute shit. I'm seriously thinking about killing myself. I will bust my skull open with this nail. Do you realize what a tragedy this adds up to?"

"God Almighty. Have you looked everywhere?" I show some interest. Of course, a vision of Melvin opening his skull with a rusty nail is far more fascinating.

Melvin replies, "A little while ago I stripped completely naked. Like Adam in the Bible. I even looked underneath my balls, man."

Normally Melvin is a lying hyena. But this time I can believe him. He looks as if he is on the verge of a nervous breakdown. His body is shaking all over. Sweat pours off his forehead. He is as pale as a sheet. I can imagine that if his knees suddenly gave way, he would collapse on top of me like a factory chimney during demolition. I'm prepared for the worst, but suddenly I have an idea that might save the day. "I bet I know who did it, Melvin."

"Really?"

"Really. It was Benny."

"Who's Benny?"

"Matt Jackson's guide dog."

"What on earth makes you think that?"

"It happened exactly like you said. First of all he jumps at me. Then he puts me in a full Nelson. As I fall, I knock the toolbox over. I lose consciousness. And he takes advantage, the bastard."

Melvin's jaw nearly falls out of its hinges. "Are you feverish? Since when do dogs steal money?"

I pull out my last trump card. "Benny is not an ordinary dog. I swear. A little while ago he was with Jackson by the window spying on some beauty wearing nothing but a negligée. I wish you could have heard them. She was out on the balcony opposite, feeding seagulls."

He hasn't been this stunned for a long time. Only a moment ago he looked to be on the verge of screwing his head into that vise of his and now he's smiling broadly at me.

But I've already turned on my heel. I'm leaving. I hear him calling after me, "Harley! Do you remember by any chance on which balcony it was exactly?"

Of course I pretend not to hear. If he's so damn clever, let him find out for himself.

17

I head straight for the reception area to tell Jacques this latest piece of news. Well, not just one piece, but two. Nor are they really connected. Or, if they are, then it's only because both concern me. First, Mr. Hornsby promises to put me in touch with his Vietnamese jungle guide. And next I discover that someone has stolen fifteen dollars from Melvin.

The Frenchman's leg is lying on the table. It looks like a twisted pine tree trunk. Jacques is painting his toe nails red. With a small brush he dips into an even smaller bottle. So as to make better use of the time spent decorating in this way, he is humming something about a nightingale—*alouette*. Currently a popular song in France. This activity, if it achieves nothing else, at least rids the world of all its banal grayness.

I shape a mouthpiece out of the palms of my hand and hoot above his head, "Too-wit-too-woo."

"*Sacrebleu!*" He jumps up. "The irresistible call of the wild?"

"Snow owl," I confirm.

"Why a snow owl?" he asks.

I refresh his memory. "I'm standing at the edge of the jungle. You know? I have no idea what to do next. And this hooting solves everything."

He's burning with curiosity. "How, Harley?"

"Quite simply. I'm calling on an experienced guide."

"Who told you that?"

"Arnie Hornsby."

"He knows of some guide?"

"Of course. His name is Hua Kua Pooh. If I hoot three times like a snow owl, he will immediately rush out to help."

"*Mon Dieu!* Congratulations. But here you are hooting like crazy and nothing. No one's around."

"That's because *Winnie the Pooh* is not at home right now. Do you understand?"

I'm not sure if he does. Even so, he is shaking his head, as if he was giving the matter some thought. Jacques takes top place (behind Amanda, and now also after Hornsby) in a privileged group of chosen individuals—people who have some idea what it is I do at night in the Royal Arms. He is fully supportive of my creative activity, understanding that it is all part of my personal therapy. Especially since he knows what I've been through in my life. The best therapy is to commit one's chimera to paper—this is his theory—rather than to exorcise it by banging one's head against a wall.

"Listen," he says. "Have you decided yet what to do with Wayne Piscopo?"

"I shall leave it to fate," I reply resignedly.

"Don't leave anything to fate," he's trying to convince me. "Get rid of him at the very first opportunity. What is it you carry... MG42? Excellent! Let him blow his brains out while cleaning his weapon. That's it. You don't want that farmer boy from Nebraska dragging you down. *Oui*, Harley? *As-tu compris?*"

"I'll think about it," I reply. Strictly speaking, I would never have expected such advice from him considering his natural sensitivity. I am beginning to wonder whether the nail-varnish fumes he is inhaling are affecting him adversely.

"Who are you trying to rescue?" he asks. "Some peroxide-blonde spy?"

Here we go. I was right. Drugged to the eyeballs, he has managed to confuse the most basic concepts. "She's not a spy," I reply. "She's a singer. When she was singing Rudolph the Red Nose Reindeer, she fell through a hole in the stage. Try to remember, Jacques. It's not the first time you've heard this story. And she's not a peroxide blonde. On the contrary. Her hair is its natural colour. Do you understand? Beautiful. Like being dazzled by sunshine at three in the afternoon."

"I see," he sighs. "A dazzling blonde beauty!"

"Something like that," I say. "She is absolutely heavenly."

"OK. OK. *L'amour, l'amour,*" Jacques sings.

"Exactly so," I confirm.

Usually I have more luck than wisdom. But this time it's the other way round. I've already told Jacques more than enough. But not everything. And now my cautiousness is paying dividends. Take the fact, for instance, that Jacques has no idea that this fictional heroine is called Blondie. Otherwise he might put two and two together and realize that the Blondie of the jungle is the same person as the one coming here from Las Vegas. That would be the last straw. I know Jacques. He would be waiting for Blondie in front of the hotel as she steps out of her taxi. And, once inside, behind the swing doors, he would gleefully inform her that Harley Davidson (his best *ami anglais* incidentally), who is madly in love with her, is awaiting her with open arms.

I'm on tenterhooks. It's five minutes to four. Within less than four hours, I will be holding my sweetest darling in my arms. I hurry to her room. I smooth down the cover on her bed. Artistically I shake out the pillows. During my inspection of the bathroom I discover the smudges Melvin has made all over the washbasin. What's more, he's even used Blondie's Grumpy soap. He's completely washed away his lovely head. I change the water for the roses in the vase. As I put them back into the closet, I almost slip on the banana Amanda gave me.

What happened next—I don't really have a clear vision of any of it. Most probably I sat down with the banana in my hand on the edge of Blondie's bed. Everything else follows from that. My exhaustion. My state of mind. My immeasurable longing to bring an end to this thirty-three-year war of nerves by announcing our engagement. No—forget the engagement. I shall ask for Blondie's hand straight away, as soon as she appears on the doorstep.

I do vaguely remember peeling the banana. I open my mouth. Perhaps I even bite into it, but I don't remember anything. Out of the blue, the flat ceiling of Blondie's hotel room above me takes the shape of a pyramid. And the horror begins. Yes. I'm in a tent. Wayne Piscopo and I erect it on the edge of the jungle. We have to consider that our first night together will now commence. Obviously we have no other choice. We are stuck together.

The moment we lie down, Wayne falls into a baby-like slumber. The tent is so small, he is snoring with his head on my shoulder and making my arm go to sleep. What shall I do? Should I strangle him? Would he wake up before turning blue? What would his parents say? Good advice is worth its weight in gold. I stare out into the void. The rustling breeze dances across the harsh countryside. The terrifying shadows of swaying rubber trees on the tent canvas are provoking me into taking decisive action. It's nearly midnight.

Suddenly I feel the call of nature. It's my own stupid fault. After supper (liver paté on a cracker) I drank over at least a liter of stinking rainwater. My moving causes Wayne's head to drop against the hard earth with a crack. But he continues snoring away as if nothing had happened. He's probably dreaming he's back in Nebraska with his mother.

I stagger out of the tent. There is a full moon. The clouds are scudding swiftly across the sky. In the distance an occasional gunshot can be heard. Or are they grenades exploding? All of a sudden I hear Blondie's desperate call—but it's more likely (I assure myself) that this is the first sign of my insanity. With swaggering gait I head for the nearest bush to pee.

At the first step a suspicious crackling sound comes from the jungle. Before I manage to open my fly, a gigantic toad jumps out of the darkness. It's about 20 feet tall and covered in warts. Its eyes are alert. Dried mud clings to its neck. In a split second I take up a defensive posture with bayonet at the ready. But it soon becomes clear that this frog's only intention is to play innocent games with me. It flirts and disappears back into the undergrowth. From time to time it makes a lovely quacking sound. It's plainly trying to convince me that if I caught it and kissed it, it would turn into a beautiful princess.

Oh well. So I begin to hop around like a fairy-tale prince. I've never seen a bigger imbecile in my life. And I would probably still be hopping around today, had Wayne Piscopo not stopped snoring quite so suddenly. Perhaps he just turned over onto his belly, I tell myself. So I wait to see what's going to happen. Slowly but surely, I feel a bad premonition coming on—one which will soon turn into ugly reality. The sounds of a death rattle come from inside the tent. At the same time the toad disappears back into the jungle with a horrifying screech. I hurry over to Wayne Piscopo. It's too late. He is lying in a pool of blood. His head is shattered. Wayne Piscopo, from the state of Nebraska, has gone to his eternal rest.

What else is there to say? I collapse onto the ground. Sobbing. Despite all the rivalry, we have become (after a fashion) inseparable buddies. Brothers in arms, so to speak. Quite frankly, Wayne paid with his life for the crime of overestimating himself. I firmly believe that, had the pair of us stood before Blondie (posing as her saviours), and had she been forced to make a choice between us, just one look at me would be enough for her to choose. My eyes are ablaze with such immeasurable longing that I know of no other person on earth who could possibly match me.

Next morning, at dawn, the saddest of all tasks is awaiting me. I must give Wayne Piscopo a dignified burial. But I only have a small military spade. It takes a full six hours to dig a hole big enough to comfortably take all of Wayne's seven-foot body. In the end I don't even have to take his boots off. Wrapping him in the tent, I put him at the bottom of the pit like a mummy. Once I've throw a few fistfuls of earth over him, strange things begin to happen. Wayne's hand breaks through the earth like a woodworm through a piece of dry wood. It beckons to me with its index finger to follow him.

In spite of my efforts to return it to its rightful place, this restless limb continues to find its way back up. There's nothing for it but to dig Wayne out again. I unwrap the tent from round him like diapers. He behaves like an unruly baby. I feel like smacking his bottom. To be quite certain he really has snuffed it, I shake him vigorously. It looks as if he has. But don't count your chickens before they hatch. As soon as I start mummifying him again, this unbelievable guy from Nebraska opens his eyes wide. "OK, Harley," he states matter-of-factly. "As you please. Bury me. But on one condition. Tell Blondie that I will not forget her until death. Promise?"

I feel a huge surge of relief because as soon as I agree, he starts acting sensibly. And his soul looks like a little blue balloon. It rises up and up into the sky, finally disappearing from view.

18

Had it not been for the heroic deed of Kevin Dorsett, my best buddy, I would have stepped on an enemy mine some four miles north of Da-Nang—and goodbye Sweet Angel Blondie! At that very moment she would have become (though quite unaware of the fact) a young, pretty widow. Kevin would have had the grim task of ringing her doorbell in Los Angeles. Blondie would have opened. Kevin (still wearing his uniform) would have stood there clutching his military cap nervously between his fingers. A whole eternity would have gone by before he could blurt out the tragic news. Blondie, of course, would not have had the slightest idea (and this is the irony) of whom he was talking about. Yet during Kevin's account—how I, practically blown to bits, had bled to death in his arms she would have fainted.

To this day I have my suspicions that he only saved my life so that he didn't have to ring Blondie's doorbell. Every time I thank him for my salvation, he just gives a nonchalant wave of the hand. Apparently it's alright. He jumped into the fire *just like that* for the sake of a friend who had a promising career as a drummer before him. That's his standard answer. By the way, Kevin is quite mad about big swing bands. He should have become a famous conductor. He will happily engage in a lengthy discussion on the subject with anyone willing to listen. Including non-English-speaking Vietnamese. No wonder his army nickname was—Arturo Toscanini.

My friend lives close to La Guardia Airport in New York. Unlike his fellow countryman Melvin, an obstinate pacifist, Kevin volunteered to go fight. Although we have this much in common, our personal reasons for becoming GIs are completely different. I went to fight for Blondie. Kevin, on the other hand, only ran off to Vietnam because of his girlfriend—Jamie. He confided this to me when we had been buried up to our necks in mud for several hours, waiting in the jungle to see our first real action. One can't forget a day like that. It happened exactly at eight minutes past four on the morning of the sixth of July. Even though we were desperately shitting in our pants, I contrived to kill one and Arturo Toscanini two skinny Commies.

Kevin is the spitting image of Louis Armstrong—a younger edition of the true Satchmo. The problem is that Jamie has a tendency to make unpredictable demands of him. For example, during their very first meeting, she started pressing Kevin to get a proper job. He had to earn decent wages in order to cover the instalment payments on a big enough apartment for the two of them as well as *at least two* children, not to mention acquire a second-hand Buick which they will drive to Louisiana where Jamie's parents live. Before each journey she has to pop into a beauty salon to see her favourite hairdresser.

Kevin raved on and on in the jungle about the band he was going to put together. He had the jingle already: Beat Me Daddy Eight to the Bar. And he intended to marry some singer like Billie Holiday.

But it didn't happen quite like that. When he returned from Vietnam, Jamie was waiting for him at the airport with their marriage licence. Three days later they were at the altar, exchanging wedding rings. Kevin got a job in the Bronx Zoo. He took care of exotic animals. They had three children, a car that was paid for and a nicely furnished apartment. Just like Jamie always wanted.

We call each other once a month. Twice a year we visit one another. I travel to New York in the spring, my friend visits me in the fall. He always sleeps in Blondie's room. It's the same room (about 12 feet by 12 feet) that Amanda vacated shortly after I moved in with her to leave me space for all my Blondie paraphernalia. I have at least three big boxes of it. Each one is capable of holding an 18 cubic foot refrigerator.

All in all, I'm very grateful to Amanda for all her kindness, although the whole thing has led to some misunderstandings. In the beginning Amanda thought that this would be a shared archive, i.e. one for both Blondie and Raúl Ibanesios, that Spanish troubadour of hers. It took a great effort on my part to convince my partner that Blondie and Raúl Ibanesios do not belong in one room together, if for no other reason than for the immense differences in their artistic aims. Luckily for us, common sense won out. With head held high, Amanda took those few things belonging to Raúl into the bedroom and put them on her bedside table. They're still there, thank God, to this day.

Each morning Kevin assures me that he slept like a dream. No wonder. I even suspect that he is a little bit envious of *my lifestyle*. It must be crystal clear to him than I am steadfastly focused on my set goal. My love for Blondie does not diminish with the passing of the years. On the contrary— it is gradually reaching gigantic dimensions. Jamie doesn't even allow him to hang a picture of Billie Holiday in the farthest corner of his own apartment—even though Billie has been pushing up daisies for quite some time now.

The last time he called me was in March earlier this year. It was shortly after Blondie's birthday. Naturally he was very interested. "So how did the celebrations go, brother?" he asked eagerly.

"You wouldn't believe it," I began. "It was colossal. First thing in the morning I went to the florist to buy thirty-three freshly cut roses. As you know, that's one for each year that Blondie and I have known each other. Well, she still doesn't know very much about me. But that's only a question of time. Just leave it to me. So I put the vase with the bouquet in a strategic spot in the living room. So that it would stay in my line of vision in the blazing sunlight all day long. And I keep on staring at it as though bewitched. Reaching out for it with my arms. Like I'm at a seance calling up a spirit from beyond the grave. I murmur—no, whisper: *My darling, so near but yet so far!* And then it happens. The roses begin to move. It's as if someone is making their way delicately among them. Blondie's face appears in the center of this fragrant floral cascade. Quite magnificent, Kevin, believe me. Of course, you might say... it's not really Blondie who's looking at me. That it's only my imagination at play. But, my friend, this vision has such a *tangible* effect, that it matters not a damn thing that it's not really Blondie peering out at me from that floral tribute! But, after all, we did agree on one thing, remember... that true love accepts no obstacles. It can walk through a wall. What do you say?"

"Come on!" Kevin barked. "Why don't you stick to harsh reality!"

I was stunned. Kevin had never spoken sharply to me like this. Up till now we have always somehow agreed on things—understood one another. Surely, we are inseparable friends. We're more like brothers.

So, I drew my own conclusion. He's in the middle of calling long distance. All the while, standing behind his back is Jamie, pulling at his sweaty T-shirt, making signs indicating that he should make the conversation brief. It's costing a lot of hard-earned money. Don't forget they have three children. There will never be enough saved to send them all to college. Dear God, I say to myself. A war hero. What has become of him? He can't even call up his natural twin.

There was nothing for it but to keep my report to a minimum. I didn't want to ruin him financially. "Oh well. Around mid-day," I continued, "Amanda breezes in from Steinbergs like the wind. The first thing she does is to take six roses out of the vase—one for every year of our being together. I must say it rather spoils my festive mood. And what's more, I have no idea that the worst is yet to come. Amanda used to go to tango classes. Can you imagine? So all of a sudden she insists that this is the time to find out if she can still remember how to do it. How hellish. She puts Burning Nights on—the latest platinum recording by Raúl Ibanesios. Imagine her gliding through the room from one corner to the next. That's all I was waiting for—her circling around me like I was some invisible imbecile. You don't know just how much it annoys me that, although she's endowed with plenty of natural intelligence, she hasn't the good sense to realize that Blondie has a birthday *only once* a year!"

"Oh my God," Kevin wailed on the other end of the wire. "I never realized that you got a bullet in your head in that jungle!"

"Listen, Kevin," I reply. "What's the matter with you?"

"Harley," he said soothingly. "I have always been on your side. Haven't I? I always admired your boundless fantasy, appreciated your stamina. Right? But if it's going to drag on and on *forever,* it could be a sign of some kind of mental disorder. Have you ever thought about that?"

"No, I haven't."

"My God! How old are you?"

"The same age as Blondie."

"And how old is she?"

"Approximately the same age as you."

"And what's that?"

"Roughly the same age as me."

"So you see!" Kevin groaned. "Why don't you say so straight away? We have entered the second half of the century. It's downhill from now on, brother. For me, you, and even for that unfading spectre of yours. Can you understand that? We're too old for these stupid things. Believe it, brother—as Arturo Toscanini is my name!"

From what I was hearing, I judged that if anyone was going downhill, then it's definitely Kevin. I'd say he's on his way out. Even if he won't realize it, he is a mental eunuch. It's as clear as the sun in the sky. Jamie had finally managed to brainwash *my own brother.*

From the other end I heard what sounded like a herd of monkeys chasing one another. "Where are you calling from?" I asked.

"From work," he answered.

"So you are calling from the zoo," I said quizzically. "You are afraid to call your own friend from home, in case

Jamie grabs the receiver out of your hand. Eh? Congratulations, brother."

Then there was a munching sound, as if the telephone wire was being nibbled on by a camel. "I must go now," he said, suddenly subdued. "I'll call you soon."

He woke me up early in the morning of the following day and announced that he would be paying me a visit in three days. I would have to make sure that my shift at the Royal Arms finished at six. Kevin would fly in from New York at five that afternoon. We agreed that he should take a taxi to the hotel. And then we will pick up Amanda from Steinbergs in our Escort.

As it happened, I had some discussions to conduct with McCarthy in the office. When I returned to reception, the proclaimed Arturo Toscanini was already seated in an armchair in our mini-vestibule. As was his custom, he was dressed as if he were appearing in a Broadway musical. He was wearing a pale-grey suit with dark stripes. A silk orange handkerchief dangled from his breast pocket. The red-cinnabar vest was complemented by a canary-yellow tie speckled with pea-green spots. A shoe of aquamarine blue dangled on his left foot (his left leg was crossed over his right one). Its shine was greater than a mirror's. Melvin, sitting opposite him and wearing jeans fading at the knees, looked like a street vagabond in comparison. With a Havana cigar in his mouth (and both sneaker-clad feet resting on his toolbox), it didn't stop him from staring at Kevin as if he were the exotic inhabitant of some undiscovered planet.

I could immediately sense that the atmosphere prevailing under the eternally gyrating blades of the fan was not ideal. Luckily Jacques Bélanger arrived to change shifts with me. He did his best to salvage the situation. He began leafing like crazy through the French-language paper Le Droit. Finding something scandalous, he attempted to translate it into English for all presumably interested parties.

Just as Kevin got up from the armchair to embrace me with a fraternal hug, Melvin stopped him with a surprisingly intelligent question, "So you and Harley are friends?"

"That would be correct," confirmed Kevin.

"How long have you known each other?"

"Vietnam... nineteen-seventy-one."

That remark about Vietnam failed to raise Melvin's spirits. He pulled hard on his cigar and turned to face Jacques. "We're fully booked today. Isn't that so, Jack?"

But Jacques is a Frenchman, and as everyone knows, the French have loved blacks ever since Josephine Baker, decked out with bananas, infatuated all Paris. "On the contrary, Melvin, we have plenty of vacant rooms today," he replied. "We could literally accommodate two military divisions along with their general staff, at the very least."

Enraged, our Hercules' tiny head turned bluer than Kevin's shoes. At the same time he had a gut feeling that if he didn't lift anchor and disappear as fast he could, he would be set upon by two GIs, both of them boasting vast experience in dealing with a mortal enemy. And so he picked up his toolbox. Before he turned the corner he dejectedly uttered, "Excuse me boys! Yabba-Dabba-Doo! Hope I haven't insulted you with my chit-chat. I didn't mean any of it!"

19

A short while later we picked up Amanda from Steinbergs. The journey home took five minutes. In another ten we had a delectable Mexican meal on the table—crispy corn tacos filled with beans, minced meat, garlic and onions, garnished with lettuce leaves and slices of tomato, and sprinkled with salsa. This gastronomic orgy was topped with grated Cheddar cheese. Kevin was soon munching on a deadlychili. It's as hot as the hellfire of Lucifer. No wonder he wept tears of joy even as he suffered. In the same breath he both cursed and praised Amanda's culinary skills.

After dinner we retired to the living room. Cracking peanuts, we talked about Glenn Miller. Now that they've finally located the Titanic, Kevin muses, perhaps they might be able to find that crashed airplane. I explained to Amanda exactly what airplane we're talking about. Glenn Miller disappeared in it without a trace during World War II over the English Channel on a flight to Paris.

We drank Portuguese wine. Until perhaps a couple of years ago, Kevin could entertain us for hours on end. He would dream about how things were going to be once he started up his own band. Today he was lucky if he was able to buy one miserable record—and only very occasionally at that. I feel really sorry for him. The conversation turned to the zoo in the Bronx. I'm quite fond of dogs and cats, but my fondness for animals is nothing compared to Amanda's. If she could, she would go out tomorrow and buy a giraffe! Kevin's job is the perfect subject for her conversation. She is interested in everything, down to the minutest details of the animals' lives. Patiently, Kevin answered every one of her questions. He is a walking, talking encyclopedia. Then it's our canary's turn. What else? Amanda inquired whether Tiger would mate or fight if he finds himself in female company. My best friend gave her an expert opinon—they may fight but in the end, as people do, they make love, feathers flying and all.

I fell asleep like a log in my seat. I had no idea how long I'd been there. When I awoke, I didn't open my eyes straight away. I had my reasons. They weren't talking about animals anymore. Obviously they waited until they heard my deep breathing before starting on a discussion about me and Blondie.

"Jesus Christ, Amanda," I heard Kevin sigh. "She means nothing to anyone today. Jamie buys the *National Enquirer*. You know? You'd have to be very lucky to find a couple of lousy lines written about Blondie these days. Like the other week, when it said she is walking about on crutches. But, don't you think, if she had broken her leg or some such thing, Harley would have told us all about it?"

"Sure," Amanda agreed. "If she had broken her leg, he would probably break his own too. On purpose. Out of sympathy—the very same day. Believe me."

"Isn't that crazy?" asked Kevin.

"Don't ask me," replied Amanda.

"Listen, has he made any progress from his spot?"

"Not as far as I know."

"So he's still stuck at the edge of the jungle?"

"As far as I know, yes."

"My God," Kevin groaned. "Sometimes I still get pangs of guilt about having once saved his life."

Through the slits between my eyelids I observed the way Toscanini leaned over me, inspecting me, obviously counting all the new lines that have appeared on my forehead. Or how many grey hairs I now have. The closer his face got, the more distorted it became, both in height and width. Even through eyeglasses I couldn't reconcile myself optically to his ever-swelling proportions. I pretended to be having a nightmare. I wheezed. That made him shoot upright.

He continued talking to Amanda in a half-whisper, "Listen, sister. Be brave. Harley isn't alright up here. He has a screw loose. Try to make him see a doctor. Of course, it might already be too late. We've recently had problems with

Greg, our favourite gorilla. Can you imagine? We put a broad into his cage... but Greg doesn't want to co-operate."

"This doesn't seem to be Harley's problem."

"Whatever you say, Amanda. I'm only suggesting he should see a shrink. What do you reckon? How would you go about getting Greg to see a vet, if you thought there was something wrong with him?"

"I haven't the slightest idea, Kevin," replied Amanda.

"Ah yes. But I found a solution. Quite a simple one. I don't feed him for two whole days. Then I wave a banana skin in front of his face... and believe it or not, Greg follows me pretty damn quick all the way to the vet, just like a dog on a leash."

"But Harley is not Greg," objected Amanda.

"I never said that Harley is Greg. But he urgently needs to see a psychiatrist."

"He's been behaving like this ever since I met him."

"A volcano smokes and smokes and suddenly erupts."

"You know, Kevin," mused Amanda, "I think Harley was born a motorcycle. He never stops revving until he runs out of gas."

"Jesus Christ," lamented Kevin. "You think he runs on gas?"

"I guess. But I don't want him to crash."

"Dear Amanda," Kevin replied. "Where do you get your wonderful patience?"

"It's nothing to do with patience, Arturo Toscanini," whispered Amanda. "I just happen to be in love with the fool."

At first my friend stared open-mouthed at Amanda. Then he took her sleek hand into his great, bearlike paws. Before I could count to three, the pair of them were sobbing as though they were at a funeral. When the last tear was shed some moments later, there was a deathly hush. I could hear nothing apart from my own breathing. Undoubtedly this meant the time had come to wake up. I waved my arms about as if dreaming and wiggled my feet. Then I sat upright in the chair and opened my eyes wide at them. "I've just finished drumming the solo in that Bee Gees track where they're accompanied by the Harry James orchestra," I announced.

"That's fabulous, Harley!" Kevin grinned. "Did you beat with brushes or sticks?"

"First with the brushes and then with the sticks."

"Did you break any?"

"Two pairs."

"You must have been thrashing like crazy!" said Kevin admiringly.

Amanda yawned and rubbed her temples. I excused myself to go to the kitchen for a glass of water. With a finger under the tap I stood waiting for the water to get cold.

Even though Kevin was trying to speak as quietly as possible in the next room, his crackling voice sounded clearer than cow bells in mountain pastures. "Mark my words. He has become a fugitive. Most of the time he's asleep. But when he isn't, he's on permanent tenterhooks. And, what's more, he's a dreadful liar. The only solo in that Bee Gees track belongs to the tenor saxophone. And Harley is drumming! Christ! You can't imagine Harry James would allow such a fundamental insult to the discipline, even in his worst nightmare. Believe me—as my name is Arturo Toscanini, I know what I'm talking about. What if Harley has already crossed the solid white line? You know, the one that if you make it to the other side... you've had it. Jesus! Have you any idea what he could be doing in the kitchen all this time?"

Amanda burst out laughing. The glasses on the shelf behind me trembled.

As Kevin got into a taxi the following morning, he said goodbye in such a manner that I got the feeling it's for the last time. When I said to him, "See you soon in New York," he wouldn't believe me. Instead he clasped me tightly to his enormous chest. I heard his heart banging away underneath that cinnabar-red vest. He mumbled something about the stinking mud. How we were stuck up to our ears in that shit but how lucky we were to have saved our skins.

20

As soon as I woke up in room 403 from my Vietnamese dream—the one where in the end I throw the last handful of soggy soil on top of Wayne Piscopo and insert a bamboo stick complete with raised American flag into his grave (the so-called ant-hill) at the edge of the jungle—I began to feel extremely hungry. On this occasion I polish off the whole of Amanda's banana in one go.

On my way down I meet Arnie Hornsby on the staircase. He is legging it upstairs, breathless, with a rucksack on his back.

"What's the matter?" I ask.

He continues trotting, on the spot. "You don't know, Harley?"

"No, I don't."

"Yes, you do. If I stop it'll be the end."

"What end?"

"The absolute end. Everywhere I look, I can see that Korean corpse floating face up in that rice field."

He waves his walking stick—and is gone. I go down to reception, arriving at precisely the moment that Jacques puts the telephone receiver down.

"That was Amanda," he informs me.

"What did she want?" I'm surprised.

"She left a message to say that she's heard Tiger singing in the tree. That's the first part. And the second is, when Blondie arrives, not to forget to ask her for her autograph."

I nearly faint. What did she say that for? Jacques, of course, looks at me inquisitively. As for Tiger it's really quite simple. I explain that our beloved canary escaped last Monday. End of story. With Blondie it's a bit more complicated. I quickly make up a tale about how Blondie bewitched Amanda when she was around sixteen, starring in some black and white epic. A little girl, Gwendolyn, had fallen into a deep well, and Blondie climbed down on a rope to rescue her. And, from the very moment when Colin from Kitty Junction took tonight's booking for Blondie at the Royal Arms, Amanda has scarcely been able to wait for me to get her an autograph.

The Frenchman asks, "Isn't this Blondie something like Catherine Deneuve?"

"Yes, yes, Jacques," I agree eagerly. "They are the spitting image of one another."

Nothing enthuses Jacques more than to find out that something North American has an appropriate French equivalent. And I'm not about to tell him that, with all due respect to Catherine Deneuve, she couldn't hold a candle to Blondie.

"Although I'm kind of interested in women," mumbles Jacques, "it only goes so far. Unfortunately, I only have one life. If I had two, maybe I would take the risk and study them in greater detail. So you just have to understand, Harley, that if I had to make a choice between Marie Antoinette and the Marquis de Sade, I would pick the Marquis de Sade every time. By the way, have you ever been to the Louvre?"

"I went past it a long time ago."

"You should have taken a look inside."

"One day I will. You'll have to believe me. Don't forget, my daughter lives in Paris."

"*Voilà,* Harley! She couldn't have chosen a better place to live. You can envy her two things—the architecture and the cultured society. You Anglos are so desperately unimaginative. Since losing your colonies you just go cavorting around your skyscrapers like embittered gnomes. And you don't talk about culture. You avoid surrealism like the plague. Abstract art drives you to despair. You are quite simply the epitome of Neanderthal man!"

I am searching for the appropriate words with which to clarify to Jacques that I'm basically not an Anglo, never mind a Neanderthal man—bearing in mind how I came to be born outside that newspaper kiosk in Vienna, where a copy of

Face of Future was on display, the one with Blondie on its cover.

But suddenly I notice something. There, staring up at me from one step before the bottom of the staircase, next to the elevator, is a rather scruffy size-14 sneaker. Immediately behind it is a twin. Above the two sneakers, two chimney-like legs belonging to a pair of faded jeans make their appearance. Somewhere in the middle of it all hovers a toolbox covered in stickers. Then, from the very last step, springs Melvin, complete and wearing a flat cap on his head. From between his teeth dangles the inevitable cigar. In next to no time he has filled the entire mini-vestibule. Before flopping with a great thud onto one of its shabby armchairs, he addresses us jovially, "Hi there, you guys. What's new? Stop fooling around and confess to me which one of you has palmed the fifteen bucks!"

Jacques takes no notice of him and carries on. "You Anglos are, if you'll excuse the expression, a touch simple-minded. If for example I draw two lines crossing one another on a piece of paper, the shit really hits the fan. You can't understand why it is two such innocent lines *have to* cross one another. And, as I know, you Anglos are prepared to go to war over such an *apparent abnormality*. Yes, yes. You feel trapped. And God only knows how you might react if I were to build a pyramid out of nothing but triangles and squares, then circle it nicely and put a prettily pointed chocolate nipple on top."

Luckily Melvin has already removed the smoldering cigar from his mouth before his jaw drops in utter astonishment. Otherwise it would have landed in his lap—and everyone knows what would happen if it had burnt a hole in his pants. He gawps at me, "Harley, Yabba-Dabba-Doo, you don't happen to know what Jack is blabbering about?"

The Frenchman answers him, "A: my name is not Jack, but J-a-c-q-u-e-s. Just remember that. And B: does the name Picasso mean anything to you?"

"Excuse me." The colossus is offended. "Who do you take me for? If, *by any chance,* I should ask you over to my place for a cup of coffee, the first thing you will see behind Micky as she opens the door, is that famous dove of peace of his hanging on the wall."

Jacques is visibly pleased. "Alright, Melvin. I was only asking, OK? That doesn't mean that I take you for a complete idiot."

"I'm greatly relieved," Melvin replies. "Do you mean to say that, as well as the peace dove, Picasso also painted a pointed nipple? A chocolate one at that?"

"Look, Melv," Jacques says in a more familiar tone. "I only mentioned the nipple as one of *thousands* of possible elements, with whose help an artist creates his immortal masterpieces. OK? It could be anything—a piece of glass, a wire or someone's nose. Perhaps yours even, sticking out arrogantly from between your eyes. *As-tu compris?*"

"Take it easy." Our Hercules looks offended. "Don't you dare touch my nose."

As soon as he says that, something incredible happens. A big fat bluebottle, until now lazily gliding about as if on roller skates around the edge of the reception desk, suddenly decides to take off towards the ceiling, heading straight for the gyrating fan. It shouldn't have done that. Knocked down by one of the chipped blades, it lands half-stunned on the tip of the sacred (and therefore untouchable) snout of Melvin's Graeco-Roman profile. For a few seconds it balances there as if on the edge of an abyss. Jacques and I watch in petrified anticipation. The tickling of the fly's legs provokes Melvin into a fit of sneezing. The colossus jolts upright and the unfortunate passenger drops one flight lower—right onto the back of the same hairy hand whose fingers hold the smoking Havana.

If what has just happened could be referred to as incredible, what we witness next is gruesome—it unravels in five sequences that follow one another in rapid succession: 1. Melvin, with a split-second movement of his hand, catches the fly in his palm. 2. He jumps out of his armchair. 3. He walks slowly (with swaggering gait) towards the reception counter. 4. He bursts into such ugly laughter that we all get goose-pimples. 5. He introduces the imprisoned fly to us with these words, "Dearest bluebottle! This is Harley, that is Jack and I'm Melvin... expert fly-catcher!"

Jacques blurts out, "Melv. Now that we're all aquainted, I hope you'll let it go. *Oui?*"

The fly-catcher puts his clenched fist to his ear and replies, "Jack, do you hear the buzzing? It won't buzz for much longer, believe me. Melvin is a nice guy, but enough is enough."

Then he inserts two fat fingers into the tunnel made by his tightened fist. He fumbles inside for a while until he feels the fly. He pulls it out, and plucks off its wings as if it were a chicken. With the wingless little ball, he marches towards the coffee table standing between the armchairs. According to the ensuing loud smack, he has obviously crushed it unceremoniously into the ashtray.

"You animal!" Jacques call out at him. "Aren't you ashamed?"

As soon as Hercules hears those words, his whole body starts to shake, as if he has just touched a live electrical wire. Before we realize it, he has collapsed, doubled up with cramps, into the armchair. He sobs uncontrollably. "You are right, Jack. I'm an animal. If that is all you wish to call me. I'm a beastly brute. I hope you guys will find enough forgiveness in you to have mercy on a poor bruiser like me. Please, I don't know what's come over me. Probably nerves. Yes, yes. I'm over-anxious. Those fifteen dollars someone stole from me was the last straw. Christ, I'm going crazy. Micky is probably already sitting by the window, waiting for me to appear at the street corner. Poor girl, she doesn't know that I won't be coming home. I'm probably going to kill myself. Though, if you can truly forgive me, guys, I won't kill myself. However, I will promise never to do it again. I will leave flies alone, even when they eat me alive. And the same goes for moths and spiders too. I will not touch them. And if I do, it will be to return them, unharmed, to mother nature. Honestly, guys, I'm not kidding. And if there is ever another war, I will volunteer for the front. I will not desert this time. I swear it. What do you say, guys? Are you going to forgive me or not?"

All of a sudden Arnie Hornsby, rucksack on his back and walking stick in hand, comes running down the stairs. He circles round the armchair where the sobbing Melvin is sitting, and while still trotting on the spot he shouts into his ear, "Fifteen!"

Melvin jumps up. "So it's you, you thief!"

"What are you talking about?" Hornsby asks, astonished. "I've just run down the stairs for the fifteenth time!"

Melvin collapses back into the chair. He hasn't even the energy left to start sobbing again. Jacques, it seems, is truly worried that Melvin really has lost the will to live. He shuffles towards him, reaches inside his own jacket pocket for his wallet, and pulls out one ten and one five-dollar bill. He thrusts them in front of Melvin's face. "Here you are," he mumbles. "I will lend you fifteen until next pay-day. Buy Micky something suitably French."

Melvin looks at him with his sad eyes. "Thanks, Jack. You've no idea how much I appreciate this. But unfortunately, I can't accept anything from you. There is much more to it than what you know. General amorality. Understand? I was robbed today. Tomorrow it might be you, and Harley the day after. I have lost all faith in mankind. I've reached rock bottom. No use in carrying on in this inhuman misery. Can you do something for me, Jack, before I breathe my last? *S'il vous plait?*"

"And what might that be?" mutters Jacques.

"A quick call to the newspapers, informing them that I'm going on a hunger strike. As a matter of principle!"

If the Frenchman was pale as a sheet at the sight of the wingless fly, he is now as pale as two sheets. "Don't be a fool, Melv. A hunger strike! What would the boss say to that? He'll be back from Montreal tomorrow and... you would be sitting here dying. Who's gonna water his little Brazil for him? Not me. And I doubt Harley will. Fifteen dollars! Is it worth it? Be sensible... *sacrebleu!*"

At the same time Arnie Hornsby appears yet again, circles twice around Melvin and shouts, "Sixteen!" to his face.

"Go and play somewhere else, man!" Colossus lashes out. "Can't you see I'm dying of hunger?"

He throws the cigar into the ashtray. Picking up his toolbox, he heads for the elevator. As the doors close behind him, Arnie exclaims "Seventeen!" but Melvin doesn't hear him. All three of us look first towards the elevator, then at one another and finally we burst into uproarious laughter.

But he who laughs last, laughs longest. At its peak the sound of our laughter is permeated by a call for help. We look around us. In the space between the two armchairs, where there is a round table, smoke is spiralling upwards towards the overhead fan. We step forward almost simultaneously and lean over the ashtray. A horribly gruesome sight is awaiting us. The heat of the stub of Melvin's cigar is slowly roasting the wingless bluebottle, as if it were turning on a spit. When Arnie pokes the remaining cinder with the point of his walking stick, it disintegrates into fine gray dust.

"Gentlemen, this is awful!" says the Korean war veteran from room 303. "If I had been able to turn that North Korean Commie cadaver into ashes, I would have rid myself of it forever."

21

Since I was incapable of not being serious about Blondie, Ilona dragged me back to Bertold's presbytery two years later, to annul our marriage. A short while afterwards she went back to Hungary with our daughter Sandor. No doubt her path has been eased by the return to power of her castrated father's red friends. These people even want to erect a monument to her grandfather in Budapest.

I accompanied the two of them to the station. As the train moved off, my eyes were filled with stinging black smoke. Making a tight little fist, Sandor kept on waving to me until the train disappeared behind the viaduct.

I should be glad it turned out like this. Quite frankly I am not suited for the demanding roles of husband and father. Instead of taking care of my family, I'm constantly wrapped up in thoughts of Blondie.

By now I was just twenty years old. And I didn't take lightly to this sudden loneliness. I kept changing hotels like they were socks. It's as if, in so doing, I hoped to find the answer to the emptiness all around me. Finally I landed up in the Excelsior. There I was put in charge of the flower arrangements on all fifteen floors. Quite a pleasant job really. I distributed irises and petunias along the corridors and in all the rooms. My relationship with the guests (I make myself out to be a little bit like Apollo, the god of light and sun, the protector of life and nature, infallible marksman and prophet) could be called close. Sometimes even intimate. Foreign visitors to Vienna often confide in me those intimate thoughts that until now they kept buried far down in the darkest depths of their desk drawers.

For a while I took great care to keep up an eccentric appearance. For example I might wear a ladies' hat. Or tie an enormous bow in my hair. Many guests laughed. Somehow my presence alone was enough to provide them with a certain satisfaction. Some took me for a harmless homosexual who made a living as a florist. But when I started telling them what

I know about Blondie (and about my plans for our future together), they soon changed their minds. There was not one person who didn't know what I was talking about—even though occasionally we had such bigwig guests like king Abdul Allah Abdul, a former Berber, Bedouin and Beelzebub, who went about proclaiming for the benefit of all who cared to listen that the territory he ruled is three times bigger than Austria and that there are 608 extremely demanding beauties waiting for him back at the harem.

Once a week I would head for the municipal library near the Liechtenstein Palace. There I browsed through all the newspapers and magazines. I really had to keep pace with all the intricacies of Blondie's staggeringly successful career. A propos, I found out that Blondie only recently had her second ear pierced, the left one, so that she could wear both her earrings at the same time. The cherry ones suit her most of all. They are indistinguishable from the real thing.

I also enjoyed reading all the news about her first substantial part in a Hollywood film. It's called *The Sour Fruit of Paradise*. They say it's rather a poor interpretation of the short story of the same name by J. J. Jericho. Apparently, though, from the very first scene, Blondie excels. It starts with an aerial view (probably taken from a plane) of someone down below running (looking like a tiny dot) in a meadow studded with Rudbeckia flowers. There then follows a quick pan across to a pig-tailed head. It's Blondie. In her hand she has a letter. Wherever it is she's going, they don't tell us. Probably to the post office. I don't know. I just read about these things in magazines.

So, as far as I understand it, the setting is a farm well away from civilization. The bone of contention as far as Blondie's extended family is concerned is her horse Tom. He recently went blind. And villain number one is Blondie's father. He gets it into his head that the following day he is going to shoot Tom with his Remington 870 Express. My Angel plays his daughter, the oldest of seven children. Her name is Rachel and she herself lives in a nearby town (called

Coleslaw) where she works in the light-bulb factory belonging
to Sullivan & Co. Blondie, alias Rachel, comes home every
week by bus to help her parents over the weekend, either by
milking the cows or digging potatoes from the field. When
she finds out, on her return one Friday night, that her father
intends to shoot her blind Tom next morning, she is
distraught. The moment the farm is wrapped in darkness,
Blondie gives three ominous coughs. That's the signal. Her
brothers and sisters (along with her half-deaf mother) hurry
into her bed where they hold a counsel of war. They all want
to think of a way of saving Tom. Some suggest stealing their
father's Remington—but they are scared. If he woke up, he
would shoot the lot of them. In the end it turns out (and this
is practically the highest peak in the plot) that Blondie will
mount Tom at dawn and gallop off over the meadow and
into the far yonder. Unfortunately all the dogs start barking
(especially that idiot Smokey), waking Blondie's father.
Terribly bad luck. From the window he takes aim (deaf
mother sleeps through the whole tragedy, lying flat on her
belly) and fires three times. One bullet kills Tom. The second
lodges itself in Blondie's body, near her pancreas. The third is
probably still flying around somewhere out there to this very
day. However, Blondie is now lying in a pool of blood next to
Tom in the meadow studded with Rudbeckia, while the rest
of her family (including the mother whose hearing has
miraculously returned) are calling the father all kinds of
names. But as often happens in Hollywood, a happy ending
will put everything to rights. The following Sunday the entire
family visits Blondie in Coleslaw hospital. My poor little
Darling is recovering from her operation. And, as Doctor
Frank Smith says, do not fear, she will come out of it all
without suffering any permanent consequences. At her
bedside her tearful father swears that as soon as he comes out
of jail he will buy Blondie another palomino and they will call
him—what else?—Tom.

I eagerly gobbled up every word the critics wrote on
Blondie's performance in this film magazine. Except for one,

who thinks Blondie with pig tails looks so provocative it's hardly surprising her father did what he did, if only out of sexual frustration, they are unanimously of the opinion that Blondie has a most promising film career ahead of her. The film itself, though, was not a box office hit. Even I have never had any illusions about *The Sour Fruit of Paradise* ever hitting the silver screens in Austria. It didn't matter; I was confident of making it to Los Angeles well before that.

And when at the library, I often profited from the opportunity to think about my own self. Who am I, where do I come from, and why is my name none other than Harley Davidson? Surrounded by all the collected wisdom gathered in the millions of tomes on the shelves around me, I would tell myself that perhaps one of those books might actually contain the key to solving this particular mystery. An inner voice told me that before the second world war my parents must have been motorcycle fans—and that's how it all began. Let us suppose, for instance, that Father (an Austrian Jew by origin) can't afford a motorbike and that he travels around Europe on a bicycle. He makes it all the way to Amsterdam where he catches a glimpse of my future mother whizzing by on a moped. He is so infatuated by this woman that he waves at her furiously to catch her eye. He succeeds to perfection. Mother nearly crashes through a milliner's shopwindow.

It looks as if Mother fancies Father too. One word leads to another. Father sells the bike and takes the seat behind mother on the moped. Together they set off for Italy. But before they can make it all the way to Rome, Father suffers from acute saddle-soreness. They are forced to make a pit stop—one that lasts for three days until he recovers. Luckily they are hanging round a gas station which happens to have a second-hand Harley Davidson for sale, including a spare tire and a sidecar. The rest is easy to guess. Since that moment, life for my future parents has been paradise on earth. One day Father drives, while Mother, with a scarf flapping around her neck, a leather cap on her head and an enormous pair of plexiglass goggles, smiles up at him from the sidecar. The following day Mother takes charge of the handlebars, with Father sitting in the sidecar, taking off his leather hat to allow his hair to blow free.

The second scenario that comes to my mind is that it is actually Father who is riding through the streets of Amsterdam on his moped. And when Mother on her bicycle waves at him, because he is such a good-looker, it's Father who nearly crashes into the shop window, with difference being that it is in a store that sells dairy produce.

The mere thought that I, as the fruit of their love, was either conceived on the motorcycle or in the sidecar (which probably has better suspension) and as a result came to be tenderly referred to as something like, *"Our beautiful sweet little Harley Davidson,"* is enough to send me into a joyful reverie amidst all the bookshelves.

Fortunately, there always happened to be an elderly librarian in there, one who had never refused to listen to my stories about my missing parents. But this time, when I finished pouring my heart out to her she whispered confidentially into my ear (although there is not a living soul around), "So you insist, Harley Davidson, that your parents were gallivanting around Europe without a care in the world just as most of us Jews were worried sick about what was going to happen to us. Of course, listening to you, it seems to me you are only interested in finding out where it happened... on the motorcycle or in the sidecar... simply to be able to tell vividly colored stories about how you came to be conceived... and why you have such a name... to that Blondie of yours... when you finally come to meet her."

Her long sentences made me feel quite dizzy. The problem was that the sentences got more complicated each time I went to the library, and the number of words in them increasd according to her mood. In short, on that particular day, I had to wait some five minutes before being able to make even a brief reply to her habitual question. "It's like that and no different," I said. "Blondie will certainly be interested."

This woman was not terribly fond of my Angel. Whenever I mentioned her, she looked as if she has just bitten into a sour cucumber. She asked, "Have you ever read the diary of Anne Frank, my little Duckling?" When I hinted, by shaking my head (at what she has already known for a long time), that I'm hopelessly ignorant of anything in which my dearest has not been given at least a minor role, she continued, "Then you should read it pretty damn quick, Duckie, so that you understand the sort of worries Anne had compared with those of your blonde, who obviously has nothing in her head apart from her ridiculous career in light entertainment."

It was an irony that this spinster, dried up like a salted cod fish, bore the name of Elfie von Ribbentrop—the same as the infamous Nazi minister of foreign affairs. She kept throwing the matter of Anne Frank's diary into my face each time I visited the library until, one fine day, I finally borrowed it just to have some respite from her.

She couldn't wait for me to come through the door the following Thursday. It was raining outside and I was still shaking the raindrops out of my hair, but she ran over to me dying from curiosity. "So what do you think about life now, Harley Davidson? What is your opinion of Blondie after all the things that Anne Frank wrote in her diary?"

I replied, "It's a very sad story. Without any doubt Anne had to live through hell on earth. Then, of course, Blondie's youth was no bed of roses either."

"Stop talking nonsense, Ducks!" Elfie von Ribbentrop threw the most voluminous of her encyclopedias at me. But she missed. "Do you remember, for example, what the wretched girl wrote in her diary on the 24th December 1943?"

"Not precisely," I answered.

"That's a shame, then," said the librarian. "You should remember that in the entry of the twenty-fourth of the twelfth Anne refers to another *ruined* Christmas holiday...

even though we Jews really don't celebrate it. Do you understand now?"

"I'm trying to," I replied truthfully.

"Well. Have you ever had *a completely ruined* Christmas, Ducks?"

On the tip of my tongue was the statement that, on the contrary, having a *not ruined* Christmas is an experience quite unknown to me, because without Blondie it can *never* be Christmas. It goes without saying that without her it's a dog's life—not only at Christmas but on New Year's day too. Without even mentioning Easter. But Elfie would not or could not understand this. And so I said, "No, I have not."

"So you see," she complimented me, "I'm talking about the entry where Anne sighs, *Himmelhoch jauchzend und zum Tode betrübt.* I presume you realize that that was written by Goethe."

"It's not possible to remember everything that Goethe wrote," I stated.

"Well, he did," the librarian informed me. "*At the summit of the world or in the depths of hopelessness,* and Anne made a note of it in her diary that very day."

I suddenly saw the light. Anne is describing the visit by Mrs. Koophuis. Although she has virtually been imprisoned in that Dutch house for two years now, Mrs. Koophuis starts talking in great detail about her daughter Corry, who plays hockey with the boys, takes long canoe trips, visits the theatre (sometimes even appearing in plays)— but the main thing is that she has a lot of friends. Anne writes in the diary that although she doesn't envy Corry, she admits that she, just like Corry, would like to play hockey with the boys, paddle through the rapids on a canoe or sometimes be able to burst into hearty laughter. But what hurts the most is that Mrs. Koophuis is so blinded by her own happiness that she doesn't perceive the suffering of others.

When I told Elfie von Ribbentrop that I did actually remember the entry in Anne's diary for the twenty-fourth of December and fully appreciated all her psychological hardships, the librarian stroked my hair in a motherly way. I hoped this was all she had to say for now, but Elfie sighed, "Imagine what that Jewish girl lived through when she was dying in the concentration camp knowing that she would never again play hockey with the boys."

I tried, as hard as I could. Of course, in the end I couldn't hold it in anymore. "Only last week," I said, "Blondie announced at a press conference in Cincinnati that, of all sports, her favorite is the long jump, followed by basketball."

Elfie stared at me through the thick lenses of her glasses. "As I can see, you are more stubborn than a mule, Ducks. But I'm slowly getting used to you. Believe me. But remember that sometimes I even have positive thoughts about you. So here is something to remember the librarian Elfie by, when she's not around any more."

She handed me a yellowing newspaper clip. On reading the the first few words my hands started to tremble. It was an account of events that took place on 2.7.1939 in Bayreuth in Germany. The story began shortly before mid-day, when a masked couple robbed a local bank. Eyewitnesses insisted that one person was wearing a leather hat and plexiglass goggles. And here I stopped dead. It said that suddenly my mother jerked her head. A strand of blonde hair fell out of the hat. It spilled out onto her left shoulder. My hatless father, on the other hand, had hair as black as a raven's feathers and his mouth was covered with a checked scarf. While Mother was guarding the door, Father emptied all three tills in the bank. The only thing they left behind was a piece of paper. On it my parents wrote that they deeply regretted their deed. If they had not been forced into it, they would not steal. However, they need money for gas in order to save themselves from the Nazis. Then there was heard the noise of a motorcycle engine revving up. Eyewitnesses swore that the machine was a Harley-Davidson. And the most riveting part was right at the end. To add to the roar from the exhaust, an infant of approximately three months was screaming its head off in the sidecar. Having witnessed the event, the mayor of Bayreuth himself made the following statement to the investigating magistrate: "The robbers shot across the square and straight over the hill on a motorcycle. They are long gone but even today I can hear that baby squealing like a stuck pig.

22

It's all Kevin Dorsett's fault. If he had allowed me to step on that mine thirty miles north of Da-nang, that first meeting with my little Blondie would have had to take place up in heaven, on some tiny little cloud, in peace and quiet.

Meanwhile, here on earth, I am going through sheer hell. I'm just hurrying on my way past little Brazil. It's almost six o'clock—nearly time to change over with Jacques Bélanger in reception. And then it happens for the third time.

I say to myself, 'Better now than in retrospect, when every common foot-soldier is a General.' I hear the elevator starting up from the ground floor. It brushes several times against the walls of the elevator shaft. The doors burst open. I'm not in the least surprised when my Angel steps out into the corridor.

"There you are!" she exclaims as soon as she sees me. "Harley Davidson!"

"B...Blondie!" I stutter. "H...how did you find me?"

"Jacques Bélanger sent me. He made me laugh."

"How come?"

"Can you imagine! He reckons me to be something like Catherine Deneuve!"

"You must realize, the French like to see things their own way."

"That's correct. So? How are you?"

"So-so."

"So-so! What's the matter with you? Put some life into dying, will you. Well? Listen to this then: Glory be on high! An end to this wandering and this tormenting loneliness! Come, handsome dark Señor, take me into your arms and say Hurray to Santa Fé, stowed away on a train between jute sacks stuffed with unroasted coffee beans!"

She waits for my response. And what I say is that this was obviously a passage from her second film *Sombrero*. It's about how she is in New Mexico, being pursued by a group of adventurers, acting on the assumption that she, Blondie (her name in the film is Rita), has a parchment scroll secreted in her brassiére on which is drawn a map showing the location of some treasure buried on one of the Galapagos Islands. As Blondie flees, she stumbles and falls off a rock. Her life is saved by Señor J.X.J., who just happens to be taking a nap beneath his sombrero in the shade of a 10-foot-high cactus. It is the very same cactus on which my Angel will land. Following a quick exchange of bullets (five hot-blooded bandits equals five quickly cooling cadavers), Señor J.X.J. will spend the rest of that torpid afternoon carefully removing all the prickly cactus thorns from the pretty behind of the lovely señorita.

It looks as if Blondie has been waiting for something to happen. She hops onto one leg and bursts into room 403 like a hurricane. Before storming in, she brushes against me with her elbow. More or less carried onward by the dynamics of the rotating movement, I lurch in head-first behind my darling. She draws the latch. I explain it thus: you learn by your mistakes. The last time, when she left me out in the corridor, she nearly suffered a heart attack. That was when she found Melvin tightening her dripping tap in her bathroom.

My miracle looks at me breathlessly to see what I'll come out with next. However, I was born bashful. Instead of exclaiming, "Here I am, my love, do what you want with me!" I just shuffle from foot to foot and make the fatuous enquiry, "Did the plane from Las Vegas fly faster than usual, Miss?"

"You know," yawns my Angel, "sometimes the plane flies quick. Another time it flies slow. The worst thing is when it stops flying altogether."

She is obviously referring to when the aircraft mechanics are on strike.

Blondie is wearing something that could be described as a man's sports T-shirt, which goes down all the way to her knees. Written in phosphorescent letters right across her chest is the legend: THE LAST DAY OF DICK HAMMERSMITH. And that's not all. When my Angel turns to face the window, starting from the first vertebra of her neck and finishing at the coccyx, this consists of a pair of crossed skis with a ski jump in the background. And across the blue horizon is written in capital letters: ASPEN. Evidently, she is advertising her most successful film to date.

Never mind. My dilemma is far from over. The entire script of everything I intend to say to Blondie has been rehearsed to perfection. But I am not yet prepared for the intimate dialogue that will subsequently take place between four eyes and four walls. So instead of taking the roses out of the closet, falling onto one knee on the carpet and declaring my undying love for her, I say matter-of-factly, "Blondie, I've been waiting all my life for this moment."

She turns away from the window and throws up her hands. "Really, Harley? That's a story that's going to take at least a week to tell."

"If only a week. I guess it could take a whole month."

"My dearest, I would love nothing more than to listen for at least a fortnight. But, as you know of course, this evening I have a performance at Kitty Junction. I must take a look at the size of the stage. Otherwise I might step off it accidentally and fall into the audience. And you wouldn't like that, would you? *A propos*, my dear, when you go downstairs to fetch my luggage, would you please be extra careful with the cage containing the rabbits. Can I rely on you?"

In the normal course of events I would like to know exactly what these rabbits are supposed to mean, but lack of time forces me to deal with matters of a more personal nature. "Have you received any one of my many letters, Blondie?" I ask.

"Oh, letters. If I were to tell you about *all* the letters I've received during my lifetime, I wouldn't need to exaggerate. It went so far that I had to choose between reading letters and my career. That I chose my career you will no doubt understand. So if that letter of yours ended with the words, '...yours lovingly and devotedly, Harley Davidson', I regret to say I have some sad news for you. I don't remember ever reading it. Of course, another possibility presents itself. I could have thrown it in the waste basket unopened. Sorry, dear, but that is the harsh reality."

She flops onto the mattress. Lying there motionless, she reminds me of Snow White poisoned by her stepmother's apple. In my mind I'm so glad that this Snow White of mine is a platinum blonde. I shuffle closer to the bed. I could never tire of beholding such beauty. My Darling's semi-closed eyelids are practically like two butterflies that have come to rest. I say to myself that they have found on her magnificent face a safe haven on their long journey from the furthest-flung corners of the earth in which to rest their exhausted wings. Seeing Blondie's smile is encouragement enough for me to kiss her back to life. I lean over her, as far as the edge of the bed allows. But instead of kissing her, I whisper, "Of course, during the last thirty-three years, at a conservative estimate, I have written a thousand letters, Blondie. Not counting telegrams and parcels weighing over two pounds."

Blondie sits up so swiftly that we almost suffer a head-on collision. "Good heavens! And what was in the parcels of over two pounds?"

I take her hands into mine and hold them against my lips. It's now or never. Yes. This is my big (and probably last) chance to express my feelings to her. I murmur Dick Hammersmith's now famous lines, "Did you ever have the opportunity, as a child, of looking inside a paperweight? You know, the ones shaped like a glass ball? When you shake it, it snows and snows and snows inside. My goodness! And when around mid-day, it finally stops and the sun reappears over New York, you'll see an old-fashioned couple skating inside. These two foolish creatures are kissing in the middle of the skating rink below the statue of Prometheus in Rockerfeller Plaza. Have you ever experienced anything like that? And, if not, I'm asking you openly, wouldn't you like to experience it sometime?"

Tears well up in Blondie's eyes. "Harley! That scene with Dick beneath the ski jump in Aspen was rehearsed seventeen times in all! Do you understand? And yet you come out with it for the very first time without one single mistake!"

"That's because I love you."

"I feel the same way."

"This summer it has been thirty-three years since I saw you for the first time in Vienna."

"My dear, it may seem odd, but I've never been to Vienna!"

"Oh yes, you have. By the way, Gertrude Steinbach sends her regards."

"Really, so Gertrude Steinbach sends her regards?"

"We met on a bench in a park."

Blondie observes me for a long time. "Listen, Harley. You really remind me of someone."

I'm not about to wait any longer. "Yes. Yes. It's me. It happened some twenty miles from Saigon. It's Christmas. You are singing Laura. In front of you on the lawn are six thousand tearful GIs. And amongst them I am just one tiny speck. I take off my uniform. And I run towards you on the stage. And that was the first time you saw me. Finally! So you do remember, Blondie!"

"You say...you were running towards me wearing nothing?"

"Yes. Yes. That was me!"

"Just when I was singing Laura?"

"Yes, Laura. I was standing in front of you completely naked."

"My dearest. *As a matter of principle*, whenever I sing Laura, I keep my eyes shut."

"What? As a matter of principle?"

"Absolutely."

"You don't even keep a little slit open?"

"No."

I'm devastated. Such disappointment! Why didn't I wait until she started to sing, say, "Jingle Bells?" I blurt out, "And I was hoping that I'd engraved myself indelibly into your memory as you stood there singing Laura. I have to admit now that all this time I've been living under a great illusion."

"I'm really very sorry, Harley," she whispers. "I can't sing Laura in any other way."

"Only with your eyes shut?" I ask at least for the third time.

"Okay, Harley," says Blondie. "From now on I will never sing Laura again."

"No please. I cannot ask that of you."

Blondie raises her voice. "Yes. To hell with Laura!"

"But I am not worth it!"

It's as if she didn't hear me. She is almost hysterical. This time it is she who takes my hands into hers. She puts them to her lips. As she cries, she wets them with her hot tears. "Listen... if you should... think, my dearest... if you should feel, that it would help *us both*... if I cancelled tonight's performance, you... you only have to say so... and I will drop everything... honestly I would... do you see?"

"Oh no, no Blondie!" I cry out. "What about your career!"

"Career isn't everything!"

"I can't stand in your way."

"Jesus Christ, where... where are you going?"

"I'm going to fetch your luggage."

"Oh. Please. Don't forget the rabbits, will you?"

"I won't, Blondie."

I shuffle along the corridor towards the elevator, feeling for all the world like a beaten-up cur. So she didn't see me!

From the door Blondie calls after me. "Tell me, tell me, my... dearest, was it very... very difficult for you to... to overcome your shyness in front of all those spectators and... and to take off... because, because of me... take off your uniform?"

I summon the elevator. "Very, very... difficult... Blondie... yes, yes... extremely, extremely... so to speak... psychologically difficult... but for you, for you I would always... always do anything. For you... nothing, nothing hurts me in any case."

Somewhere behind my back I hear a sob. "Tell me, tell me... my dear... if you would do... do for me... anything... do you think, think... that you could wait for me... here... when I come back tonight... from Kitty Junction... and we will try, try it again... again, only this time without... Laura?"

I wish I could answer: YES, YES, YES, BLONDIE!, but I am already heading relentlessly towards the ground with the elevator. Not in a long time have I experienced anything so exhausting. My shirt is soaked with perspiration. After such a rehearsal, I will be fit and able to land in Normandy today at any time. I am quite pleased with my performance. And Blondie, she was so sweet and natural. One can only imagine how she is going to be in reality. Her lips, her eyes, her hair—everything! The way she held my hands in hers. And when she said something it was as if coming from the ether.

All of a sudden I stop in my tracks. *She* could also be *the real* Blondie! Quite simply, the plane has arrived early and this is not a dress rehearsal, this is an actual performance. D-Day! I have indeed landed on the shore of France!

Reaching the ground floor I don't even wait for the doors to open. With unexpected force, considering the pathetic state of my otherwise useless arms, I pull them apart. Briefcase in hand, Jacques is already waiting for me at the reception counter with one foot stretched out pointing at the exit. He's right. It's five minutes past six. I should have changed over with him some time ago.

"*Sacrebleu*, Harley," he lisps. "Has Melvin being trying to murder you again upstairs?"

"No one wanted to murder me!" I shout at him. "Where is Blondie's luggage and the rabbits?"

Jacques takes a step back. He examines me as though I was the newly completed Eiffel Tower. "Do I hear you correctly, Harley? Blondie's luggage and the rabbits?"

"Yes, yes," I run round and round. "Blondie's luggage and the rabbits!"

"*Mon Dieu,* Harley, is it really you?" he enquires carefully.

"Who should I be, you Frog!" I throw the insult to his face.

"If I'm a Frrrog," he rolls his R, "then you are Harley IV, king of English idiots! *Bonsoir!*"

He storms out into the street. I want to shout after him that it was he who sent Blondie upstairs to me. So what's so strange? But I leave him alone.

I'm starting to think about whether I should really ask Blondie to cancel this evening's performance. In fact it would be an enormous help to both of us. We would have the whole night to ourselves. And that's time enough to be able to get to know one another just beautifully. After all, true love knows no bounds. And what could be more important in life than two people loving one another? Being in each other's arms, making sure that nothing ever comes between them?

I start legging it upstairs like a bat out of hell.

"Blondie!" Already, from along the corridor, I am shouting. "Let's cancel today's performance and that'll be that."

I burst into her room like a hurricane. It's completely empty. As I take a deep breath, I realize that Blondie's Erocascade perfume has been replaced by the stench of a Havana cigar. And that's not all. The drawer of her bedside table is half open. I step closer. The Bible is in its usual place. But my book of poems, called Blondie, along with the letter which I wrote with such zeal to welcome my sweet Angel, has disappeared.

23

Some nine years after I vouchsafed my undying love for Blondie in front of that kiosk in Vienna (and five and a half after I split with the Hungarian Ilona)—I tried it for the second time. I married Helga. She was born in Germany to Canadian parents. At the time I was working in a night club in Frankfurt. Mostly American and Canadian soldiers came there looking for entertainment. Apparently anyone who knew the house in the medieval heart of the city, where Goethe was born, would find it impossible to miss the Concordia.

Every Friday, Helga appeared there, chaperoned by her parents. Usually she sang and danced a few numbers. Her childish face was in complete contrast to her already womanly figure. For six months, ever since her very first stage curtsy, I had been admiring this little nymphette. But each time she would hurry away from the Concordia before I had a chance to speak with her.

One April, or possibly the beginning of May 1965, I succumbed to the temptation to wait for the family. Their name was Henderson. It was shortly before midnight. When they began to leave for home, I stood as if by chance on the sidewalk outside the door.

"Do you know Blondie, young lady?" I asked, catching hold of the nylon sleeve of Helga's blouse. It was white and see-through and underneath I caught a glimpse of a velvet brassiére with lace trim.

All three of them stopped. The parents were guarding their offspring like a lamb from a hungry wolf. They frown at me. Mrs. Henderson held an umbrella. Should it be necessary, I was ready to jump sideways. Helga, on the other hand, smiled at me with girlish innocence. "Of course," she answered. "Blondie is my idol. I own all of her records."

It had started better than I could imagine. "Could I come and listen to them sometime?" I asked.

Helga's eyes roamed between the sidewalk and the star-studded sky. She avoided her parents' gaze. If they were not with her, she would have asked me to visit her there and then.

Finally her daddy cut in. "Listen, young man," Mr. Henderson growled. "Doesn't it matter to you that we haven't met?"

"So, why don't we introduce ourselves," I replied. "My name is Harley Davidson."

Mrs. Henderson bursts out laughing. "Harley Davidson! Like the motorcycle?"

I feel hurt. "Excuse me, Madam! And what about Hen-der-son?"

"Hen-der-son?" repeats the father if as in a trance.

"You hear correctly... Son of a hen!"

My interpretation was rather loose but it had the desired effect. The Hendersons stared at me aghast. I can imagine how very proud they had been of this name for generations past. It looked as if I was the first person to have had the courage to analyse it to such a degree. In order to disguise their embarrassment, they started sniggering unconvincingly, as if they hadn't heard a good joke in years. Helga giggled more than anyone. She blew warm kisses at me from behind her parents' backs. Evidently I had conquered her with my inventiveness. I winked at her.

They turned to leave. Mrs. Henderson could not refrain from remarking, "Unless you play hockey, *lieber Herr*... you have no chance. We are returning to Canada and only a first-class pro will be good enough for our daughter. Understand? Someone who can shoot the puck right across the ice and into the net for Montreal or Toronto. And makes a killing for doing it."

Mr. Henderson added more fuel to the fire. "Do Bob Forham or the Stanley Cup mean anything to you, Mr... Blondie?"

They turned the corner. I could hear Mrs. Henderson sighing about how she can't wait for the time when the first puddle in her Canadian garden will freeze over. She was complaining that in Germany it hasn't frozen over for at least ten years. The local children probably don't even know what an icicle is. I'd never in my life heard anyone be so desperately sentimental towards something so self-evidently unsentimental. This lopsided sense of values seriously pissed me off. "I don't play hockey!" I yelled at the neighboring street. "I'm not interested in it. I beat the drums... if you care to know! I don't pretend to play like Gene Krupa. But I'm working on it. That will certainly be of interest to your daughter. Much more than your pucks and hockey sticks!"

Mrs. Henderson's voice suddenly chased after me like a yodel around the Alps. "Forget about Helga... waiter boy. We certainly aren't looking for a second-hand motorcycle for our daughter. You bald coot, you!"

This rather scared me. I touched my head. My frontal hair was receding like shallow but swiftly forgotten fjords. On the crown of my head I felt a small island of hairlessness. At twenty-six I didn't consider this to be anything out of the ordinary. OK, my nocturnal lifestyle and the constant worrying about Blondie didn't exactly preserve my youth. People thought me ten years older. But I considered it an insult that any old parents should write me off as a potential suitor for their daughter.

Then and there I swore that I would get Helga. If for no other reason, then out of revenge. I kept going round and round like a vulture circling its prey, until the Hendersons lost their nerve. The moment they let me into their apartment for half an hour to allow Helga to play me Blondie's records, I had won and they lost.

Three weeks after the famous discussion on the street I taught the Henderson's daughter how to swim in the deepest of oceans. And right in front of her parents' very noses at that. They were reading *Der Spiegel* next door in the living room. Subconsciously I blessed my Hungarian Ilona (I admit, not for the first time) for all those swimming techniques.

The senior Hendersons soon realized that chaperoning Helga to the Concordia every Friday was like taking coal to Newcastle. When the time came for them to return to Canada, Helga stayed in Germany with me. I taught her not to be afraid of water, and then made sure she got a full-time engagement at Concordia. It suited us both extremely well. We lived around the corner. On our way to the bar we would pass Goethe's birthplace holding hands. When we returned tired to our little nest at dawn, we made love and slept until lunchtime.

During her breaks Helga would sit before me on a barstool. As I mixed drinks for the guests, we talked as though we had never met before. Not one evening went by without her asking me the same question, "So you are originally from Austria, Sir?"

"To tell you the truth, I feel like a wandering Jew."

"How come? I thought you came from Vienna."

I was halfway through preparing a third *Polish Sidecar* for some inebriated Sergeant. I rattled the ice cubes above my head in a silver shaker. "I came to life for the first time in Vienna, Miss. I was seventeen at the time. As to what went before... I can only guess."

"That sounds interesting," Helga sipped her lemonade through a straw. "And how did that happen, please tell?"

"My awakening to life?"

"Yes."

"Well, it's like this. One fine summer's day I see Blondie on the front cover of *Face of the Future*... and at that very instant I am born."

"Oh, I've heard that somewhere before," Helga sighed dreamily. "You're not by any chance Harley Davidson?"

She shouldn't have said that. As soon as the drunken Sergeant heard "Harley Davidson," he took off from his bar stool with a perfect motorcycle roar and was gone.

24

Helga and I got married in the spring of the following year.
At the beginning of summer we went on our honeymoon.
For a long time now I'd been meaning to go to Portugal, with
or without Helga. There were two reasons. The first one was
basically trivial. I knew a hotel receptionist in Albufeira,
which meant that we could stay in the hotel for practically
nothing. But money was not the issue. I was propelled there
by the thought that Blondie spent the happiest time of her
life in those parts.

It really is unbelievable, the things that can happen to
a person. It all started with Blondie's mother Doris falling
into the bone crusher in a Chicago slaughterhouse shortly
after Blondie was born. Her father (his buddies call him
Frank the Drunk) got killed in an amusement park, riding on
the so-called Devil's Run. What follows is that Blondie found
herself kidnapped from a Los Angeles orphanage by a jealous
Portuguese. He mixed up the beds at Saint Theresa's
Orphanage, where she had been abandoned as a baby of a
few months by her relatives.

The Portuguese happened to be married to a woman
who wanted to become a film star. All her longing after fame
and fortune drove her to run away to America with their
daughter (also a baby). When her scorned husband eventually
found out that his child ended up in Saint Theresa's
Orphanage, he too set off for America. He decided to kidnap
his little daughter. But instead of grabbing the baby sleeping
by the window, he stuffed the one by the door into his bag.
He didn't stop until he reached Portugal. Everything was only
revealed to him when his wife, who did not become a film
star, returned home several years later, begging her husband
to take her back and clutching their real daughter in her arms.

By now Blondie had grown used to Portugal.
Everyone loved her very much. Especially the children, who
adore her blond hair. They played at being Indians in the
Wild West. They would shoot corks on a string at each other

with pop-guns. Or else they ran on the beach without a care in all the world. It was veritable earthly paradise. But it can't be helped. All good things must come to an end. In Blondie's case it meant returning to that orphanage in L.A. Goodbye Albufeira, she wrote in her diary. (She would have written more, only she couldn't see properly through all those tears.)

I was telling Helga all this on the plane during our flight from Germany to Portugal. We were landing now, though I'd hardly reached the middle of my tale. Our hotel was called the Boa Vista. I continue the moment the door to our room closes behind us. We unpack the few things from our suitcases and hang up our clothes. I knew Helga was only half-listening in any case. For a while after we met, she used to follow my Blondie stories with avid interest. But as time went by, she realized just how deadly serious I was about Blondie, and her tolerance rapidly began to diminish.

Before I had time to smooth down the creases on both pairs of trousers, she had already downed half a bottle of cognac behind my back. She fell onto the bed like a hewn-down tree.

I felt sorry for Helga. Just like Ilona before her, she fell victim to her own illusions. She found it extremely difficult to get used to the idea that living with me also means living with Blondie. One cannot change that. I kept trying hard to get her to understand me. For example at this point I tried mentioning Sisyphus. I mumbled something about pushing a stone up the mountain. As soon as it reaches the top it rolls back down again. And there's nothing for it but to start again. It is my damnation. And if it's not a curse—then it's the only acceptable way of having a tolerable existence.

But I was wasting my time. Helga slept like a log.

I set out from the hotel to get some fresh air. With my trouser legs rolled up I waded on the beach, leaving my footprints in the wet sand. Occasionally I picked up some pebbles. I battered the waves with them. A flat one skimmed the surface like a frog, only faster. I hadn't felt such happiness for a long time.

After two hours I went back to the hotel. On my way from the vestibule to the elevator I glimpsed the latest edition of *Le Figaro* lying on a chair. Blondie was smiling at me from the front page—just like that time in Vienna. My French was good enough to understand that my Angel was at this very moment performing in Paris. They described her every step, everything she did from dawn to dusk: What she had for breakfast yesterday, how long she spent in a Montmartre bookstore, how it started to rain afterwards and the fact that she opened an umbrella to cover her head. An all-yellow one. Eyes ablaze with hunger, I was lapping up every word.

I hurried upstairs to share this latest piece of news with Helga. When I left her, she was lying on her back and snoring, but now she'd turned onto her tummy. Her wedding-ring hand hung limply over the edge of the bed. She had managed to empty the rest of the cognac bottle.

I ran for the telephone as if my life depended on it. I was put through to the Hotel Esplanade in Paris (where Blondie was staying). I tried to explain to the receptionist that I was actually a colleague of his from Germany who just happened to be on honeymoon in Portugal and that I was calling with some very important news for Blondie. It didn't work very well. He insisted that he always takes messages to his guests personally. I understood. This was how he got his tips. I resorted to an old trick. I told him that it concerned a sudden death in the family. In such cases nobody minds losing a tip.

"Hello," Blondie answers on the first ring.

It takes some time before I manage to stutter, "T...this is Harley Da...Davidson."

"Really?" she replies. "This is Blondie."

"I...I've called you a million times already."

"A million times!" she breathes out. "That's absolutely wonderful!"

"And this is the... first time I found you in."

"That's because I normally don't answer the phone, Mr..."

"Ha...Harley Davidson."

"Yes... Harley."

"So who... answers it?"

"Take today for example... Alfonso. But he's taking a shower. And I just happened to go past when the phone rang. If Alfonso wasn't in the shower, he would have answered it. You see?"

As if I didn't. She sings as sadly as a bird in a cage. Alfonso is a Chilean soccer player. In Le Figaro they say that he's been stuck to Blondie's heels ever since the Santiago Film Festival last month. And he hasn't unstuck himself yet. He simply proclaimed himself Blondie's manager—without her even asking.

"So Alfonso is taking a shower," I repeat cluelessly.

"Where are you calling from?" she asks.

"From Portugal."

"From Portugal!" Blondie calls out happily.

"Yes. I'm calling from the Hotel Boa Vista."

"Boa Vista? Where is that?"

"In Albufeira. I know a receptionist here."

"Wait a minute," she exclaims. "Did I hear correctly? In Albufeira?"

"Yes. From the window I can see the sea."

"Listen. Do you know what that place means to me?"

"Of course. That's why I'm calling. I returned from the beach a little while back. I was throwing pebbles into the waves. It all depends on how flat they are. Some are more and some are less. According to their flatness they jump on the surface of the water. Like little frogs. You wouldn't believe it. Some jump twice, plop... and then they're gone. Some bounce on the surface as if they were on fire. Plop, plop, plop. Fifteen times in a row—plop! Quite simply I am behaving like a little boy up to no good. And then I realize I'm walking on the very same sand that you used to walk on as a child. I begin to tremble all over... I'm not exaggerating."

"I am also trembling!"

"Why are you shaking?"

"Because I would like to be there with you. I..."

She doesn't get any further. Somewhere a door slams. That's Alfonso coming out of the bathroom. He grabs the phone from Blondie's hand. He barks at me, "What d'ya want?"

From the tone of voice I could tell the kind of person I was dealing with. He introduced himself as Alfonso Lopez, Blondie's manager, agent and press officer, all rolled into one. He was not in any way interested in who's on the other end or where I was calling from. He began to lecture me on responsibilities and irresponsibilites. He couldn't comprehend how I would dare bother an artist a few hours before her much-trumpeted performance. I should realize that a first-class star, like Blondie, needs to concentrate if she is to give a solid performance. For the next fifteen minutes he explained how it was that persistent fans such as myself did nothing whatsoever to help him in his difficult task. In the end he threatened to sue me for no less than a hundred thousand dollars should I *insist* on calling again.

A polite person would have made some sort of effort to listen to me—show interest in what it is I have to say. But not Alfonso. He didn't forget to warn me to be careful and not to phone again or—I end up behind bars. Then he immediately hung up.

It's Blondie I felt sorry for, though. This ugly scene only testified to the desperate nature of my Angel's predicament. When one hadn't the least idea where to turn, one could easily fall into the trap of having to rely on an absolute brute like him. Obviously she (my sweet little Blondie) was in desperate need of someone who would not only put her on the pedestal where she belonged, but would also be capable and intelligent enough to help her rehearse the new scripts she had to learn by heart. But it's some kind of Murphy's law that instead, she crossed paths with a Chilean soccer player—albeit one who years ago played for the national team (though only as reserve goal-keeper)—who happened to be completely brainless.

As I paced up and down the room talking with Paris, I got more and more wrapped up in telephone wire. Finally, so tangled up that I couldn't move, I fell onto the bed next to the sleeping Helga. She wasn't snoring anymore. As a matter of fact she was smiling beatifically. I seriously doubted that I played any significant role in her pleasant dream. All of a sudden I realized that the telephone cord, now stretched tight across the bed like a bowstring, was cutting into my wife's neck.

Two things immediately entered my head. First, that she had recently put on a lot of weight. Thirty pounds at least. And second, what would happen if I strangled her? For a moment I imagined her with her tongue sticking out, completely purple. However, as has happened many times before, I swang from one extreme to another. In this case, it was from murderous thoughts to feelings of great shame that anything like this should ever have crossed my mind. After all, we were still on our honeymoon. Furthermore, I didn't really have anything against Helga. She was very kind to me. If there was one thing I could dislike about her, it was that she drank more than she should. That aside, if I killed Helga, it would automatically mean having to say goodbye to Blondie forever. And I was not such a fool as to dig a hole and then to fall into it.

As I breathed, the telephone apparatus sitting on my chest moved up and down. Instead of sinking into the deepness of sleep, I rose spirally, twisting like a corkscrew, heading for somewhere near the ceiling feet first. Before I could fly through the window of the first castle in the air, there was a sound of ringing.

"Hello," I said.

"Hello, you there," whispers Blondie almost simultaneously. "Harley Davidson?"

"That's me!" I sit up.

"This is Blondie. What a stroke of good fortune this is, is it not? Remembering where you're staying in Albufeira. I'm not this lucky every day. Usually the name of the hotel evaporates from my head the moment I've set foot in it. Goodness! And I have stayed in many hotels. Believe me! Boa Vista! Boa Vista! The name really has engraved itself in my memory. But now to the point, Harley. Alfonso has just gone out to fetch some cigarettes. We haven't much time, understand? First of all, many thanks. Your telephone call from Portugal really lifted my spirits. I'm very grateful to you for returning me to my almost forgotten childhood. I have long been suppressing that happy episode inside me. Can you hear me?

"Yes, I can."

"So what do you say to that?"

"I say that I will fly to Paris at once to see you!"

"I cannot ask anything like that from you."

"Nonsense. You're not *asking* me, you are fulfilling my long-standing dream!"

"Really?"

"I swear it. On everything holy that exists in heaven."

"Are your seriously coming to see me?"

"I've been longing for you so very much."

"Can you make it by this evening?"

"What time is it?"

"That is something I would like to know as well."

"One moment," I say. I struggle out from the telephone cord and run to the bathroom. My wristwatch should be lying next to the toothpaste tube. No—that was this morning. Since then I wore it to the beach. Who knows, maybe I lost it when I was throwing those pebbles into the water. I hurry back. Helga is wearing her watch. But the way she has been lying on her belly, she has overlaid the arm I need. I'm worried sick in case Alfonso returns with his cigarettes before I can turn Helga onto her back. I huff, puff and moan at her about why she's eating and drinking so much. She nearly falls off the bed. "It's exactly three thirty!" I shout out breathlessly into the mouthpiece.

"At what time does the plane leave?" Blondie asks.

"I haven't the faintest idea."

"Can you please find out, Harley? I hope you will manage to be here as soon as you can."

"What about Alfonso?" I enquire.

"Oh him! I'll get rid of him somehow."

"I have an idea."

"What's that?"

"Kick him out the door."

"Excellent! I'll kick him out with his cigarettes."

"In my opinion, he's a lout," I say.

"I agree with you entirely, Harley. I loathe him. I only reached out towards him the way a drowning person clutches at a straw. I hope you get my drift. When I'm depressed and homesick, I feel like crying. But I say to myself, Dear girl, you must go on. The audience have bought their tickets. It can't be helped. You can't disappoint your admirers just because something is bothering you. That's why usually I grit my teeth and bear it. Isn't that so? But inside I'm hurting. Like recently in Santiago. I felt terribly low. And all of a sudden Alfonso appeared holding a football. He threw it into the air, let it fall onto his head. He threw it against the wall, then up towards the ceiling—from his head onto mine and from mine back to his. And so we played ball together for fifteen minutes at the very least. My God! We were playing headball. I started wondering about it. But the truth is, I wasn't feeling sorry anymore."

"What do you miss most of all, Blondie?"

"Oh. Right now I'm missing you terribly, Harley."

She sniffs. I have to promise her that I will hurry. But I won't have time to make that promise. I can hear the door open in Paris and Blondie hangs up.

Here in Albufeira the telephone cord tickled Helga under her nose. She sneezed so hard that she jumped up into a sitting position. The cord was wrapped around her neck.

She hiccuped. "So you're trying to strangle me?"

"What makes you think that?"

"I don't think. I know it. What's the time?"

"You have a watch on."

"Three thirty five?" she said, bleary-eyed with sleep. "In the morning?"

"Morning! No, in the afternoon."

"Afternoon? It's dark outside."

"You make me laugh. The sun is shining."

"The sun! Do you think I'm stupid, or what? I can tell the moon from the sun." She yawns. Only then did she notice that I was holding the telephone receiver in my hand. "Is there someone on the line?"

"Blondie has just called."

"Really? And what did she want?"

"She wants me to fly to Paris to see her."

"So when are you leaving?"

"She begged me on her knees to be there by this evening."

"And? Are you going to make it?"

"I will try my best. She is desperate. But, of course, first she has to ditch Alfonso."

"Who the hell is Alfonso?"

"Oh! She has some Chilean footballer after her. She took my advice and promised to kick him out. Along with his cigarettes."

Helga yawned again. She put her slippers on and headed for the bathroom. As soon as she got there, she began to vomit, emitting animal-like sounds. For the next five minutes she gargled with a mouthwash.

When I opened my eyes, my wife was standing above me by the bedside, a glass full of water in her hand.

"What were you dreaming about?" she asked.

"Can you imagine? Below me the Champs-Elysées glitters already."

"Harley Davidson," she stated. "Please, can you at least leave all that in peace on our honeymoon?"

She threw the water in my face. She immediately ran back to the bathroom to get a refill. I looked for somewhere to hide. First I tried under the bed, then on the balcony. Helga was at my heels. We ended up out in the corridor. I

153

called for help. Helga screamed with demented laughter. Of course, the guests were already opening the doors of their rooms. For once she was right. It was four o'clock in the morning. Dawn was just breaking.

Two days later the newspaper headlines announced that, before leaving Paris, Blondie kicked the Chilean soccer player out, along with his football. I showed them to Helga. She couldn't believe her eyes how Blondie really took my advice.

We were just leaving for the beach when my receptionist saw us coming from the elevator and called out to us. His name was Olaf Parmesan—like the Italian cheese.

The first thought that crossed my mind was that perhaps Blondie sent me a telegram. But Olaf had something else on his mind entirely. He suggested that Helga sing a few evergreens in the bar this evening. He'd already told the pianist—and I would have the chance to play the drums. Helga whispered something into his ear. Olaf grinned.

"What is it?" I asked him.

"Harley. It is my honour and duty to inform you, as the first person on this planet to have the opportunity, that your dearest, beloved wife is pregnant. Allow me to congratulate you both on the successful beginning of you honeymoon. Keep up the good work, my friends!"

Joker. Tears rolled down our cheeks. That very same year I became a father for the second time in my life. We celebrated Christmas in Germany. Helga presented me with daughter Ingrid under the Christmas tree.

25

When I imagine that in order to shoot *The Last Day of Dick Hammersmith* in Aspen, they had first to construct (and then demolish) a gigantic ski jump, I don't know whether to laugh or cry. Such a pointless effort and waste of money on what will be such a flop. The only person in this movie who shines like the sun through grey skies is of course Blondie. She is unbeatable. It goes without saying. Her performance is like that of Marilyn Monroe in *Some Like It Hot*. But at least that was a side-splitting comedy. This hotch-potch (about this hopeless jerk D.H.) is a rather desperate affair from beginning to end.

In the film Blondie plays Dr. Martha Baker. As is well-known, she gives Dick practically two-and-a-half hours of encouragement (in her function of a doctor-psychiatrist) to help him overcome his fear of attempting a certain ski jump. According to the screenplay (written by none other than the crowned king of Hollywood kitsch Alan Albatross), it is supposed to help him stand on his own two feet. Good. Dick will finally jump, but instead of seeing the light, he gets killed. The title of this masterpiece alone should make it perfectly obvious to the average cinema-goer that it will scarcely be worth the admission price. In short, although he's already flying through the air, Dick, a complete crackpot, can't actually tell where his skis are. And it is precisely this *detail* that will prove fatal. Normally this would be a tear-jerker, but in this case it is more likely to be a tooth-grinder.

Dick is impersonated on the screen by an actor called Clark Boatner, a veritable bighead. I bet the first time he saw snow was here in Aspen, Colorado. When the producers offered to substitute a double—a stunt man—for the deciding jump, he nonchalantly waved his hand. This could be called a gesture of bravado, made without considering the catastrophic consequences. In this specific case the fictitious Dick will break his neck in the fall and will not live to enjoy his lunch (that same morning he was like a small child looking forward to his salmon in wine with almonds, garnished with vegetables and heaps of garlic), while the actor Clark Boatner will break both his legs. Oh well.

My poor angel Blondie! What she has had to endure! Just to recap, she now has plenty of productions behind her, including *Pearl Harbor* (that six-part TV series)—but what is a war with millions of treacherous Japs when compared with this nerve-racking horror about one incurable schizophrenic. To this day Blondie hasn't recovered from the massacre at Aspen. And strictly speaking, neither have I.

But this is not all. The mystery remains as to the identity of the impertinent dandy who bursts into Blondie's room at night, *in real life*. Each time, exactly twenty-five minutes and thirty-six seconds from the beginning of the picture, the door flies open—and I, although thoroughly prepared for this intruder, jump with fright. The same goes for Blondie. She is singing "Ciribiribin" in the shower (it is currently her favourite song), when someone bangs on the bathroom door. Blondie's blood curdles. She turns off the shower. She slips into a robe. My God! In the middle of the room, as if springing out of the earth, appears an unbelievable scarecrow. At first glance it is clear that above all else he needs to comb his hair. His windbreaker is hanging off him like a potato sack full of holes, sprayed with orange colour. Under his nose he has something like a false moustache. A complete vagabond. And he is as bold as brass. He is appearing in the film for the first time, and his arms are already reaching out towards Blondie. "My sister!" he calls.

I nearly have a heart attack. As I recall, Blondie has no brothers. But this smartarse (I guess he is no more than twenty-three) apparently has nerves stronger than the anchor chains on a deep-sea liner. He gets very angry when Blondie stares at him like a silly goose, as if she were supposed to herself round his neck, conquered by fraternal love. "Jeez, don't you recognize me, Blondie?" he asks. "It's me, Jimmy, your younger brother, missing for so many years!"

Blondie just blinks her eyes. She really could do
without this visit. Then she remembers that she is primarily
an actress, whose job is to act in even the most precarious of
situations. So she lashes herself into a super-human effort.
"Jimmy!" she calls out. "You're kidding. Where the hell have
you come from, my golden boy?"

"What the fuck does it matter where I've come
from," hisses Jimmy. "The fact is I need a hundred bucks."

"A hundred?"

"OK. If you insist, I'll have two hundred."

"Two hundred?"

If I hadn't seen it with my own eyes, I wouln't have
believed it. Firstly, I cannot understand how someone can call
Blondie Blondie, when her name is Dr. Martha Baker.
Wherever I go I worry about it. Amanda can't stand it
anymore. She has come out with an idea about Jimmy being a
hotel burglar who has become mixed up in the filming by
accident. Because he plays the part so well, the director makes
the most of it, also since it helps wake up the already nodding
audience (apart from Blondie's singing in the shower, nothing
much is happening in the film around this time) and he will
leave the scene in. Well, I don't know. Amanda's imagination
sometimes runs riot. But I am beginning to have my doubts
on this matter. What if she is right this time?

To my considerable surprise Blondie allows herself to
be talked into it. She picks up her purse and coughs up ten
crisp twenty-dollar bills. Her so-called brother Jimmy,
without saying as much as a "thank you Ma'am," "my
compliments" or "good evening," exits lower screen left,
even faster than he entered upper screen right just a few
moments earlier.

Of course I am losing plenty of sleep over this. I vow
not to cease my investigations until the mystery is solved.
Unfortunately, Blondie, with her contradictory statements
(they are printed in full the following day on the front page of
the tabloids), does not help me very much. In one interview
she announces that Jimmy is in fact her real brother, who, like

herself, was once kidnapped from Saint Theresa's Orphanage in Los Angeles. The only difference is that while she ended up in Portugal, Jimmy made it all the way to Nepal. He spent his youth there in an aristocratic family (they are Albanian by origin) and then he became a sailor with an Anglo-Greek shipping company. In the second interview she categorically denies everything. Apparently she only *adopted* Jimmy as her brother when he was eleven. She made up the scene with the money herself, so that Jimmy can get noticed by some important producer who will give him a better role in his next film. But no one notices him so he will never make it as a movie actor.

Instead Jimmy puts together a troupe of jugglers. They are called Seven Incredible Boys and a Girl with a Wig on Roller-Skates. Something like the Globetrotters, only instead of basketball, they all play pingpong on roller-skates. In the third interview, this time for the Italian *La Dolce Vita*, Blondie denies knowing anyone called Jimmy, although he literally robbed her of two hundred dollars in front of millions of spectators. Everything is topsy-turvy. There are moments when I have to force myself not to worry so much. And for the first time in my life I start thinking seriously about consulting a down-to-earth psychotherapist (at least about my more *serious* problems).

26

Once I'd heard that Seven Incredible Boys and a Girl with a
Wig on Roller-Skates were touring in Buffalo (such a
sensational act would never get as far as this town) and that
the show also would be live on television, I decided to take a
bus there. My plan was that, having found Jimmy, I would
press him to own up to how exactly his alleged brotherhood
with Blondie came about. It soon transpired that quite an
army of other, no less remarkable performers, did not get
their names included in the lengthy title of Jimmy's
minicircus. For example, along with Jimmy, who commanded
the whole operation like a captain (wearing a beautifully
shining brocade uniform embroidered with gold threads), and
the remaining six more or less not-so-credible boys and a girl
with a wig on roller-skates, there was a chimp called
Samantha, a bear, a seal and an ostrich. All in all, quite
splendid entertainment. The fact was that when this colourful
team flew to and fro on their roller-skates, we, the audience,
doubled up with laughter. Consider that these clowns played
almost uninterrupted table tennis—without any tables—with
the pingpong balls crisscrossing in the heavy air like so many
sweet little clouds under the cupola of the Buffalo Memorial
Auditorium.

When after an hour or so they announced something
called the window of opportunity, I thought it was kind of a
funny name for an intermission. Sort of like what they have
when they broadcast from the Metropolitan Opera to change
the set and give people the opportunity to go to toilets and
buy refreshments. So, I decided to visit Jimmy in the
greenroom. When he saw me, he immediately started to
behave like I'm some great fan of his—the sort of admirer
desperate for a pingpong ball along with his autograph. I bet
he would go to the end of the world if he could teach me
how to roller-skate as perfectly as Samantha the Chimp.
Jimmy was therefore beside himself with astonishment when
instead I pounce on him with the question, "How come

you're Blondie's younger brother when her mother Doris could not have possibly conceived for the second time so soon after Blondie was born, especially since she had already fallen into a bone crusher in Chicago?"

"You cannot be serious, man," Jimmy was almost offended. "Has it never dawned on you that Blondie's and my mother survived the bone crusher?"

"You're crazy. Is she still alive?"

"Not anymore," he replied. "But she lived long enough to have me, even though she lost both her legs all the way up to the hip joints."

"It seriously escaped me," I admitted.

"Now you know. Next time be more careful not to miss out on the most basic episodes from my life. Capish?"

"I'll try."

"Good. What did you say your name was?"

"Harley Davidson."

"You're kidding."

"I'm not."

"OK, Harley. I'm not going to argue with you. What made you think that?"

"What?"

"That I'm *not* Blondie's brother."

"You robbed her of two hundred bucks."

"Wait a minute. Where did you get that from? I robbed her! She gave it to me of her own accord. No? Voluntarily. Which clearly proves that we are brother and sister."

"Brother and sister! But only in the film, Jimmy!"

"So what?" he asked. "What is a film, for Chrissake? Allow me to explain that much to you. A film is real life, only captured on celluloid. Capish?"

"It depends."

"You are getting on my nerves, man! When I ask my sis for bread and she counts it out from her purse, that's something real, don't you think?"

"No, I don't."

"So what is it then?"

"A film scene."

"Have you gone mad?"

"No, I haven't."

"Look at these patent leather shoes."

"And so what?"

"I bought them in Aspen for the same two hundred I got from Blondie."

"I don't believe you."

"So go to hell. As Jimmy is my name and I am Blondie's brother, I bought them for those two-hundred bucks. When I say something, it's true. And if you don't believe me, you can tell me straight into my face that you take me for a pathological liar. Out with it!"

Jimmy made his chin protrude like a boxer's and waited for my next piece of self-expression. One thing was certain. I wouldn't be able to delay my answer for long. So I played it diplomatically, "Blondie cannot have a brother who is a pathological liar."

"Harley!" he exlaimed happily. "As soon as you came in here, I knew I would not be disappointed in you."

Apart from this phantasmagorical discussion, Jimmy was attractive enough. His uniform fit him like a glove. In his right earlobe he wore a little earring; on the left, the tattoo of a tarantula. I didn't doubt that somewhere, under his shirt or pants, he has even more curious engravings.

Because at present he appeared to be extremely friendly, I took undue advantage. "Jimmy," I said while scratching my ear, "listen. What you're telling me here, about those patent leather shoes and so on, is all very well. But nothing doing, this whole business of you bursting into Blondie's room like you were the big cheese, takes place in the cinema and on the screen. You can't deny that. But I haven't come to Buffalo to indulge in a detailed discussion of your acting ability. First and foremost I want to know whether you are also Blondie's brother in real life. Understand? I mean, outside the silver screen."

"Excuse me," Jimmy got annoyed. "I would never accept a role which was not one hundred per cent autobiographical. Capish?"

Samantha the Chimp, who, up till this point, was sitting on Jimmy's lap trying to stuff four pingpong balls into his nostrils, jumped across into my arms and tried to stuff the balls not only down my throat but right into my belly. When I began gasping for breath and changing color (out of politeness I did not dare to protest), the chimp put on a gloating expression and leapt onto Jimmy's shoulders. There she began picking something small and bouncing from her fur, which she then planted lovingly among Jimmy's thick curls.

Come what may, my conversation with Blondie's wishful-thinking brother took place between the four walls of a room, which must have borne witness to all kinds of loonies, neurotics and cranks over the years—from hockey players to concert pianists. But an eccentric of Jimmy's calibre? Probably never.

Without warning, Samantha forgot her fleas and started screaming her head off, because the seal had just stolen her pingpong ball. The bear and the ostrich were having similar problems. They were fighting over the pingpong paddle. The remaining six jugglers on roller-skates kept on gliding non-stop around us as though they were on fire. And, when the girl finally removed her wig to scratch her head, she turned out to be a bald man (who, apart from this particular handicap, was incapable of conversing in anything other than Turkish). I was not in the least surprised.

Such pandemonium had broken out that, if I really wanted Jimmy to hear what I'm saying, I'd need to shout right into his ear, "If you seriously are Blondie's brother, you can prove that you're not kidding by arranging a date with her for me. The fact is that I've been crazy about your sister since 1956 and I would be eternally grateful to you if you could bring us together, because mine is as undying a love as this world has ever seen!"

I was wriggling and rolling my eyes, awaiting his kind response, so it escaped my notice that the hullaballoo all around us had ceased. But that wasn't the end of it. As if someone had waved a magic wand, hordes of paparazzi and TV cameramen emerged from the darkest recesses, aiming their flash bulbs and telephoto lenses right into my terrified face.

Then Jimmy gave me the sort of look which told me another surprise lay ahead of me. "Excellent, Harley!" he crowed enthusiastically. "Just plain superb! I am positive your narrative was just the greatest ever to be told live on TV! Welcome to the family, my boy!"

I had never been so upset in a long time. First of all, I wanted him to clarify exactly which family he was talking about. And secondly, I was fed up to the teeth with him.

I almost screamed, "TV? What TV? I thought this was an intermission!"

"Hey, buddy! For some it's an intermission. But for others, who come to show me their stuff, it is—a window of opportunity. Capish? People have the opportunity to perform for millions of viewers. Instead, you have just declared your red-hot love for my sis on a TV show which is broadcast across practically the whole of North America. My sincere congrats, Harley. You have just made my day!"

I rushed from the chair and reached the door. "OK, Jimmy. If the program's still on the air, allow me to inform your dear viewers how appallingly you have cheated me. You never once gave me the slightest hint, not even a sly wink, that this meeting was going out into the ether. And that's not fair. To tell you the truth, if I was Blondie I would be ashamed to have such a brother, believe me, and next time I would not even give you two bucks and fifty cents."

Oh well. If nothing else, I managed to bring tears to the eyes of this famous animal-tamer. He got up and puts his arm around my shoulder. Then he escorted me into a long corridor, from where I hoped an exit to the street would soon appear. But instead we wound up in a circus arena. The blinding glare of the spotlights was so strong that I needed all my powers of observation to see one step ahead. Judging by the intensity of the applause I guessed that we were creating indescribable elation among what must be a crowd of several thousand. I did not even have time to ask if this was still the so-called window of opportunity, an intermission or the show itself. I was totally confused.

We were standing under the bar from which Samantha was swinging. She threw some objects at us, which appeared to be ordinary figs but also looked rather like something she ate some time ago—and was now expelling from her body piece by piece. So as to create an authentic atmosphere, Jimmy stood with a long whip in his hand, which he occasionally cracked loudly.

Then suddenly he darted away someplace. I stood there alone not knowing what to do with my hands. When he returned he was more friendly than ever. "Look, Harley," he said. "I'm really sorry, man. You must realize that when you stormed backstage in such haste, I didn't expect you were so eager to tell me what's eating you from the inside out. So now I know. And it got out of hand. But my God, you were so great in being crazy about my famous sis—it's unbelievable! Wanna hear something? I was just told by the producer who spoke to his boss and the boss spoke to somebody else at the very top, who told him that this Romeo and Julliet stuff of yours simply knocked him out of his armchair in Beverly Hills. He swore on his dying grandmother that our TV ratings will go not only through the ceiling but through the roof. In fact, the head honcho said, the way you conducted this window of opportunity surpassed the show itself. And to confirm that, we are receiving hundreds if not thousands of phone calls. Yeah. What a blast! The other day a Pakistani guy came to see me. That was in Toledo. And you know what? He started to juggle four eggs but then he became fanatical about being a vegetarian. By bull's balls! He spent fifteen minutes just talking about how he hates beef. Sure, it was a big flop. An unsurpassable disaster. So all said and done, I owe you one, Harley. If I can repay you sometime, do let me know. Capish?"

"Jimmy..."

"Wait a minute. Are we one big happy family or not, for Chrissake?"

I leaned over towards his ear, "OK, Jimmy. Whatever you say. But do you think Blondie's watching?"

"On this one, I have to disappoint you, Harley," he replied. "Right now she's on one of the Caribbean islands. Our television signal doesn't reach that far yet. I'm so sorry."

I was not aware that Blondie was where Jimmy says she is. And so, to be certain, I asked, "Do you by any chance know which island it is exactly?"

"She called yesterday from St. Lucia. She's there with the Jimmie Lunceford Band."

"Jimmie Lunceford died a long time ago."

"Really? Then it must be some other band."

"Arthur 'Sour' Honey?"

"Maybe. Shall I find out?"

"I'm mainly concerned with Blondie."

Jimmy understood straight away. He assured me that he would call her for sure today. He would tell her all about my serious intentions. He swore that he would relay the *traumas of my soul* to her, word for word and down to the exact letter. He would also put in a good word for me so that she doesn't delay giving an affirmative answer. She should be astute enough not to miss the chance of a lifetime. According to his judgment—and I have to rely on his reporting everything accurately—I seemed like the type of person she has been pining for all this time.

I almost flung myself round his neck in gratitude. I was on cloud nine. In view of what Jimmy has just told me, it appeared I've made it to Buffalo in the nick of time. If I had only been late by a hair's breadth, Blondie would probably have gone crazy. Only yesterday she was crying to him over the telephone about how she would gladly exchange all her glory (including the Caribbean islands) for the reassuring arms of a devoted partner with whom, at long last, she could experience true love. And that partner was none other than myself—at least Jimmy would make certain on that count. I should bet that Blondie was right now staring into the distance waiting for the moment when I, finally, appear over the horizon as her life's saviour. His prediction was that I would make my first appearance before her like some mysterious silhouette, one which will then assume a concrete form commensurate with the speed with which Blondie and I run towards each other.

"Man, the pair of you remind me of two gigantic magnets," he said, ending his prognosis.

"Please, can't you ring her right away?" I pled with him.

Jimmy cracked his whip. "Have you lost your marbles? In the middle of my show? When you are given an inch, you want a mile. Boy! Can't you see that we're going out live? Who would be in charge of this mayhem if I popped out somewhere? Capish?"

"I'm sorry."

"Don't be alarmed. I will give her a call tonight. Some time after eleven. When the charge is two-thirds cheaper. I bet a thousand bucks that you have already won her over. Have you got that much on you?"

"Do we have to bet?"

"Okay. If you don't want to we don't have to. But, believe me, my words are soon to be confirmed. You and Blondie are so made for one another, it needs no repeating. What did you say your name was?"

"Harley Davidson."

"Oh yeah. Harley Davidson. A beautiful machine. I too used to own one, once upon a time in Florida. Would you be interested in knowing some more?"

"Let's leave it for another time."

"I quite understand, Harley. The main thing, I beg you, is to take good care of your nerves. You're going to need them. Now that you and Blondie are so close."

"Thanks for everything in advance, Jimmy."

"Don't even mention it. Aren't we one big family?"

At that moment the lights in the arena went out. Jimmy gave me a push. As I stumbled towards the exit, he called after me to ring him at the Four Seasons Hotel. He will know more by then—like the date, place and time when Blondie and I will finally be able to embrace one another.

I could hardly sleep a wink the whole night. Impatience was killing me. The following day the Buffalo newspaper carried my photograph on the front page. It was a profile shot. Samantha was stuffing a pingpong ball down my throat. At eight-thirty I called Jimmy at the hotel. The receptionist informed me that Seven Incredible Boys and a Girl with a Wig on Roller-Skates checked out around 6 a.m. Apparently they were on their way to catch the flight taking them on a long tour to India and Saudi Arabia. And they were still awaiting the necessary permission to perform in Iran.

The receptionist seemed to be well informed. And when I asked him kindly to look inside every slot to see whether Jimmy had left me a message from Blondie, he did so willingly but could not find anything to cheer me up.

27

At this very moment the Boeing 737 (Flight Number 815) is (in all probability) circling over the airport. In a short time they will push the stairs across the tarmac to the plane and— *my darling Blondie, my Angel, it has been thirty-three long, extremely long years, but now, when you are inexorably and at long last coming closer, it seems as if the suffering of my endless waiting has metamorphosed from a deep wound into an insignificant scratch, which, although still hurting a little, is bound to stop doing so the moment we fall into each other's arms (my-forever-mine-dearest), leaving only a small, negligible scar (something like that funny little wart hidden behind your ear), like some memento, lest we should ever forget, that all good things come to he who waits, that he who really loves will be rewarded with a love more fervent than the boiling lava discharged from the crater of Kilauea in Hawaii, and that he who believes in miracles will discover (sooner or later) what he is seeking, and, in a form so stunning, that mere words pale before the inferno, turning to ashes all the burning desires from before his very eyes*—but while I am raving deliriously in fever, here in the Royal Arms time has stopped as if forever.

Nothing new under the sun. For a change it's me who's now looking for Melvin. In my bones I can feel a terrible catastrophe approaching. It's very nearly six-thirty p.m. The pilot of the Boeing 737 is in all probability in the process of communicating with the control tower. He is requesting permission to land. But here—once I have escorted Jacques to the door practically without a hitch— Melvin appears to have vanished from the face of the earth. As a matter of fact I have two reasons for looking for him. First: he has to return the book of poems he stole from me. Second: if he doesn't get the hell out of the Royal Arms immediately, it will be all the worse for him. Because in that case I will have to get rid of him forcibly. Most likely kill him. Can't help that.

While deliberating over how best to dispose of his body as I hurry past McCarthy's office, my search draws to a sudden close. From around the corner I can hear Melvin in reception talking to the Boss over the telephone.

"The weather here? Fine, Donald. What's it like in Montreal? Really? Isn't that strange? Only two hours away by car. Here the sun is setting. And over there it's as if it was rising. What? Oh yeah. Don't worry. I have everything under control. Of course, one never *knows*. I have to have eyes like a hawk. The Amazon has been watered. It smells just like Brazil in the spring. I'm not exaggerating. And this afternoon I changed a light-bulb in the bedside lamp of 401. Pardon me? Oh, that's great! Congratulations, Boss! What an experience! That Rousseau must be a genuine genius! Isn't that so? You do have a nose for such things. Eh? And your dearest wife too. What an artistically minded couple you are. One more thing. Don't forget to give my regards to that nutty prof. You know... what's his name? Correct. Berkowitz! My advice to him is to use his loaf. Why shouldn't we survive when it's quite obvious we can do so perfectly well as it is? Am I not right? You can't imagine, Donald, how much we are looking forward to hearing all about it on your return tomorrow. Believe me, we miss you here. It's so sad without you, like at a funeral. Honestly. We are wandering round like a bunch of abandoned orphans. At least that's what it looks like to me. If you were here I would cry, Yabba-Dabba-Doo, on your shoulder. No, I'm not exaggerating. Oh, before I forget. I would have gone home already except that the TV set in 202 has broken down. I'm working on it downstairs in my workshop. I'm mending it with a hammer. Ha ha ha! A good joke, don't you agree? There are so many wires inside that my head is spinning. What? Very well. Me too. And give my regards to your other half. Have a good time. You know what I mean. Cheerio!"

Before putting down the receiver Melvin gives it a look of utter disbelief. Then he looks over at me in exactly the same way, staring as if he were dreaming. I speak very quietly, so as not to frighten him, "Melvin. Don't you recognize me? It's me, Harley."

"Oh, stop it. I would know it was you even if you were standing in a bathtub taking a shower behind a shower curtain. But you're in luck, because I heard the phone ringing all the way from the basement. The Boss rang from Montreal and you are slacking God knows where!"

And he starts running. I'm trailing at his heels, all the way down the staircase. Across his workshop table are strewn the insides of a television set. Before I have time to recover, he crawls inside the half-empty box. For the life of me I can't imagine what he could be looking for in there. To the best of my knowledge, his understanding of electronics is on the same level as his understanding of the Mongolian language— to give but one random example.

Due to pressure of time, I take an offensive line. "Melvin," I cough behind his back. "Believe it or not, I found your fifteen dollars."

"Really?" he mumbles from inside the box. "And where were they?"

"They were smiling at me right at the edge of the jungle."

"Well, that's a coincidence," he says. "I found them too."

I gasp for breath. "In the same place?"

"Oh no. You see, the other day I rolled them up and put them inside the hollow handle of one of my screwdrivers. That's my secret hideout. But don't say anything to anybody."

"Don't worry, I won't."

"You know how it is. And then I forgot where I hid the secret hiding place. Can you explain that to me?"

"No."

"I can. My brain is going soft. The worst thing is, I'm beginning to suspect everyone around me of being a thief. Yet in fact, such people generally turn out to be honest."

As I listen to this, it occurs to me that if I were to insert the plug from the TV set into the socket, I would be rid of him once and forever in a matter of seconds. What's more, it would look like an accident and I wouldn't need to explain anything to anyone. But just at this moment Melvin crawls out from inside the box.

"You know, Melvin," I say. "I made everything up. From A to Z."

"What did you make up?"

"I didn't really find the money."

"Jesus, so where did you take it from, Harley?"

"I took it out of my own pocket. Look. Like this."

I take out all the creased five and ten dollar bills. Then I wave them in front of his face."

"Jesus Christ, why are you taking them out?"

"To buy the book of poems you *borrowed* from the upstairs bedside table."

"Oh yeah, my friend. That's too bad. Some things cannot be bought, not even with gold. Their price is quite simply immeasurable. Astronomical. Do you understand that? I just went to 403 to check if that blind I mended this morning is still okay. I was looking out of the window and all of a sudden I felt the urge to pray for the world as it is today. Because today Micky and I celebrate our silver-wedding anniversary. I also wanted to say a prayer for our two wonderful daughters. For the Boss, Donald McCarthy, who gives us our daily bread. And for you and Amanda, so that God might give you both his blessing at last. And for Jacques too, to stop him from varnishing his toe nails red. But, when I reached inside the drawer, my hand came out with some strange verses instead of the Bible, and I was so shocked I commmpletely forgot my Christian duty. Tell me, Harley. What, if I may ask, is it all supposed to mean?"

"What are you getting at?"

"Do you really write poems?"

"Why not?"

"Does Amanda know about it?"

"And so what if she doesn't?"

"I see." Melvin emits a whistle that sounds like a locomotive arriving at a level crossing. "So she has no idea whatsoever of their existence!" He removes the lid from the toolbox. The book of my poems to Blondie, inspired by an eternity of waiting for my darling, is lying on top, amongst a mixture of screws, hammers, pliers and wires. Melvin presses the dirty ball of his thumb against the edge of the book and rifles carefully through the thirty-three pages, in quick succession, one by one. "Poor Amanda. She's in for a shock when I tell her what's going on behind her back. And, can you please explain to me, who the hell is this... Blondie?"

I have the feeling of having been cornered. Quickly I reply, "Blondie is a symbol of all that's miraculous in the world. For one person it could be a spider's web floating free in the autumn air. For another it might be the froth on a freshly pulled glass of beer."

He is staring at me as if through two of those cardboard tubes that inhabit the centre of a roll of toilet paper. "That's wonderful, man. And where have you been gathering all this wisdom?"

"That's my own affair."

"But you also write letters, don't you?" Squeamishly, with just two fingers, he begins fishing out my welcome letter to Blondie by one of its corners. Then he hurls his personal opinion in my face. "Aren't you ashamed, Harley? This is called adultery!"

"I beg your pardon," I protest. "Those few innocent lines?"

"Innocent! You are cheating on Amanda like there was no tomorrow. You should be hoping that the ground will open and swallow you up! Are you?"

"No way!"

With this he feels no further compunction to wait. He grabs hold of the creased-up bank notes, smoothes them down with his fingers and puts them in his pocket. "Well," he says. "My initial thought was that I should hand this doggerel over to Amanda as clear proof of your appalling infidelity. But for these fifteen dollars I will *only inform* her that you write poems to girls and send them obscene love letters. Because fifteen plus fifteen equals thirty, understand, and that's more than enough to take Micky out to dinner. What do you say, buddy?" Without waiting for an answer he hands me the book and the letter. But he doesn't miss the chance for one parting shot. "I must say I had a quick glance at it, buddy. And I really feel sorry for you. It doesn't even rhyme!"

Melvin is the last person in the world with whom I would discuss literature. I'm quite sure that if I asked him what *according to him rhymes* with the word grass, he'd say brass, and with the word roof he'd suggest hoof. Or something equally clever. "Melvin," I say, "Do you know what time it is? Micky is waiting for you at home, dressed to the nines. And here you are, playing with a broken TV set."

He looks at me as if he had just woken up from a hundred-year slumber. "You're right," he says. "Damn Sony. Why do I even bother? Let the genius who invented it repair it."

As if to show that he is not full of hot air, he kicks the lid of his tool box shut. Then, with the same foot, he pushes it into the darkest corner of his workshop. Soon after, hands in pockets, he makes for the door. Obligingly I accompany him upstairs, along the corridor, past McCarthy's office, the reception counter and the mini-vestibule.

At the swing door I say politely, "Give my best regards to Micky, okay?"

It would have been wiser to hold my tongue. As is generally well known, Melvin uses every available opportunity to push himself as the savior of mankind. This time, though, he even goes so far as to suggest he can't possibly live without me. "Thanks, Harley," he says. "I will pass it on. I promise. And you can count on it that, all the time I'm devouring my meal in the restaurant with Micky, I will be thinking of you. You know, you are basically a good sport. But you commit so many sins. And you should cleanse yourself of them. You know what? I will volunteer to be your personal confessor. How about a cocktail together at the Banana Split? I swear I won't interrupt. What do you say? Are you interested? How about next week?"

173

If only he knew that by tomorrow I will already be gone with Blondie, God knows where, he would have a heart attack on the spot. "What about Thursday?" I enquire.

"Thursdays are perfect!" he rejoices. "Wednesdays are worse. And Tuesdays impossible. Micky is a member of the Friends of the Tour de France Club. They meet every Tuesday. And I have to chauffeur her."

"Why doesn't she cycle?"

"She would if her bike hadn't been stolen."

By now we are standing outside the hotel. Melvin is aiming kicks with his sneaker at the first of the two steps leading up to the entrance.

"So long then," I say.

I've reduced him to tears. He shuffles over to me and puts his bear paws on my shoulders. "Harley," he says. "You can't imagine how much I'm looking forward to next Thursday when you will have your long awaited opportunity to unburden your conscience. What about you?"

"Can't wait," I reply.

I watch him as he walks off, a little bit hunched over, as though he is sorry we never had this cocktail together a long, long time ago. Before turning the corner, he waves. I reciprocate. I feel a touch of melancholy. That's when I realize that this is the last time we will wave to each other.

A few seconds later I lock the door to the Royal Arms. For the first time in my life I live for the moment. I can feel an enormous weight being taken off my mind. Now there is nothing in the way for the two of us—Blondie and me.

28

Three months after giving birth to Ingrid, Helga got bored with living in Germany. Her biggest complaint was having to look after the baby. She blamed me for never having discussed the desirability of having children with her. It seemed that now, with Ingrid's arrival, neither of us had the time to look after her.

I couldn't understand it. First of all, people cannot simply argue over children as if they were chattels. Children should be born—the fruit of fervent love—spontaneously. Secondly, Helga spent all day at home. To use lack of time as an excuse in her case was, to say the least, most curious.

The changes that overtook Helga are gradual. At first I ignored any unusual fluctuations in her moods. I blamed her sullenness on the weather, PMS or on the fact that during lovemaking, she seemed to miss the bus before she could get on. And then one day—quite out of the blue—my wife stopped singing and dancing. She never set foot inside the Concordia anymore. She sat at home and watched television, with eyes in which one could see that she was mentally elsewhere. She was neither here nor there.

If she ever came out with anything spontaneously, it was only to say that she missed her parents. She started pressing me, initially about once a week, but after a month every single day, to move to Canada with her to be near them. The Hendersons had something of a small chateau near Ottawa. It stood on several acres of land near the river. All day long she kept on repeating that there should be plenty of room for all of us there. She begins to sound like a broken record.

The photograph on her bedside table confirmed her words. A big house stood on top of a hill. A reflection of the sun shone on the surface of a river. Mrs. Henderson was weeding the garden. My father-in-law had chosen a most unflattering moment at which to snap her. As he called across to her, she stood up, an armful of wilted dandelions in her hand, and smiled into the camera lens as if she couldn't remember what day it was.

In less than three months, though, we did find ourselves on the other side of the ocean. Mother Helga, little Ingrid and myself, the father. Throughout the preparations for this journey I pretended that I was being forced against my will to undergo this terrible upheaval—just so that the three of us could stay together. In fact the opposite was the truth. In my mind I was rejoicing. In Canada I would be much closer to Blondie (at least according to the map) than ever before.

And, from the outset, it looked as if exchanging the European continent for the North American one would really turn out to be the sought-after balm needed to soothe Helga's aching soul. She kept telling everyone how well she sleeps at night. During the day she sang. She hardly ever wanted to put little Ingrid down. And soon she even took a renewed interest in dancing. Instead of watching TV she listened to the radio. From her room (for we now had separate bedrooms) it was possible to discern the sound of a typewriter.

Before three weeks passed, the first deep crisis began. I first became aware of it when Helga started to spend nearly all her time in her room. Sometimes she missed lunch, other times dinner. For hours at a time, and sometimes even days, she kept playing the same record—Puccini's opera *Madame Butterfly*. Then there were the special Sunday matinées, as she decided to call them. Usually she waited until after lunch, when the Hendersons took Ingrid out for a walk. As soon as the door closed behind them, my wife started to take her clothes off.

I felt awkward. I sat on the sofa, trying to focus my eyes on something that would provide moral support. I tried the ceiling, the surrounding walls, through the windows. Helga was all the while wriggling before me like a fakir on burning coals. Her exposed body, heavy with surplus pounds, inspired pity rather than erotic desire. On top of everything else, she accompanied her crude movements with singing.

And what a song! My uneasiness grew greater the longer it went on. The only light note in these proceedings was the blond head of our sweet little daughter. She was scampering through the long grass like a salvation-bearing firefly.

By December of that year things had gone so far south that Helga didn't even bother to undress at the start of her Sunday routine. She hopped in front of me wearing a red jumpsuit. The second weekend of that same December, in order to hide my embarrassment, I reached for the first book I could find on the bookshelf behind me. R.H. Northon called his work *The Real Soldier is Never Thirsty*. Quite frankly, after reading the first few lines, it occured to me that the author could well be my own father-in-law, Mr. Henderson. While Helga pranced about on the carpet, rattling the whole house, I read on page forty-five that some guy called Henri Closson, a Belgian paratrooper, survived for three days buried in the Sahara Desert sand like a lizard, hiding from the Moroccans.

It took a while for me to register the fact that Helga had completed her performance and was now sitting by the window scrawling something in her sketchbook. Only when she rushed out of the room in tears did I get to judge her approximately ten-minute effort. It consisted of the silhouette of a man with his trouser legs rolled up, standing on the beach and shading his eyes with the palm of his hand. It could be in Germany, anywhere to the north of Hamburg. But intuition told me that my wife could well have Albufeira in Portugal on her mind. Another figure, high up on a rock and visible against the sky, held her arms out like an angel descending from the clouds. Her long hair was flowing in the wind. Next to her bare feet I deciphered the initial letter—B. That proved without the shadow of a doubt that it was she whom I so admire. In the sand beneath the rocks, written by a shaky hand in gothic script: *I, the wretched terrestrial worm, look for the way out of th*e *stray circle of my somnambulic madness.*

A few days later I got a job as a barman in Vinny's Chuckwagon Motel. On my first night I met a group of musicians. I could hear them at their table discussing how they would like to set up a septet but had no drummer. When I confided in them that it was only an unfavorable stroke of fate that prevented me from becoming the second Gene Grupa, they welcomed me with open arms. We decided we want to resurrect the melodies of the greatest bands from the war era—my musical domain. I was really starting to enjoy myself. We began to meet regularly on Mondays and Thursdays.

I slept wherever I could—sometimes even in the bar. Or perhaps at the place of one of my musical colleagues. Slowly but surely I was becoming estranged from my so-called home. It was a bit like an ice floe—once it has cracked, the fissure inexorably grows bigger and bigger. It did not, however, mean that my occasional visits home were greeted with any animosity. I was not made to feel in the least like an undesirable outcast. I found the doors always open. Strictly speaking we all met once a fortnight for Sunday lunch. The resulting comedy was enough to reduce one to tears. We all pretended nothing out of the ordinary was happening. Mrs. Henderson sometimes prepared roast goose, or duckling with red cabbage. The amount of caraway seeds on the roast (and the way in which she made the sauerkraut) was proof that she had passed through the German school of culinary arts.

Mr. Henderson could never escape the retired soldier in himself. His only interest at the table was who is at war with whom and who is going to win.

"Listen, my good Sir," he addressed me on a certain occasion around Christmas, choosing, as is his custom, a moment when my mouth was full. "Why exactly are you here?"

I took my time before answering. Prior to swallowing the next morsel I chewed over it twice as long as normal. "And where should I be, General?" I asked.

"Where else," he raises his thick eyebrows, "than on a battlefield, young man. Don't you suppose?"

Little Ingrid sat opposite me, imprisoned on a high chair. Usually it was difficult to see her among all the teak furniture. But at the table she was a head taller than the rest of us. The only person with sufficient authority to force her to take a piece of meat into her mouth was Mrs. Henderson. But it was a pale sort of victory. Ingrid usually half chewed the morsel and spit it out anyway.

Helga was not much interested in the chirping round the table. When not staring into her plate, her gaze was directed somewhere out in the unknown.

"Which battlefield exactly have you in mind?" I asked the General.

"There are thirty-six wars in the world today," he answered. "Of course, the one that poses the most immediate threat to us is the Vietnamese war!"

Mrs. Henderson sighed deeply. "When she grows up, Ingrid is going to be a figure skater. Don't you think, Helga?"

My wife put her knife and fork down. Leaning against the back of the chair, she raised her arms above her head as if she were lifting an invisible hat. "When my daughter grows up, she will be a stage artist," she replied without any hint of a smile.

"You mean an actress?" her mother asked.

"You must be out of your head," Helga snapped. "An opera singer."

The first person to push away his empty plate was Mr. Henderson. "Singers are like begging birds," he declared. "If you don't feed them in the winter, they drop dead from hunger. I would recommend the army for Ingrid. There she would have a chance to get inside a tank. Or make a living as a radio operator."

I could not believe I had withstood three years of this.

It had been some time now since Helga discarded her sketch book. She'd begun to paint even bigger and more absurd canvasses. Ingrid was growing up fast. She seldom saw me. Sometimes I had the impression that she didn't know quite where to place me. By this time I was earning a good wage. But when I brought my money home, it looked as if no one expected anything from me.

Our band broke up before we even had had enough rehearsals to be able to play in public. During this episode in my life I wrote, without mailing, several letters to Blondie. To be exact, they were more like unfinished essays. One, the last one, went on for over fifty pages. In it I discussed the tragic situation that faces children who grow up without their parents. I obviously wrote from my own experience. I was unable to find peace. Wherever I happened to be I was on tenterhooks. I was searching for human happiness and love with an intensity bordering on obsession. And at the same time I gave my children so little—it was as if I didn't exist for them.

On one occasion I returned home in the small hours (usually I finish around one-thirty a.m., but this particular time I cut my finger on a piece of broken glass and had to spend another hour in the motel's bathroom) and found Mrs. Henderson sitting in the living room. She was holding a magazine. As I walked past her, she stopped me with the question, "So this is your beloved Blondie?"

The manner in which my face immediately lit up did not escape her attention. Of course, smiling up at me from the very centre of the two-page spread which she held up to my face, was none other than—*my* Blondie. It was a still from a film called *Reality*—some pale Hitchcock imitation. In it, Blondie burns to death under suspicious circumstances in a San Diego bus shelter.

"Yes," I sighed, bewitched. "That's her."

"According to Helga, it's apparently not over *between the two of you.*"

"I would lie if I told you otherwise."

"Don't you think you are exaggerating *somewhat*, Mr. Davidson?"

In all the time we had known one another, she had not once called me her son. "I don't know how best to explain it, Mrs. Henderson," I said.

"What do you want to explain?" Her replies showed greater and greater displeasure. "You are married to my daughter. Isn't that enough?"

After a whole night working my shirt off in the bar, I could hardly stand upright. Without making the slightest attempt to suppress it, I yawned. "I'm not doing anything that Helga hasn't known about from the beginning."

"Please, stop talking nonsense!" The small lady with one strand of purple hair on her otherwise graying head gets agitated. "When are you going to behave like an adult? Or a father!"

Wearing her nightdress, little Ingrid appeared in the doorway. The nightie had miniature trains, cars and boats printed all over it. Ingrid dragged a large teddy bear by his leg. Soon she would be four years old. Before I had a chance to pick her up she took refuge on Mrs. Hendersons's lap.

The following Sunday was my father-in-law's birthday. As was his custom during lunch, he started discussing war. Helga painted a picture for him as a present. In it, Mr. Henderson, wearing a freshly spruced-up uniform, sits bolt-upright on a horse at the top of a hill, surveying the troops assembled in the valley below. This is exactly how he would have looked (so his daughter imagined) had he been a General in the Napoleonic wars. In real life he was wounded in 1944 near Assen in Holland. He almost never made it home.

Having inspected the oil painting thoroughly, he leaned it against the opposite wall so as to be able to look it over during the course of the meal.

He began mumbling something between mouthfuls of food, seemingly to himself. But I soon realized what he was getting at. He was talking about a country where there was a house similar to ours. But if we looked through the window into this second house, the people sitting around the table *there*—as opposed to us *here*—were all dead. No one could talk him out of his certainty that, if the world continues the way it is going, the same fate awaits us. What happened to *them* today, was waiting for *us* maybe tomorrow. The only way to avoid destruction was to stand up to the enemy. The question was, who, at *this* table, would raise the flag to give the order for the decisive offensive? The veterans were now long past it. Mothers should stay at home and look after their children. Had he stayed behind when it was his turn (instead of fighting in Holland), who knows what would have happened.

"Helga," he turned to his absent-minded daughter. "Your excellent painting is my idea of the way real art should look."

The General used a napkin to wipe his greasy mouth. Before getting up he threw it onto the table. On his birthday he always put on his best uniform. It only differed in a few minute details from the one he is wearing, on his horse, in his daughter's painting. The buttons on the canvas were slightly bigger. So were the epaulettes.

This Sunday was different from others not only because it was the General's birthday. This was also the first time he has showed us the shrapnel scars on his belly. He put his jacket over the back of his chair, pulled his khaki shirt from his pantaloons and, before our very eyes, exposed his belly hanging like a balloon over his belt. Little Ingrid laughed. She stuck her little finger into his navel, as if she were hoping to burst it.

I wet my lips on the glass of red wine. Then I excused myself, saying that I would come back shortly. I went into the garden. Spring was in the air. Intoxicating scents filled it. The birds were singing. The earth under my feet felt soft; at each step water oozed to the surface.

I reached the fence. Animals' territorial limits can be set by an impassable obstacle, but when it comes to self-preservation, humans know no bounds. My effort does not need to be great. I kept walking along the fence to the closed gate. I took the footpath to the main road. An hour and a half passed before the first car stopped for me. In less than twenty minutes I was in town.

That same evening I telephoned Helga telling her that I was sending her a list of my personal belongings. I strongly hinted that I would appreciate it if she could prepare them for immediate dispatch. Three days later I sent a taxi to the Hendersons' house. The driver was instructed to deliver the cargo to my new address. I was lucky to have found lodgings with the bass player from the band, with whom I get on very well. His record collection was without peer, in volume as well as quality.

For the first six months, I drowned in the musical improvisations of players I had never even heard of. It looked as though, apart from Blondie, music was the only thing that kept me going. During this time I wrote another letter to my Angel, this time forty-five pages—but just like the preceding ones, I didn't send it. In it I expressed my great sadness at so often being reduced to feeling like a mountain wolf, howling words of love into the night—whose echo doesn't even bring one single bark in return.

When, at the end of summer, I called Helga to say that I am going to war (matter-of-factly I mention that perhaps we might not see each other again), her reaction did not surprise me. She handed the receiver to the General. He was beside himself with joy. For the first time ever he addressed me by my name – "dear Harley." In a rousing speech he spoke of how much he appreciated my heroic decision. By this unparalleled deed I was manifesting my responsibility not only towards my threatened family, but also to the continent which had seen fit to accept me as one of its own. In all my life I have never before received so many sincerely meant compliments. After this the General gave me his promise that, since such a significant journey is involved, he would take care of all the necessities. Even as I listened to him, I kept wondering how great his enthusiasm would be if he only knew that the main reason for my going to Vietnam is Blondie.

In a fortnight the whole family gathered at the airport, as if they wanted to touch me while I was still alive. Mrs.

Henderson gave me an apple strudel. Several times she even calls me "son." Her husband had a different kind of surprise for me. From a shabby leather pouch he took out a short bayonet. Apparently it saved his life on more than one occasion on the battlefields of Europe.

Helga turned up just the way she always was—with nothing. Just her mysterious smile. She held our daughter firmly by the hand. Once released, Ingrid launched herself into my arms. I lifted her up above my head. She kicked out with her legs and waved her arms, as if the air was water and she was swimming in it.

Our goodbye had all the idyllic mood of a Monet painting, at least in as far as the lighting was concerned: shades, colors, even the grim ostentatious figures spread around the airport tarmac like bowling pins.

Far more puzzling was the emptiness of the streets two and a half years later upon my return. Helga found another father for Ingrid, the owner of a well-known art gallery in Montreal. When I called the Hendersons to enquire about the one suitcase I left with them (for the most part it contains photographs and newspaper cuttings relating to Blondie) and offered to return the General's precious bayonet, my former father-in-law replied grumpily that he knew nothing about any suitcase. And I should keep the bayonet. As far as he was concerned, the war from which I returned was effectively lost. It came as no surprise to me when he asked what I was doing there all that time anyway.

29

Around 3 p.m. one mid-October Monday afternoon the Boss sent me to his country summer cottage, situated on the shores of Golden Lake, to fetch his briefcase. Normally he would have asked Melvin to do this. But Melvin, as he typically does around this time of year, had gone to the Bahamas with Micky for ten days. He wouldn't dare go to Florida. He is afraid of the exiled Cubans in the bars, who might just punch his face in after a few drinks were he to tell them he was a draft dodger. They would love him just the way they love Jane Fonda. As for McCarthy's briefcase, he left it behind at the cottage the previous weekend. It contained irreplaceable documents, without which the Royal Arms, according to him, would simply become unmanageable—and who knows what would then become of the rest of us. My mission was therefore of the utmost importance.

I sat behind the wheel of our Escort. A few miles from Renfrew the landscape grew hilly. The smell of freshly ploughed fields permeated the car. My thoughts soon turned to Blondie.

I mulled over what might have happened had I married her right at the outset—instead of Ilona and Helga—and we had had four children together. I envisioned various scenarios. First of all I imagined that we had four little girls—four little Blondies. Then I became upset because we at least should have one boy, the spitting image of me. So, in the end I pictured mother Blondie, her three miniature replicas, a boy who looks like me and myself bursting with joy in the role of proud father.

During all this fantasizing I nearly had an accident. That brought me back to reality with a jolt—and my thoughts turned to Amanda. The moment she found out where McCarthy was sending me (I would not be back before nightfall), she started lecturing me on not catching a chill, not falling asleep behind the wheel and not getting lost. And the main thing was about being sure to read other people's minds. There are a lot of maniacs on the roads.

I turned the radio on. To make the journey go quicker, I wanted to tune in to an ever-lasting (if possible) drum solo. Instead, I came to the sound of broken glass. Agitated voices confirmed the fact that I was bearing witness to some kind of domestic argument.

"So you won't give her up," said a woman.

"How do you mean?" a man enquired.

"You are cheating on me."

"Don't be silly."

"What time is it?"

"I couldn't get the car started."

"Why do you think they invented the telephone?"

"It was busy."

"I wasn't talking to anyone."

"Come on. You were flirting with Garry."

"Nonsense."

"Liar!"

"Womanizer!"

Quite simply, this was just a *normal* quarrel between two partners of the opposite sex—the kind which could go on for hours without solving anything. It soon became evident that this melodrama was aimed at the *sophisticated* listener. The window pane shattered because the house (which happens to be situated at the edge of a forest that, according to the narrator, looks exactly like the landscape through which I am driving at this very moment) was being broken into by a burglar intent on stealing a television set. Once all the clatter stopped, the thief could hear voices arguing in the living room. He was about to flee when he realized, just like myself and a thousand other listeners, that the sound was coming from a *love thriller* being shown on the very TV set he wanted. In fact the owner forgot to switch it off in his rush to get to work.

Our gangster was hungry, too, and once he climbed in through the broken window, he headed for the refrigerator (meanwhile the marital *ménage á trois* in the drama is turning into a *ménage á quatre*), where he made himself a sandwich, opened a bottle of Molson Ale and relaxed in a comfortable armchair. Should the owner of the house return suddenly, he would find the intruder grinning stupidly at an ad in which Victor Kiam is so impressed with his Remington shaver that he intends to buy the whole company.

Approximately half an hour later, the burglar, his stomach full to bursting, and well fortified (after the first beer he had another two) dragged himself, along with the TV, towards the door. To his considerable surprise, he found a black dog lying outside on the mat, baring his teeth and growling. There followed an experiment with a piece of leftover salami from the fridge. The dog ate the salami, stopped baring his teeth, but continued growling menacingly. The robber's plans were foiled by the presence of this monstruous creature. Since he was not so foolish as to risk having his trousers ripped or losing a chunk of his ass, he left the television set and quietly disappeared through the bedroom window.

Before I could find out who wrote this trash or was responsible for broadcasting it—and what sort of moral the listener was expected to draw from it—I switched the radio off. Quite frankly, I was not in the least bit interested.

I swerved round the first sharp corner and a dense forest grabbed me from both sides like a pair of forceps. Then, I noticed a strange man standing at the roadside. He waved his arm as if he wanted a lift. What was more terrifying was that, going by the narrator's description in the radio play I was been listening to, this inividual looked exactly like the failed burglar.

Normally I would not dream of stopping for such a vagabond in the middle of a forest. But my foot suddenly hit the brake pedal, the door opened and before I realize it, the unknown passenger was wheezing in the back seat. I was unable to avert my eyes from the rearview mirror. I felt cold sweat pouring off me.

He began to reveal the entire story of the robbery (word for word, just the way I heard it on the radio), including the shattered glass and the TV set which had been left switched on. The only difference in this case was that he wasn't frightened off by the black dog—because, when he switched to another channel, he saw none other than himself, sitting in the armchair, chewing on the sandwich and washing it down with a Molson Ale.

But it didn't end there. All of a sudden he burst out sobbing. He begged me to accelerate. He wanted to give himself up and confess his crimes. And, once having served his time, he vowed he would to return to society a new person. He wouldn't even steal a toothpick from a restaurant, let alone the salt or pepper shaker.

Of course, I wasn't able to talk him out of it. I dropped him off at the nearest police station. They greeted him with open arms.

As I arrived at McCarthy's cottage the sun was setting. Once it dropped beyond the horizon, I started shivering from the cold. I soon found the briefcase, but I was not in any hurry to return home yet. In the refrigerator I discovered everything needed for a light snack. Although the TV set was within easy reach, I chose not to turn it on.

The moment I lit the fire in the fireplace my eyes closed. I found myself at a funeral. Both my wives had died within a few years of each other. In this dream they were being buried at the same time. The chapel smelled as if their bodies had been decomposing together there for a long while. The lids of the coffins were raised. I walked round the cadavers on tiptoe. First I kissed Ilona's forehead. Then Helga's.

Obviously such a funeral ceremony could not take place without the presence of members of the family. In the first row on the left, my daughter Sandor was sniffling loudly. Behind her, drowning in tears, was what looks to be a large delegation of uncles and aunts. Judging by their clothes, they must have come all the way from Hungary to be here. And on the right, Ingrid was staring blankly into emptiness. Her eyes were dry. In the row behind her, trailing away like the train of a bridal gown, was the Henderson family clan complemented by a staff of military bigwigs. Their formation grew symetrically the further back it went, so that the last echelon (like a pyramid base) took up an entire row.

When I woke up, I was not exactly in a cheerful mood. Ilona actually died in mysterious circumstances a few years after our break-up. While boating in the middle of Lake Balaton, about 70 miles from Budapest, she fell overboard and drowned. There were no witnesses. They only started searching for her when the empty boat was washed ashore the following day. My second wife was killed in an automobile accident in Vermont not long after I returned from Vietnam. Her then husband also met his end a few hours later in the operating room. Before breathing his last, he managed to affirm that Helga was driving. Apparently she hit that rock on purpose.

The logs burning in the fire made pleasant crackling sounds. The sparks coming out of the chimney fell towards the surface of the lake. It could also be the reflection of the stars in the sky that I saw.

On a sudden impulse I decided to place a call from McCarthy's summer house to Sandor in Paris. The last time we exchanged any words was last Christmas. And in March of this year I received a letter. The address on the envelope corresponded with mine, but the letter was destined for someone else. It began: "Dearest Jennifer..." I did not read any further. Instead I returned it to her with a note saying that she must have mixed up the addresses. I still haven't had an explanation.

As I dialed her number, the moon emerged from among the trees. The first sounds I heard in the receiver appeared to be coming from somewhere like—the Moulin Rouge. On my second attempt a woman's voice said: "Hello" - but it was not Sandor.

Nevertheless I asked, "Sandor?"

"Who is calling?"

"Harley Davidson."

"Oh... one second, please."

"Sandor," my daughter said.

"Here is Harley Barley."

"You're kidding. Are you in Paris?"

"I'm calling from the boss's summer cabin."

"That's interesting."

"He's left his briefcase behind."

"What else is new?"

"I've just had a dream. I was at Ilona's funeral."

"Great. You should dream about it more often."

"Why do you think that?"

"So you don't forget that my mother killed herself because of you."

"She drowned in Lake Balaton by accident."

"With your letter to Blondie on her."

"Aren't you confusing her with Helga?"

"Helga had a similar letter in her purse. My mother had hers in the pocket of her summer dress."

"I'm calling to tell you some good news."

"I doubt it will be good."

"I suggest that we all move in together once Blondie and I have a permanent address. You know? You and Ingrid. Blondie and me. I will try and make it up to you for all those lost years when you had no *real* home."

"Jesus, Harley," replied Sandor. "Have you been drinking?"

I was silent. I didn't know how exactly to explain, without sounding absolutely pathetic, how much I longed for us all to be able to sit down at one table. I imagined us all having dinner together (first having said a prayer of thanks for all God's gifts) and afterwards perhaps everyone would go to see a movie. Something completely ridiculous, just for the fun of it—let's say some schmaltz like *The Last Day of Dick Hammersmith.*

But before I could come out with anything comprehensible, Sandor told me not to waste any more money on meaningless telephone calls. She hung up before I could utter: "Hold on a moment."

I would not going to let such transparent failure discourage me. Immediately I called Ingrid at her Oconomowoc rabbit farm in Wisconsin.

"Ingrid." She had a pleasant, velvety voice.

"Harley," I said.

"Daddy! What's going on?"

"Important things."

"How come? You only called the other day."

"Really?"

"Three days ago. Don't you remember? Late at night. You apologized for my mother's suicide. And what it'll be like when you and Blondie have a permanent address."

"Excellent. So you know about it?"

"Of course."

"And have you made up your mind yet? Are you interested in living with us?"

"Without the slightest doubt."

"Hold on a minute," I replied. "I've lost my train of thought. Are you married or single?"

"I'm living with a guy."

"And would he be moving in also?"

"I'll ask him."

A smacking sound came down the telephone. I thought to myself, My God, it sounds as if the two lovebirds are exchanging a quick kiss in passing. I cleared my throat. "Very well," I said. "Bring him along with you. If things turn out the way I plan them, then we'll be seeing you soon."

"You're a wonderful Dad," replied Ingrid. "But don't worry about a thing."

"Like what?"

"Like blaming yourself and all that crap. Don't forget that, when the accident happened, the art gallery in Montreal was on the brink of bankruptcy. I suspect it was my stepfather who jerked the wheel towards the rock. He was banking on his own survival and having all the debts paid from mother's substantial life insurance policy."

"You just want to console me."

"No I don't."

"Yes you do."

"You know what, Dad? Good night."

30

My psychotherapist's name is Dr. Hugo Wasserman. If only
Kevin, alias Arturo Toscanini, knew about me seeing a shrink,
he could breathe a great sigh of relief. As everybody knows,
he worries himself to death imagining I have finally gone as
crazy as a March hare. All because of that jungle hell I went
through—or else from my never-ending hassles with Blondie.

I don't treat Kevin fairly. I know that. Instead of
coming clean and telling him about my occasional sessions on
the couch, I pretend nothing has changed. It must be because
for the life of me I just can't imagine our friendship without
seeing his tormented face—without being aware of his
genuine sympathy towards me.

Dr. Hugo, as Amanda and I call him, is a
psychoanalyst to the letter. We alternate our bi-monthly visits
to him. If I have a sitting in June, Amanda has one in July.
My next visit will then fall in August. Amanda's in September.
He is a nice fellow whom I discovered by sheer luck. One
spring day, more than six years ago now, I stepped on my
glasses. And his office was in the same building as my eye
doctor's. As soon as I entered the waiting room, feeling my
way with my arms out in front of me, I realized that
something is amiss. My opthalmologist had a squeaky voice.
But what I heard was something more akin to a bear
grumbling, standing on his hind legs and cordially inviting me
in. Instead of taking to my heels I followed him like a dog on
a leash.

"How are you keeping?" he asked halfway to his desk.

"I can see you double," I answered. "Sometimes even
treble."

"Well done!" he exclaimed. He clearly took me for
someone with a multiple-split personality. "Sit down, please."

"You must understand. I came to the wrong door!"

Dr. Hugo waved his hand. His gesture was meant to
make me understand that he had many years' experience and
knew best. Two chairs line both sides of the desk. Over a

sofa by the window there is a map that takes up the whole of the opposite wall. I gathered from the familiar, if hopelessly out of focus, shapes of the various continents, that it was a map of the world in all its glory. The shores of the main landmasses were surrounded by a deluge of blue. I could almost hear the splashing of the bottomless ocean. I flopped into the armchair as if pushed by some supernatural power.

"So... let us start from the beginning," my counterpart said kindly from the opposite side. "Your name, please?"

"H-a-r-l-e-y D-a-v-i-d-s-o-n." To be sure that he could hear properly, I spelled it out to him.

"How many c.c...?" he asked.

"I beg your pardon?" I enquired, surprised.

"You know, the cubic capacity... Is it twelve hundred?"

"Nothing like that. I stepped on my glasses."

"Alright... Mr. Harley Davidson..." he writes in his notepad, "...has run over his glasses. With the front or the back wheel?"

"He hasn't run over anything, I said. He stood on it!"

"Please, calm down. You're not the only one with these problems."

"Has it happened to you too?" I was delighted.

"Almost the same thing! I fell down a manhole. While crossing the street. My glasses were never found. Can you imagine? I lost them... in Vienna!"

"*Himmel Herrgott!*" I jumped to my feet. "In Vienna... you say?"

"*Ich wurde in Wien geboren!*"

If the desk wasn't in the way I would have thrown my arms around him. "Isn't this a coincidence!" I screamed. "I was also born in Vienna, in front of the kiosk with Blondie!"

Dr. Hugo Wasserman squinted at me. I concluded that this was the moment when all the fun stops and the serious work begins. For the next five minutes he examined the shape of my earlobes, the lines of my eyebrows and the curve of my nose, all the while huffing and puffing like a weight-lifter who will soon try to swing the barbell up and over his head. All the signs indicated that my appearance was quite unprecedented. From his Virginia cigar he puffed out a half-dozen white smoke rings that headed for the ceiling. He spoke to me like a father to his prodigal son: "Harley. You aren't going to believe this. But you are the most interesting case to come into this practice in the last fourteen months. Be brave."

"And who was that earlier lunatic?" I could not refrain from asking such an impertinent question.

"Oh. He called himself Yamaha. And that is exactly how he ended up. *Verstehen Sie?*"

I was burning with curiosity to find out what happened to the wretched Yamaha (probably he failed in his negotiations with a sharp curve and crashed), but Dr. Hugo had already started to fill me in on the details of his curriculum vitae—obviously with the intention of reassuring me as to what good hands I am in. Just a few words and I quickly realized that I was in the presence of one of the world's leading experts. He was nurtured by Freud, Jung, and his favorite composer was Gustav Mahler. Dr. Hugo expanded his psychoanalytical knowledge from conversations with abnormal individuals (the snag is that at first sight they look quite normal) in exotic places during his numerous round-the-world trips. The places most infested with sex maniacs, exhibitionists or psychopaths were, first and foremost, the infamous lovehouses of Thailand, followed by the tennis courts of Wimbledon and then the outskirts of Palermo in Sicily during the screening of Fellini's *La Dolce Vita* in the full heat of summer.He will always remember the moment when young Marcello Mastroiani stepped out from the silver screen and caused a mass hysteria.

Before long we behaved as if we had known each other for ages. When I informed him that my parents most probablydiscarded me on the doorstep of a farmhouse near Bayreuth in Germany (so that I might not end up in the gas chamber like they did), his eyes filled with tears. He had the experiences of two concentration camps behind him. Once he even waited for death for two and a half hours in the extermination camp at Auschwitz. But on that particular day they must either have run out of zirkon-B or else the gas-supply pipes were blocked—the devil only knows. In short his life was saved by a technical defect of such utter banality, one would scarcely dare imagine oneself in such a desperate situation. *Eine schweinische Komplikation!* What's more, it was Friday the thirteenth.

Thereupon we agreed that it might be enough for today. Before saying *Aufwiedersehen* to one another, he suggested that in the event of my being overcome by a personal crisis of any description, he would be very pleased to chat with me again.

He did not realize just what a godsend his offer was. The almighty alone knew what I was going through. Psychologically I had almost hit rock bottom. Rumors had it that an Arab oil tycoon and sheikh Prince Hussein ibn-Salal had proposed to Blondie. And only yesterday she asked him for three days to think about it. My nerves were in tatters. Luckily, I could breathe one sigh of relief, as I now had this nice Jew to turn to for help and don't have to travel the four thousand miles to Austria.

31

This time I managed to enter the correct door the first time. Only one person was sitting in the opthalmologist's waiting room. Of course, I did not yet know that her name is Amanda, or that the greasy-looking lounge lizard grinning at her from the front cover of a magazine (she is holding it piously in her hands like a monstrance) is Raúl Ibanesios – who, as it turns out later, is perhaps the worst-ever performer of the ghastliest of all the soppy songs ever to have been conceived in Spain.

While Amanda caught my attention from the very first moment, it seemed as though I did not exist for her. I tried coughing. When she did not react to my query as to whether she too has stepped on her glasses (she was not wearing any), I pulled out a plastic yellow duck from the box of toys intended for the use of myopic children. It had a blue beak and red wheels. I dragged the toy to and fro through the waiting room by its string, all to no avail. Only when I purposely tripped and almost fell into Amanda's arms did she burst out laughing.

A skinny secretary, nesting in the coop in the corner by the window, slammed the drawer of the filing cabinet that contains the patients' records. She asked harshly, "Do you have a problem, Mr Davidson?"

"That goes without saying," I jumped at this opportunity. "I can't even see two yards in front of me. And you know why? Because I have nobody who will help me not to trample on my glasses. Do you know of anyone by chance?"

"No, I don't," she snapped.

"Pity. If you should hear of somebody, let me know please."

In the ensuing silence I added: "I have a good eye for picking out a future Samaritan. First of all, she must be a very nice creature with big, kind eyes. Dimples in her cheeks would not go amiss either. She must be a kind of fairy godmother with an innate understanding of all my weaknesses. She would always remember that, whenever I fall asleep in the evening, my glasses drop from my hand and end up next to my slippers by the bed. Basically she has to become my guardian angel. In the morning she should wake up before me. She should lean over me and wait lovingly until the first warm ray of sunshine tickles me under my nose. And when I blink my eyes, she should whisper into my ear: 'Sweet good morning, my little teddybear! Don't forget your glasses are lying next to your slippers!' Then I will stretch, yawn and she will wave an admonishing finger at me: 'You naughty Harley! You've had some wild dream again, haven't you?' Tactfully she should infer that I called out something about Blondie during the night. Could you cope with such a situation, my dear lady?"

"I could not and I certainly would not be interested," retorted the secretary.

I swung the duck round in the air. As the string wrapped itself around my finger, I watched Amanda from the corner of my eye. It seemed she was hooked. Her head followed the path of the circling toy.

"I suffer because of Blondie, even in my sleep," I added. "It's like that. Quite frankly, my eyesight took a rapid turn for the worse in May the year before last. That's when the terrible news shook the world."

"What happened?" An instinct of irrepressible curiosity caused the secretary to shudder.

"You haven't heard? My God! It caused quite a stir. Absolutely everybody was talking about Blondie's rumbling appendix and that she might need an operation. What more can I say? On the Monday I was able to read about it in the newspapers without any problem, but by Tuesday I suddenly found I needed a magnifying glass. On Wednesday, in my panic, the magnifier fell out of my hand. I couldn't even read the headlines! It has had a dreadful affect on me. How long do I have to wait?"

"Wait... for what?" The secretary looked flabbergasted.

"You know, to have my eyes tested!"

"Oh. A few minutes."

"Five?" I demanded.

"Maybe ten," she bristled. "What's your hurry? There is no one out there waiting for you anyway!"

I gasped. Before I could respond, Amanda slapped her magazine down on a chair. "How dare you!" she shrieked at her. Then pointed a finger at me. "Why do you think I'm sitting here? Well, guess! Three guesses if you want! I, Amanda, am waiting for him! Understood?"

Her eyes blazed like a raging dragon's. The secretary went as silent as a mouse. She retracted her head like a tortoise hurriedly retreating into its shell. Amanda hissed through the corner of her mouth, "Serves her right. Don't you think? And to imagine that I myself have no business whatever here. My eyesight is fine. So are my teeth, by the way. Only, occasionally... I get short circuits up here in my head. That's because of Raúl. You know?"

"Raúl?" I repeated.

She held the picture of the greasy lounge lizard up to my face. He was spread over two whole pages of the magazine. "Isn't he wonderful? So far he hasn't answered any of my letters. That's why I'm seeing Dr. Wasserman. I only came into this waiting room to pluck up some courage before my session. Do I look as if he might send me straight to the loony bin? What do you think?"

"Not at all," I assured her.

"And what about you?" She smiled at me and I could see dimples in her cheeks. "I sure don't envy you your troubles with Blondie."

"I try to pull through somehow," I replied.

"These things require amazing patience. Am I right?"

"I do what I can."

Amanda's pupils widened. "Listen. Haven't I seen you on TV?"

"Oh," I do my best not to think about it. "That's several years back."

"Yes, yes!" she cried cheerfully. "It's you! Isn't it? You know, the classic scene with the monkey. In Buffalo, where it tried to stuff four ping pong balls down your throat. Or was it five?"

Her laughter was infectious. Amanda started jumping around the waiting room on one leg. I laughed so much I almost choke. Just when we were at our peak (I'm eagerly anticipating asking Amanda for her telephone number or something), out of the eye specialist's office came a little old man bent over double like a wicker chair. With a white stick he tapped in front of him. But he was not that experienced at being blind. On the way to the door he collided with my chair. That made him terribly angry. If I hadn't first jumped to one side, he would probably have kicked me on the shin. At that moment I heard my name being called. I did not even have time to say goodbye to Amanda.

The eye doctor welcomed me with open arms. The last time she saw me was the previous autumn. First she wanted to hear the latest news of Blondie.

She had a big nose, tight mouth and hair brushed up into one of the most recent creations. It looked like a wasp's nest and as if sparrows had recently moved in. Her own glasses had at least six dioptres. She sat me down at her miraculous machine. I always got the impression that she could see right down into my intestines. She did all the talking. This way I discover, not for the first time, that her son Eugene has a daytime job as a real estate agent. In the evening he turns into a theater director. Recently he rehearsed *Othello* in Hamilton. Due to the unsuitability of the cast (Desdemona was played by Kathleen Brown, a local hairdresser), the critics marked the whole spectacle down as an attempted look at life backstage rather than a serious theater piece performed onstage.

Oh well. When I staggered out my head was spinning twice as fast as it was when I entered. The main thing was that I now had a pair of glasses perched on my nose. These were only temporary ones. I could pick up the real ones some time next week. They said they would phone me.

32

The moment I stepped outside I caught a glimpse of Amanda waiting at a bus stop. Even if we had never met before, there was no way she could fail to grab my attention. She was wearing a red anorak and a Scottish hat with a pompon on top. In her hand she held a magazine rolled up into a tube, which she was waving as if chasing away flies.

The buses come and go every five minutes. I was incredibly lucky—she had not caught any of them. Fate must have been on my side. No doubt this all follows the definition by Euclid that the present, appearing positively at the geometrical point of intersection of what are otherwise termed negative circumstances, guarantees a far rosier future than that suggested by the attainments of the immediate past. Shivers went down my spine just thinking about how all this stuffwas thought up by people so long ago, even before the birth of Christ. Those were prehistoric times, when people didn't wear hats with ridiculous pompons on their heads.

Without wasting a single moment I hurried towards this lovely creature. I bumped into passersby and extended my apologies. When I reached Amanda I smiled. "At l...last I'm h...here. So...sorry, I've kept you wa...waiting for so long, M...Miss." I manage to stutter.

"Ex...excuse me, M...Mister," she replied. "I've been wa...waiting for the th...thirty-six bus more than twenty mi..minutes!"

I stood there in shock. "You didn't stutter before," I said.

"Before? Are you hallucinating? Do we know each other from somewhere?"

"From the eye specialist's waiting room," I reminded her.

"Really?" she said. "You didn't leave your glasses behind by any chance?"

I wasn't sure what she was talking about. "Blondie!" I blurted out. "Doesn't it mean anything to you?"

"Are you nuts?" she asked. "Blondie? What Blondie?"

This pompon hat obviously wanted to toy with me. Then the thirty-six bus came, and Amanda clambered onto it. I squeezed in behind her, almost leaving my only pair of trousers stuck in the door.

We were heading south somewhere. Soon I was trying to elicit some specific information from my fellow passenger on the subject of our *mutual* destination. She was not very keen. Probably she didn't consider there was anything *mutual* about our trip. This fact was soon confirmed when she told me that if I don't know where I'm going I'd be better to get off before it's too late. A curt and cold reply—but, the moment two seats became vacant we sat down.

"Dear Madam," I began, like some letter from the tax auditor's office. "First of all you are full of enthusiasm. You insist that you know me from television. But less than an hour later and... it is as if I've fallen from the dark side of the moon and landed at your highness's feet. Like that Blondie business. Do you not recall? Like how her rumbling appendix nearly made me go blind. You were very interested. Admit it. And now this. I mention Blondie and you look as if she could take a running jump. Are you listening to me at all?"

"It goes in one ear and comes out the other."

"You're just saying that to make conversation. In fact you reckon I shouldn't take all this so seriously. I'll tell you something. My whole life's mission is my fellow citizens' peace of mind. Like now. You can't imagine how relieved I am to see that Dr. Hugo didn't send you directly to an institution. That way at least we can ride together on the bus. And exchange opinions on matters of mutual interest. For example, as you already know, I am at a complete loss without Blondie. And you? Have you ever experienced anything of the kind?"

"Of course. I'm going through it right now with Raúl."

"What happened?"

"He vanished without trace."

"My God! Where could he have gone to?"

"Not even his parents know that."

"Do you have any idea why he is doing this to you?"

"He's not doing it deliberately *because of me*.
Understand? He is doing it... because he's had enough."

"Of... what?"

"Everything. The worst thing is... he would like to get settled at last. You know? Start... a family. To have lots of children... My God! Just believe me. I would give my life for his address."

Amanda's wailing did not escape the attention of the driver. "What address are you looking for, Miss?"

I answered promptly: "We're not looking for anything, driver! Kindly concentrate on your driving. Or else we might end up in the counterflow and that would mean a head-on collision with many dead and injured."

"Charming passengers we have today!" he snorted.

Amanda quickly pulled the cord above her head to let the driver know she was getting off at the next stop. I found it hard keeping up with her. She glided ahead of me like a ballet dancer. When we were standing up or sitting down it never occurred to me that there was any great age difference between us. But as she moved briskly onward, she smiled casually while I scowled darkly. Perhaps it's because I was so ashamed of the wheezing sounds coming from my lungs. And, on top of this, while her womanly contours could be termed erotically stimulating, my principal characteristic was my slovenly appearance, giving me the look of an eternal wanderer and dreamer. In other words, I looked somewhat eccentric. I resolved then and there to do something about this at the very first opportunity. Perhaps I would take up yoga. I haven't had a haircut recently either.

On the other hand I was able to console myself with the thought that, as an older person, I had one great advantage over Amanda—I would be able to offer her much advice on many subjects. Should she, for example, find herself in an impasse, not knowing how to proceed (for example, the problem with Raúl), all she ever has to do is turn to me and I will pick her out of the gutter and put her back on the narrow path I long ago mapped out for this very purpose. And well trodden it is too. I know every stone on it.

A few more steps and we turned down a side street. It was garbage-collection day. Rather than go round the burgeoning plastic garbage bags, I jumped over them. Damn refrigerator! I pretended that I was just about to spring lithely over it, but at the last minute I changed my mind. I'm not such a complete fool as to break my leg for the sake of a dash of bravado.

We skipped around parked cars. Amanda went to the left, myself to the right. Over the shining roofs of Fords, Toyotas and aerodynamic pick-up trucks of all types, we watched carefully so as not to lose sight of one another.

To enable her to hear me I raised my voice. "I've lived through a hell of a lot to be able to see inside the belly of the human megastructure's evolutiorary mechanism. Revolution may subvert the rotting process of stagnation, but I'm in no hurry. I advance inch by inch. Evolution is my principle. I have followed Blondie here and there. To one end of the world. And then the other. Several times, but for one small step, we would have met already. A baby one. Ha ha ha. But something always thwarts us. Do you know what I mean? At the very last moment. Like reaching for an apple on the tree, only to find the tree has suddenly grown six feet. Ha ha ha. Is that not so?"

I heard Amanda let out a deep breath. I figured that she was not yet one hundred percent with me. Never mind. Let's try something else. I deliberately tripped over a long box. Tubes of fluorescent lights protruded from within. Then there was the sound of breaking frosted glass. I fell flat on my face. I uttered a moaning sound so as to draw her attention to my plight—like a crashed plane sending out an S.O.S.

She came to my side with all the speed of a hurricane. She knelt down and put her hands all over me. I closed my eyes. She kept asking me whether I've hurt myself. I didn't want to torture her unnecessarily. I stopped groaning and rose to my feet, dusting off my trousers.

I watched for her reaction. It would be a litmus test. It wasn't too bad. She was quite obviously worried about me.

Another couple of steps and we crossed the lawn leading to a brick house. By the entrance door there were three letter boxes. Amanda reached inside the middle one. I held my breath. I could see from the sign that her name was Amanda Beiderbecke. I could not believe my eyes. Bix Beiderbecke was a famous cornet player. He drank himself to an early grave at the age of twenty-nine, in 1931. Once I had a little look round Amanda's place, I would impart this riveting news to her.

I doubted she even suspected such a sensational connection. As we climbed the staircase, I kept repeating to myself: "Goodbye Harley Davidson! Hello Harley Beiderbecke!"

Suddenly I found myself in the middle of the kitchen, loitering there like a vagabond—like someone just plucked from the gutter who now feels all dusty, sweaty and a bit of a burden to himself.

Amanda rushed to the canary's cage over by the window. "Hi, Tiger," she said tenderly. Tiger stretched lazily through the open cage door and pecked at her nose. Finally my turn came. "Coffee or tea, Harley?" she asked.

This was the first time she had addressed me by my Christian name. It felt like a fairy tale come true. I overflowed with gratitude. Quite honestly, my first impression was of feeling completely at home in the environment in which I found myself. This doesn't often happen. "Coffee, please," I answered.

I would have loved to ask for tea as well as coffee. But that would be too extravagant. I would also have to explain that my greediness was no more than a natural reaction to not having been offered anything by anyone for such a very long time now. If I had to tell her who the last person was, I would need to rack my brains for at least a week and still not remember. It's like that. I would have been grateful for absolutely anything—even ordinary tap water. And even if Amanda had not offered me anything, I would thank her politely all the same. I swear it.

Before realizing it, I was seated at the table. I sank my head in my hands. All of a sudden I began to sob. I did not even know why. Or perhaps I did. It had been a long time since I had the certainty of having a roof over my head.

Amanda tip-toed around me. Finally she plucked up the courage to stroke my hair. "My name is Amanda," she whispered. I could hardly hear her. "Amanda Beiderbecke."

I lifted my tear-stained face. "Harley Davidson," I said. "Pleased to meet you."

The aroma of coffee pervaded the room. Then the entire kitchen began to swirl around me. I lost all perception of what was happening. As far as I could tell, I was staggering away, following my nose. Somewhere or other I vomited on the carpet. The thought crossed my mind that I might just be dying.

The only thing that interested me was the bed. I flopped onto it like a sack of potatoes. I don't remember anything else.

For her part, Amanda Beiderbecke (my new Muse), knows the entire story of our encounter from A to Z and back to A again—and, from my point of view as well as her own. To this day she keeps regaling me with unbelievable tales that sound almost like Aesop's fables, about my shyness, helplessness and even my suicidal tendencies.

She untied the laces on my hole-ridden shoes. Then she unbuttoned my shirt with its two missing buttons. As she slid my trousers down she noticed that they needed mending, somewhere around the crotch. I don't know—these are insignificant details. On top of all this—apparently I bit her several times. Where, she never did say. In her ear? Her ribs? Her thigh? Her breast? The Devil only knows. She claims I was mumbling deliriously at the time, *"Stop looking for your fortune out in the world. It awaits you at home."*

33

After that memorable conversation with Melvin—the one in which we solemnly promised to have a cocktail together the following Thursday at the Banana Split, where I am to tell him absolutely everything about myself without his constant blather (that was the only way to get him out from The Royal Arms) my first act is to call the airport. Thank God for that! I finally have the confirmation that the plane in which Blondie was hovering high above the clouds, has safely landed.

Of course, when I make a *specific* enquiry as to whether *my fiancée* has also landed (so as to make it all sound sufficiently dramatic), those on the other end of the line become petrified. My question has caught them completely off guard. Apparently they do not provide such information to the general public as a matter of principle. Best that I should turn up in person at the airport with a bouquet of flowers, like any other bridegroom. Then I will see with my own eyes if there is any bride looking for me. If not, I can try my luck again, with a different fresh bunch of flowers, another time. They wish me good luck in my amorous quest. Something like—*go break a leg.*

I thank them for their advice. But I cannot refrain from remarking on how, when Blondie and I next travel (in all probability tomorrow), it will be with reliable Lufthansa. I am dead serious—you flying wise men.

I don't waste any more time. I hang up and set about straightening out my dilapidated appearance. After a whole day of such nerve-racking experiences I must look like General Grant after the battle at Appomattox. Some time ago I saw him on TV in a black-and-white movie. He was a complete wreck—smouldering like a piece of unidentifiable something-or-other in the embers of a dying fire. Amanda could have cried her eyes out. Really, she could.

I make for the trio of battered metal lockers huddled together on the corridor around the corner from the boss's office. The middle one has "Harley" scrawled over it with a black marker. The one on the left says "Melvin" and the one on the right "Jacques." Before the time comes for me to welcome Blondie I will put on all the things hanging inside this locker. I bought everything at Sears the other day with Amanda. It took the whole afternoon and part of the evening too. Kevin Dorsett would be green with envy. Such a palette of colors!

I begin with the shoes. They are sort of India ink. The socks, by way of contrast, look as if they've been soaked in the disappeared Tiger's canary-yellow color. When I look at the trousers, I can think of only two words: Lapis lazuli.

Finally, in the men's room, in front of the mirror, I slide my arms through the sleeves of a red jacket. All the while I am whistling "Mood Indigo." Duke Ellington used to wear exactly the same jacket during his celebrated concerts. He was even buried, I hear, in a similar jacket in New York to the strains of "Take the 'A' Train."

With the aid of a comb I smooth down my hair, adjust my tie (it is studded with miniature tortoises) and splash myself with cologne. And then I rush back towards reception, worried sick lest I miss Blondie's arrival.

From a distance I already hear the phone ringing. It's Amanda Beiderbecke calling. First of all she has some wonderful news for me. Tiger came back home during the afternoon. Great! Now my partner will at the very least have some company, especially in those first and most critical months after my departure, during her period of absolute loneliness.

The second thing she does is to appear interested in whether or not Blondie has arrived. When I reply not yet, she is astonished. "It's already 7:15, Harley. What's happening? Don't you know?"

I feel hot and cold. She is right. Time is passing by. And my Angel is nowhere to be seen.

Amanda is in the middle of taking a 15-minute break at Steinbergs. She is sipping coffee from a styrofoam cup. Do I realize that this is the last time we will ever speak together?

Like for the rest of this *crazy* twentieth century. She herself
has mixed feelings on the matter. She wanted to buy me a set
of drums for next Christmas. So, now I know. She has a small
fortune put aside for it. Never mind. But she had to tell me.
So now, instead, she will be able to buy herself a new washing
machine. Or something to wear. Maybe a fur coat—but of
course, only one that is not made from real animals. And
what is more, I must forgive her for all those times she
unwittingly made my life unpleasantduring our six years
together. Six years, eight weeks and five days, to be exact.
And, should I be interested, she has even counted the
minutes and seconds.

    From what she is saying and the way she is saying it, it
is clear that she has grown accustomed to me. She will miss
me. On the other hand she understands perfectly what I've
had to go through during my life and if I hadn't acted the way
I obviously have to, I would not be alive today. Or, if I had
been, I would be a totally different person—someone
completely unsuitable to be her sweet little foolish lovely
Harley Davidson. It's a Catch-22 situation—living with me
meant she had to live with Blondie. She quite understands
that. But for her it was all a terrible risk. She knew that from
the very beginning.

    All said and done, I should realize that she (Amanda)
also has a great understanding of my weaknesses. Bearing this
in mind, she has no intention of putting a stick in my spokes,
so to speak. She will not be in my way by making scenes in
public and so on, like many other women would do. No, one
partner is succumbing to the feeling that the rug is being
pulled from under their feet (Amanda), while the other one
(Harley) floats somewhere up in the sky like a bird who has
just sprouted a pair of wings. She babbles on about some
kind of intertwining fusion of two bodies and souls
(sometimes we have a job untwining ourselves, don't we,
honey?), the fragility of human emotions and finally our
animal instinct, which, she expects, will awaken in herself
once she realizes that she *really* is alone. She becomes

possessed by her exaggerated (she admits calmly) sexual lust. "You know, darling, I will try to cope without you," she insists in a shaky voice. "But I will have to *manage somehow.* Don't worry. Above all, please don't fret about me, or what I might be doing here, abandoned and at someone else's mercy. Be a sport. Promise, Harley?" She asks me to let her know, at least initially, if I am alright. And let her know if there is anything from our apartment I would like her to send me— something I will have left behind in the whirl of so many turbulent events.

I am about to reply but I must have hesitated too long. Amanda concludes that I have nothing to say. Without as much as another word she hangs up.

I would like to kick myself somewhere, if I could. I already had, on the tip of my tongue, a list of a few of the items from our apartment I will most certainly be requiring.

In any event, this telephone call from Amanda hardly makes any great contribution towards my peace of mind. Or, more specifically, her remark about what the time is—and there being still no sign of Blondie. She was right. Something is definitely amiss. Perhaps on the way from the airport there has been a terrible accident. The taxidriver has been smashed to smithereens. Blondie has been thrown through the rear window and onto a lawn. Right now life is oozing out of her, drop by drop. I immediately set about calling all the hospitals, police stations, mortuaries and undertakers. I even dial 911. In vain. I am no wiser than I was before. During the last twenty-four hours there have been no dead or injured. I look outside into the street. There is not a soul. Only the flickering of the stars in the sky.

At the moment the phone begins to ring about two yards away. It's as if something has bound my legs. Instead of jumping, I fall. It's Colin, calling from Kitty Junction. My darling would like to confirm her reservation. My eyes are immediately flooded with tears. Blondie is here! Alive! If it were at all possible, I would embrace Colin. But I'm not going to tell him what I'm going through. Not only does he know nothing about it, he wouldn't understand all this business between Blondie and me.

According to Colin, all Blondie's plans—such as taking a shower in the Royal Arms after her long journey, redoing her make-up and generally smartening herself up before her performance—were thwarted when the taxi had a flat tire on the way from the airport. Such a ridiculous affair. But that's not all. The replacement taxi, just to be different, was involved in an accident. And by the time the third one arrived, it was getting dark outside. Right now, if I am interested, Blondie is in the cloakroom at Kitty Junction. Colin tells me she is smoking like a chimney. He counted five cigarette butts in the ashtray. Her hands are shaking from all the excitement—from the journey, etc. But she's pulling herself together. And that just about sums everything up, Colin reports. That's Blondie's message. Well, not really her message. Anyway, he's taking care of it all. Now I must excuse him. He would love to spend the whole evening talking to me, but he is in a terrible rush. There is a lot of work to be done before all hell breaks loose at Kitty Junction. Yes. Oh! He bangs his head. He almost forgot the most important thing. I should reckon on Blondie turning up at the Royal Arms quite late. "Understand, Harley? It's difficult to say when. Let's say between eleven and twelve. Yeah. That would figure. Around midnight. It all depends on how everything goes at Kitty Junction, what sort of atmosphere there is and so on. You can rely on me, buddy."

Colin can certainly be trusted. He understands these things like no one elsedoes. No one elseon earth, that is.

On the other hand he likes making mountains out of molehills. Were it not for that I would be sure to believe his every word. I mean, that story about the flat tire on the way back from the airport—damn bad luck. Even if he has no idea just how bad that luck was.

34

Colin usually comes to stay at the Royal Arms whenever he's picked up a new broad. Obviously the latest one is always the most wonderful of them all. His occasional visits are really no more than a testing procedure, to see just how deep his feelings for this or that beauty really run. And whether, by sheer coincidence, something more permanentmight actually develop from this momentary passion. Seriously, his intention is to marry one of them, he claims. Why not? But only when he meets *the right one*. As far as I'm aware, none of his amorous liaisons ever did see the light of day.

I mull over this latest news. I feel like a cat walking on a hot tin roof. I can neither sit nor stand still. I'm sick with worrying over whether or not Blondie will be able to perform after all this commotion. I am possessed by terrible visions—like, for example, her having a sudden memory lapse at Kitty Junction, or that she won't be able to move her left or maybe her right arm. That her limbs will become well and truly paralyzed just when she most needs them. I can see doom and gloom.

By about ten minutes after nine my nerves are in shreds. I literally throw myself at the telephone. I call Colin. As is generally known, he is in charge of the glass and bottle emptying in the bar at Kitty Junction. It's an eternal life cycle. At Colin's bar these metabolical changes happen principally in the lavatory. What Colin pours down people's throats in the bar gradually trickles out in there. But why am I talking about all this? Colin's work station is next to the stage. If it comes to the crunch, he need only stretch his arm and touch Blondie. And that is my main concern.

On his lifting the receiver I hear complete pandemonium. I have to stretch my vocal cords right to the limit. "Hi Colin."

"Hi, Harley." He recognized me immediately.

"So, how's it going?" I ask.

"What, my tooth?"

"What tooth?"

"Don't you know? I had my wisdom tooth out yesterday."

"Really?"

"Sure. It's out. Including the root. Can you imagine that?"

This always happens. I call somewhere. I try to extract some vital information. Instead, I get tangled up in a web of other people's private problems. Usually they start complaining about their health, or about the socio-economical situation or the environment. Perhaps it's the uncertainty of international current affairs or a marriage on the rocks. The smooth trajectory of my conversation with Colin is not helped by the fact that we have to yell at one another like baboons. "Listen," I try to change the subject. "You're lucky that it's over."

"Sure thing," he agrees. Then he laughs strangely. "I only know of one other pain in the whole world that is worse than a toothache. Guess which one that is?"

I play stupid. "I can't think of anything offhand," I say.

"Harley, my God!" he moans. It really sounds as if he is writhing in terrible pain at the other end. "Haven't you ever been kicked in the balls?"

I can almost see his tormented face. "L-look, Co-Colin," I begin to stammer. "Such a thing has occurred to m-me, you know, but I'm c-c-calling mainly because I w-would like to ask you, h-how is it going over t-there?"

"You mean today's show?"

"Yes, of course. Today's show. How is B-Blondie doing? You get my meaning? Please."

"What?" Amid all the noise he misheard me completely.

"I said, how is Blondie getting on?"

"Oh, that's difficult to say, buddy."

"What do you mean... difficult?"

"No need to ask. You only have to look around."

"And what do you see when you look around?"

"Well, what do I see? The success of every show depends on two basic factors, buddy. A, on what's happening on the stage. And B, on how the audience reacts to it."

"And how are they reacting?"

"In their own way. Usually they get plastered. Idiots."

"Okay. But how do you see it yourself... personally?"

"It depends," he replies.

"On what?"

"On whom Blondie is impersonating at this precise moment."

"And whom is she impersonating?"

"Nobody right now. But when she was, I think her greatest success was Albert Einstein."

"Really?"

"Yeah. It was very convincing. Then she was reincarnated as Elvis. Of course, she should never have done that."

"Elvis Presley?"

"Yeah, that one. The guy who drugged himself so high in Memphis that it killed him. But most of these local morons insist that Elvis is still alive. To tell you the truth, Blondie as Elvis was unbeatable. She really impressed me. But for these people... it's like talking to a brick wall. They will tell you why should they get excited by some poor imitation when at any moment the real Elvis might appear in the doorway. You know, the one who can prove on request that he is the *real* Elvis."

"Are they crazy or what?"

"Don't ask me. According to them last Friday Elvis Presley came to the Zanzibar. You know, the bar across the river."

"You mean to say that Presley was there alive?"

"Those here will swear by it."

"Jesus, Colin. Is this normal? Where is mankind going? Have you any idea?"

"I wish I knew the answer, buddy. If I did, perhaps I would already be the owner of this joint. And you could be the manager. Would you be interested?"

"You can rely on me," I assure him.

"And then she imitated the Italian perfectly."

"Which Italian?"

"You know, the film actress."

"Claudia Cardinale?"

"The other one," he says.

"Which other one do you mean?"

"You know... the one. What's her name, dammit."

"Gina Lolobrigida?"

That doesn't ring a bell. I feed him names like Sophia Loren and Monica Vitti but without success. I'm referring to some faded stars of the sort of post-war films I used to go to see in Austria with Ilona or in Germany with Helga. At exactly the same time, Colin here across the ocean was identifying with John Wayne on his horse, imposing vigilante justice in his numerous westerns.

In the end he gives up with a sigh. At that moment I do a double take. I realize that I wouldn't have been able to hear his sigh if it wasn't for the miraculous dead silence over in the bar. Perhaps Blondie fell down and grazed her knee. Or it's possible that my Angel has such stage fright that she has become glued to the spot. Perhaps the drunken crowd is now gaping with open mouths and waiting to see just how she'll get out of this shit. Colin's next remark doesn't help any. "You know, Harley," he says, "she hasn't got an easy life."

"Who, Blondie?" I ask.

"Exactly. Off stage when she talks to you it seems like her attitude is basically *encouraging*. You know what I mean? As if she was encouraging you to behave naturally, to take it easy. Not to pretend you are somebody else. She can't stand that. If, for example, you're a philanderer, it's no use acting like a celibate priest. Or take this. Suddenly you catch yourself deliberating over various topics with her. But soon you realize that Blondie has a certain knowledge about everything. First and foremost she knows all about Hollywood. That goes without saying. And her grasp on world history—like what is what and who is who. For example, the American presidents. All that's fine. On stage, of course, it's much worse. She has a tough job making people swallow what she gives them. Do you know what I mean? No? She has a rather measured slow-foxtrot pace. You know what I mean? I don't mind it. But people demand greater speed. Everything flies that has wings and so on. Understand? Something like that. Or concerning the latest hits. She is about as conversant with them as with the craters of Mars."

"My God, what sort of hits you're talking about?"

"You know. Something like Material Girl, eh?"

"They wanted her to do Madonna?"

"Exactly. Fools! Can you imagine! But you don't know Blondie. She grits her teeth and bears it. A little bit shaky at the knees, yes. But she doesn't give up."

"That's a tragedy."

"You don't have to mention it. And then it was that Janet Jackson's turn."

"Christ!"

"Exactly. I knocked back two cognacs. But it didn't turn out too well."

"They booed her?"

"Something like that. She had to stop half an hour earlier than scheduled. You can trust me. I know. I was discussing it with her in her dressing room. Understand? Every little detail. The whole program. Like what was the best way for one number to follow the next. And suddenly— crash. Do you understand?"

"You were discussing it with Blondie in her dressing room?"

"I don't understand why you're surprised, Harley. You know, here at the Kitty Junction I sometimes double as principal organizer. Didn't you know that?"

"You don't say! And what do you organize?"

"Why are you asking? Practically everything. So that all goes smoothly, like when VIP guests arrive. They might come from somewhere very far away, like Las Vegas, man! You need to realize that. Eh? OK, to make a long story short, I am consoling Blondie in the dressing room, telling her not to worry. People, when inebriated, are basically animals. Also, there is a generation gap. People used to sip lemonade through straws and lovingly hold hands. They were grateful when someone stepped onto the stage to strike up a few chords on a guitar. – "It's A Long Way To Tipperary." Yeah, those were the days! Colin can confirm that. He knows it all. Believe me. Today it's only a B-52 here and a B-52 there. A few of those and people become legless. And then their entertainment requirements become all the greater."

I gulp. "And what did Blondie say to that?" I ask. "Did she understand the context?"

"Oh yes. She burst into tears in my arms."

"She burst into tears in your arms?"

"Okay. If you insist. Almost."

I am clutching the handset like it was a 200-pound leadweight. "My God! And what is she doing now!" I cry. "Why is there such a deathly silence there? Answer me, Colin!"

It takes ages before he manages to get it out. "Now? She has just brought a cage onto the stage."

"A cage?"

"With a pigeon inside."

"A pigeon in the cage?" I repeat mechanically.

"Yeah. A gray one, with a white chest."

"Jesus. What does she intend to do with it?"

Colin knows everything. And, even if he doesn't, he has no difficulty making something up. According to him, Blondie hasn't a cat in hell's chance—unless she can turn the pigeon in the cage into a dove, the dove into a smiling chick and the smiling chick into an appropriately endowed naked beauty. He emphasizes that last point—total nakedness. And then all that remains to be done, when the nymph is

sufficiently disrobed, is to let her out of the cage and throw
her to the disorderly rabble. Only by doing all this will
Blondie show the drunkards of Kitty Junction that she is no
amateur, but a first-class professional entertainer.

All in all, if she followed his advice, Blondie's greatest
success so far would be guaranteed. All hell would let loose in
Kitty Junction. It would be even wilder than in the Zanzibar
last week when, out of the blue and alive and kicking, Elvis
Presley made his appearance with a guitar over his shoulder
even though the guitar was in very bad need of tuning.

I alternately faint and regain consciousness. "Listen,
Colin," I can hear my fading voice. "And what is she doing
with the pigeon?"

"One moment," he replies. "Excuse me. I'm busy
right now."

The receiver falls onto the bar counter with a crash. I
can hear people are starting to get rowdy, like fans at a
hockey match when a player aims his puck unstoppably
towards the goal. Obviously I can only guess what is going on
there. Perhaps Blondie really did succeed in turning the
pigeon into a naked girl. Perhaps now she is in considerable
difficulty trying to get her out of the cage. And everyone is
encouraging her.

I don't know. It really makes me mad. My fantasies
are racing ahead at full speed. All of a sudden a crackling
comes from inside the receiver. I'm thrilled at the prospect of
Colin being back and about to explain the reason for all the
racket. Instead, someone barks at me, "Hey, how is your
Eustach pipe working?"

It's the kind of question that labels the questioner
automatically as one of life's persistent pests. So at least I
know the sort of person I am dealing with. "And how is
yours?" I take up the counteroffensive.

"Excellent, under the circumstances!" he yells. "Do
you hear the mayhem? This ain't no bar, it's a lunatic asylum.
You couldn't find so many loonies together if you tried." He
hiccups three times. "So what the hell are you doing there?"

"Waiting for Colin."

"For Colin?" he bursts out laughing. "Are your crazy or what? He's long dead. Didn't you know?" He is now hiccuping after every word. "I was telling the idiot not to go to San Francisco. The seismograph needles shake for twenty-four hours a day there. So I kept on telling him how they jump up and down on that checkered paper like Go Go Girls. But the idiot didn't listen to me and went to see his sis. Serves him right. The next day he was standing on the sidewalk in his jacket, tie and hat outside a shop selling religious literature, when suddenly the ground opened and swallowed him up. The devil himself probably took him to hell. Anyway, since the earthquake no one has ever seen him again. All that remained was a hole in the ground. It's not as if I didn't warn him. Do you get me? He was my friend, wasn't he? I won't meet a fool like him again as long as I live."

"But this is a different Colin," I try to convince him.

"You must be crazy. I only knew one. He had a wife and two children. Yours has how many?"

"None," I say. "He's a bachelor."

"Good for him. This one had a wife and two children. Do you want to know their names?"

The telephone makes a humming sound as though it has just fallen out of his hand and into a bucket of melting ice. Once the line clears again, I thank God upon hearing my Colin again, "Sorry," he coughs. "I had to pour another large round of B-52s. So you two know each other?"

"Who do you mean?"

"You and Blondie?"

I hesitate. Finally I manage to come out with, "That would be a l...long s...story."

"Really? I don't make too much of a fuss about it, though. Understand? I just peck away at it like a woodpecker and when I finish pecking, I leave it alone. That's my proven technique. The way that suits me. How old is she by the way?"

"You mean... Blondie?"

"Yeah."

"Same age as me."

"Jesus, and how old are you, Harley?" he exclaims.

I risk it. "How old would you say?"

"Sixty-two?" he guesses.

I burst out laughing. By doing so I at least disguise my gritted teeth. "You do have a sense of humor, Colin."

"Humor! What humor? I'm not kidding, Harley. Certainly not. The last time I saw you, you looked pretty wretched. Sorry. When was that? In February? Are you suffering from a tapeworm or something? Come clean, now. How old are you? Jokes aside."

"I was fifty in May," I reply. "Can you imagine, Colin? Only *fifty*. In May."

He says nothing. I bet he is ogling Blondie. "Yeah. That would figure," he says. "It depends on which side the light falls on her. From the left I would guess she is forty-seven and a half. From the right side it's a little bit worse."

"Forty-eight?"

"Phew! You're kidding. Forty-eight! At least fifty-five. But don't let it spoil your good mood. All the blame rests with the colored spotlights. Trust Colin. Mainly those two pale blue frontals. Pale blue doesn't suit artists. They look like death warmed up. It belittles them before their audience. Tomorrow morning I will change them. What color would you suggest? Pale pink? Would that help? What do you say?"

"I don't understand too much about colors."

"You don't? I thought you did. So what are you good at? Do you own any bathroom scales?"

"Why do you ask?"

His voice is hushed. "You know. Just like that. Between you and me, if you had some bathroom scales, you could put this lovely lady on them and see to it that she sheds a few pounds. Believe me. If Colin understands anything, then it's this—when the time has come to get rid of a few rolls of fat. Colin understands that even better than he understands a few stupid light bulbs."

"You don't say," I pretend to be astonished. "Are you really such an expert?"

He chuckles. "Really, buddy, really. Better than a health farm! Or that so-called grapefruit diet! Fuck! Give Colin a plump little imp for one night and you won't recognize her the following day. I'm surprised that you've never noticed, Harley. The next time I visit the Royal Arms, keep your eyes peeled!"

It comes as a relief when he has to go to serve another customer. There is a familiar crackle in the receiver. Then silence falls, just like the time in San Francisco when hell swallowed up the other Colin in his entirety.

35

This episode could be presented to some international symposium on the theme "Friendship and Sheer Naivity" as a classic example of a person who falsely pretends to have an acquaintance somewhere (in this case at Kitty Junction). He seems like the sort of friend you can rely on 100 percent— someone who will help when you find yourself in dire straits. But the truth is far from it. It actually transpires that I would have been far better off never having met Colin. I certainly liked him better before our telephone conversation. Now I don't like him at all. Not even a tiny bit. He boasts a lot and is rather pretentious. Add that to the fact that he's a common womanizer. He has disappointed me to no end. Colin is simply going downhill. As far as I'm concerned, not even Dr. Hugo Wasserman could help him now.

I would like to run all the way to Kitty Junction and rescue my Angel from the clutches of that gang of ante-diluvial louts. But it's now too late. Suddenly I hear a great hubbub, as if the Royal Arms was Notre Dame and the organist had just fallen out of the gallery. As I immediately realize, this racket is all Arnie Hornsby's fault. So great is his hurry to see me, he almost kills himself coming down the stairs.

"Harley," he is almost breathless. "It can't go on like this anymore."

"What can't go on, Arnie?"

"I can't sleep."

"Why not?"

"You should ask. Have you hooted?"

"Hooted?" I am puzzled.

"Yes, yes," he is agitated. "Hoo...hoo...hoo! Like the snow owl! The way to summon Hua Kua Pooh. Remember? The guide who knows the jungle like the back of his hand."

He yells at me as if I was deaf. But he means well. The thing is that he could have saved his insomnia problems for another time. Right now, I don't know where my head is.

And that's no exaggeration. There are days in which life seems to catch up with all it ever missed out on.

"I really have other problems," I try to wriggle out of this hooting business.

"Rubbish," Arnie resists. "There is nothing more paramount than love. Arnie knows best. Love not only crosses mountains, but is the salt of life. You wouldn't throw such a chance away!"

"What chance?"

"You know! You love Blondie. People want to listen to great love stories. When two sweethearts are billing and cooing, that's the only thing they want to believe in. At least in books. You wretched fellow! All that remains for you is to write the final chapter. Isn't that so? Why are you hesitating!"

"I wouldn't hesitate if I knew what I had to do," I sigh.

"Are you kidding? Don't know how to do it? And what about Arnie?"

"Arnie?" I look at him wide-eyed.

"Have you something to write with?" His request almost knocks me out.

Before I realize it, I have a sheet of paper in front of me and a pen in my hand. Arnie is dictating. From the very first words it's obvious to me that it's not just love he is interested in, but in the last few pages of my work *la nouvelle vérité vietnamienne,* where he can engrave himself into the hearts of the readers as their indispensable hero. He will all but appear in the right place at the right time and prevent the derailment of a train.

He introduces himself: "As my name is Arnie Hornsby, I sure can't watch this any longer" – and he informs his cheering fans that his main motivation for walking across the North American continent is his love of women, which is what keeps him in such tip-top condition. So he makes it all the way to the Royal Arms, where he meets a man by the name of Harley Davidson. Apparently I'm a bit of a nutcase, but otherwise a nice enough guy. The thing is, I've been through my hell in Vietnam while he also underwent his share of suffering in Korea. So, wherever we go, we are pursued by dead bodies. On top of this, Arnie tells the breathless readers, I happen to have writing ambitions, while he is a bookworm. On every one of his journeys he takes a harmonica in his rucksack, which corresponds with my being a drummer—even though at the moment I don't own a drum kit.

In the next paragraph it becomes clear that, while Arnie loves all women without any regard to their complexity (alas, he usually has to make do with what the wind blows his way), he considers me to be a martyr. I am one who has dedicated his entire life to the ideal of one love above all others—i.e. Blondie—with whom everything in this world begins and ends.

After these words Arnie drops a hint, for those interested in my lot, that Blondie is currently the prisoner of some bloodthirsty blackmailers. I am in great desperation at the edge of the jungle, ripping the last hair out of my head. Because I have no idea what the hell else to do, he appears out of the blue and gets me out of my goddamn mess.

At the same time he shapes a cornet from his palms and begins to hoot, hoo...hoo...hoo. Like a snow owl. Before he has even hooted his last hoo, before us sprouts a magnificent white-haired old man accompanied by an even more captivating secretary-stenographer of about seventeen. His name is Hua Kua Pooh and he wants to spread the idea around that the only good commie is a dead commie. Her name is Chichita and, because her outlook on life is still only developing, she loves the entire population of the world.

"Hi!" Hua Kua Pooh greets us. "What can I do for you guys?"

"Harley and I have a serious problem," Arnie Hornsby replies.

Pooh turns to face me. "Hello," he says. "Which Harley are you? I know several."

"Harley Davidson."

"Oh yeah," he retorts knowingly. Then he turns towards Chichita. "Chichita, are you taking all this down?" Turning back towards me, he says: "Harley. Wait a minute. You had a flat tire in the jungle, didn't you?"

"Something much worse," I reply.

"You don't say."

Now Arnie Hornsby cuts in, "Harley here joined the army because of his great love. And now he's in absolute schtuck."

"You guys must be kidding." The white-haired old man can't believe his ears. "And who is this great love, Harley?"

Arnie nudges me. "Out with it for godsake, you ladykiller!"

I wave my arm in the direction of the jungle. "Blo...Blondie!" is all I can utter.

"Oh yeah, Blondie." The renowned expert on the whole spectrum of most intricate situations is not disconcerted. "I heard it on short-wave radio from Los Angeles. Isn't that so, Chichita?"

"We listened to it together in the tent," purrs Chichita.

"That's correct, Chichita. In the tent. But don't write that in." He turns back to me. "What do I hear, Harley? You are head over heels in love with Blondie. And she's gone. Eh? Hey presto!"

Hua Kua Pooh knows practically everything there is to know about Blondie. He even met her once at a film festival in San Diego. His friend Randy, an independent producer, introduced them. He has also seen *The Last Day of Dick Hammersmith*. I consider asking him what he thought of that film, but Hua Kua Pooh already has his well-worn military map spread out on the grass. After five minutes of meditation he wets his finger with his tongue, then rotates it through the air. "It's looking good, guys," he announces authoritatively. "The kidnappers have a lead of fifty miles, plus or minus a bit. But fear not. I know all sorts of short cuts through the jungle. If we step up our efforts, we will catch up with them before dusk."

Taking the leading position in our rescue mission is the unbeatable secretary-stenographer Chichita, who is traipsing ahead like a rubber cat. Perhaps this is because she has the best eyesight. Chichita is a multi-national mulatto. She has inherited something from each race. From the Puerto Ricans comes her elegantly shaped and aggressive little waspish butt. It obviously impresses Hua Kua Pooh. He is constantly treading on her toes. And my toes, in turn, are trodden on by Arnie Hornsby. Nevertheless, the journey goes quickly—nobody knows how. Of course, my hurry is the greatest. I am worried sick about Blondie, and whether I will be able to rescue her before it is too late.

Arnie tells me that his throat is dry from all the dictating. We will carry on just as soon as he has been to the washroom for some water. But my writing hand is gliding over the paper (I have just begun the fifth page) so swiftly it is impossible to stop. All of a sudden the jungle thins out. A fragrant meadow is spread out before me like a carpet. On the horizon there is smoke. Not far from me two gangsters are dragging Blondie by her platinum hair towards some half-ruined building. I leap ahead without any regard for the consequences of my action. And it happens. For some reason I black out.

On regaining consciousness, I discover I am bound and gagged like a trussed-up chicken, lying on a pile of bananas in some underground warehouse. Of course it is pitch dark. As far as I can make out, Blondie is also tied up. I can scarcely believe it. We are propped against one another's backs. Above our heads near the ceiling there is a small barred window.

"I am Blondie from Los Angeles," my darling whispers to me.

"Ha...Harley Davidson... a cosmopolitan," I sibilate through the corner of my mouth.

"What are you doing here, Harley?"

"I... I came to rescue you."

"Me?"

"Yes. You."

"How do I explain this to myself?"

"Simply. You are my everything. I am so dreadfully in love with you. It began a very long time ago. While I was still in Vienna. Really. I saw you on the front cover of a certain magazine. *Face of the Future*. I was seventeen. Suddenly I hear someone's voice. It is telling me that I am seventeen and that I have only just been born at this precise moment. Maybe God himself uttered these words. I don't know. But the voice was right. If I really had been born before, I would surely have retained some memories from my childhood. Like where, for example, I went to school. And other things of that nature. What my parents looked like. But I don't remember a thing. From the moment of my birth in Vienna, every little detail about you has engraved itself in my memory. Blondie. Believe me. From that very first instant my life revolves only around you. By the way, as a Catholic, you won't mind marrying a Jew?"

"Why should I mind, Harley?"

"I don't know. Maybe because of that."

"What?"

"You know... that... that I am circumcised."

I feel like a complete idiot. Both our lives are at risk. And here I am blabbering on about circumcision. I drag in matters that we could discuss—all day long—once this terrible danger has passed.

Then the keys rattle in the door lock. Before Blondie and I realize it, two macabre silhouettes are leaning over us. We can't see their faces. From time to time their eyes glitter. We can also hear something like the swishing of a whip against leather boots. Then we are told in broken English to prepare ourselves for the worst. The first guy says that we will be executed at dusk, but the other one proposes that it is far better to shoot one's beasts at four in the morning, when one can see exactly what one is doing. They express interest in our last wishes. Just as I'm trying to explain how nice it would be if they could marry us, my darling tells them something not very polite—something I can't even repeat. This naturally thwarts my plans for an early wedding.

As soon as the door creaks shut behind them, Blondie whispers, "I've lived through a heck of a lot, in movies, on stage and elsewhere, but this is the absolute limit."

"Don't worry, Blondie," I say. "I won't allow matters to remain the way they are."

"Thanks in advance," she answers. "What have you got up your sleeve?"

"I don't know yet. But I'll be sure to come up with something."

"I'm grateful for your optimism, Harley."

"I never thought I would be so near you, Blondie."

"Neither did I," she mutters. "Could we kiss somehow before we breathe our last?"

I'm choking with happiness. We start wriggling, jumping and shuffling our buttocks, in order to get into a position to be able to kiss one another for the first time. Just as our lips are on the point of converging, a terrific explosion shakes us. Everything around us lights up. The earth splits apart before our very eyes. We are falling directly towards the fires of hell. And on top of all this comes the barking of automatic weapons. From time to time there is a deafening mortar explosion.

And when we think that we have surely reached the end of our existence, the ceiling above us opens. In the opening I recognize three familiar faces. One belongs to Chichita. The second one to Hua Kua Pooh. And the third one to—who else but Arnie. Chichita, with a dagger between her teeth, jumps nimbly between us. She snips through the ropes, cutting into our skin. In a trice Blondie and I are running through the corn field. We alternately keep falling down and getting up. In the background a helicopter with propeller blades already turning awaits.

Arnie returns from the bathroom. When he finds out that I wrote another three pages during his absence, he wants to hear them. "My God, that's excellent, Harley," he exclaims. "You know what? Once you have transcribed it on the typewriter, I will sell it to Walt Disney for a handsome fee, I guarantee that."

He boasts, but the fact is that without his efforts I would still be stuck somewhere around the edge of the jungle. I thank him for everything. Then we wish each other good night. Back in 303 he will sleep like a log.

As soon as Arnie has disappeared upstairs, the helicopter lifts off. Blondie and I are huddled together and whisper inaudibly to one another through the noise of the roaring engine. Just when our lips are inexorably closing in on each other, there is a screeching of brakes outside the Royal Arms, the slamming of a car door—and the pen falls out of my hand like a boulder.

36

I come to about five seconds later. Maybe six. Throwing all the handwritten pages into the drawer, I hurry towards the main entrance. To start with, the situation is a teeny-weeny bit confusing. In the darkness outside it's even rather eerie. At this advanced hour, the moon is reigning supreme. If the street was a dense forest and I was a child, I would certainly shit my pants.

But I wasn't born yesterday. I gather all my wits about me and try to explain logically all these frightening events. What I see before me is nothing but a normalwhite hand in the process of dipping inside a lady's purse. It is simply handing the money over to a cabdriver. Nothing more than that. The taxi then weighs anchor. The silhouette out on the sidewalk turns slowly. It takes a few steps in my direction. And now the real hell begins. Goose pimples start to scurry down my back. Only a few steps more. I hold my breath. My God! The light from above the entrance door lifts the veil of darkness. The face, until this moment shrouded in mystery, shines forth. I think I'm going to faint. Three times yes. It's my sweetheart—Blondie!

Colin should definitely consider visiting an eye specialist for a re-test, just in case he has a cataract or something of the kind. No other explanation is possible. By this light (an ordinary 150-watt bulb screwed into a light fixture that looks just like a gigantic strawberry), which falls directly onto Blondie's face, I would guess she is no more than forty-four. Yes, Colin. You hear correctly. *Forty-four!* If I were to breathe on the glass and polish it with my sleeve, maybe forty-five. But to hell with Colin and his eyesight. My miracle is standing behind the door. And that's all I care about.

The real martyrdom begins. I cry out *Darling forgive me!* I apologize for my unreadiness, stupidity, slovenliness and reprehensible apathy. I also have a tendency to give in to idle fancy. I'm an irresponsible procrastinator. I put on sackcloth and ashes. Ever since this morning I've been preparing for this one moment (let alone my whole lifetime of preparations). But at the critical juncture, instead of kneeling down by the door of the Royal Arms, I find myself going berserk somewhere in Indochina along with Arnie, Chichita and Hua Kua Pooh. Oh well. In my eagerness to remedy the situation I cry out again *Darling forgive me!* and pull the door handle. I very nearly fall right through the thick glass. In all the excitement I have completely forgot that I locked the door behind Melvin. I make a pleading grimace—for her to be patient. I dash back to the reception area. But it's complete panicksville down there. Where the keys should be hanging, there is nothing. I look through all the drawers and shelves. Nothing. I step onto the chair. Also nothing. I crawl under the table. Zilch once again. Then I hear a tinkle from inside the pocket of my red Duke Ellington tuxedo. Aha! I rush quickly back. Blondie has pressed her face against the glass of the swing door and is making ghastly—one can almost say monkey-or even gorilla-like—grimaces. Oh my sweet little comedienne, I think. Clown! Aren't your ideas fascinating!

To find the right key from a bunch of ten amidst so much excitement is obviously no Sunday promenade down Fifth Avenue. This is a typical example of one of Melvin's super inventions. And McCarthy even recommends having this sort of trash patented. His blind tolerance of these ridiculous gadgets only serves to confirm the fact that those two could never truly have found themselves until they found each other. According to our Hercules, placing all the hotel keys onto one ring would speed up the evacuation process should a fire ever break out in the Royal Arms. Any deeper analysis on my part of this clear-as-the-sun-in-the-sky idiocy would be a waste of valuable time. As is patently obvious, should the hotel be on fire now, I would already have been transformed first into ugly embers and then into fine velvety cinders, right in front of Blondie.

My hands are shaking but, at the ninth attempt, the lock clicks. Nobody would ever have believed what would happen when the swing doors suddenly swung open. My poor little Blondie! She is leaning with all her weight (according to my guess, a *mere* hundred and forty two pounds) against the door. She falls inside like a torpedo and knocks me to the ground. Holy mackerel! How I have always imagined this very thing—that one day we would be rolling together on the carpet. We would not stop until we reached the armchairs in the minivestibule. There we would remain, lying on our backs, breathless, happy and laughing. All of a sudden, like two small children, we would start to tingle in anticipation of what will happen next.

What follows cannot be described even with a paint brush. "Good evening," my miracle whispers.

Two ordinary words, uttered every day by millions of people from the Pacific to the Atlantic—but coming from Blondie's mouth, their magical power is overwhelming. "G...good evening," I attempt to say. Alas, I find it quite impossible to stop stuttering.

She leans on her elbow and flutters her eyelids impishly. "Is this really the Royal Arms?"

"You haven't hurt yourself?" I blurt.

"Oh! Falling down is my forte. That's why I'm an actress."

I hoist myself up. Blondie's trembling mouth is nearer to my hot lips than my own nose. "What happened with the pigeon?" I try to find out.

"Don't mention it. He turned into a rabbit. How, I haven't the foggiest idea."

"Thank God he turned into something."

"Into something, yes. But the people still wanted to lynch me."

"That's because Kitty Junction is not a suitable environment for artistes of your most versatile qualities."

Blondie sighs sweetly. "Thank you for your appreciation. But you know what? Let's not worry about all that. We have other problems now. Or joys rather. I don't know how, but all of a sudden I feel I'm in seventh heaven."

Sure she should feel that. And this is only the first act, taking place in the somewhat reduced circumstances of the gloomy interior setting of the minivestibule, under a forever spinning fan. Wait until we get to the fourth floor, where I will declare my undying love to her without delay. No need to emphasize that I am burning with impatience. But I try to control myself. *I know everything about her, but she knows practically nothing about me!* I must remember this fact. In no way should I push my luck and risk frightening her away before I have definitelywon her over.

"Do you wish me to accompany you to your room or would you prefer to manage on your own?" I ask.

"On my own! You must be joking! Don't you realize?"

"What should I realize?"

"That I can't go to sleep without a fairy tale first."

Of course I am perfectly well *aware* that she never goes to sleep without a fairy tale first. I get onto my feet, so as to help her up. She is wonderful. She is without peer. She is wearing a white suit. Elegant, immaculate, virginal even. I would like to bite into her earrings. In each ear lobe she has a couple of delightful real-size cherries. Their color matches that of her nail varnish.

When Blondie fell over earlier, she dropped a medium-large suitcase onto the floor. This, in its turn, is an exact match for the brown carpet. But I am not waiting any longer. I grab the suitcase and with Blondie at my heels I head for the elevator.

As soon as it jerks upward with us inside, I introduce myself, "My name is Harley Davidson."

"Harley! Of course!" she exclaims.

I clear my throat. "I called you once in Paris from Portugal. Do you remember?"

"From Portugal to Paris! As I recall, the last time you phoned Las Vegas. And Harry James answered the phone. didn't he?"

"The trumpet player?" I can think of nothing better to say.

"No, you're kidding! He's been pushing up daisies for years. I mean Harry, my masseuse. Sometimes he answers the telephone. And he told me, 'Can you imagine, Blondie, a guy named Harley Davidson just called. It was so funny, we roared with laughter!"

I transfer the suitcase to my other hand. Although she doesn't elaborate as to what was so funny, I can tell. Naturally, I don't bear Blondie any grudge. Laughter is simply contagious, like a cough. Or yawns.

Evidently this particular Harry has a senseof humor. But as with all the things in the world, humor is divided into good and bad. Bad humor then branches into further categories. One example that can serve for all is so-called primitive humor. This is obviously the type which this Harry enjoys. It's enough to tickle his sense of humor if someone calls, and introduces himself as Harley Davidson. Such a clever dick as Harry puts two and two together. He nearly ruptures his diaphragm as a result.

Oh well. One has to remain calm. If this Harry James only knew what was in store for him, that smile would freeze right there on his goddamn face. I reckon that he is definitely done with massaging. As from this moment I am going to take over all responsibility for Blondie's welfare and all matters relating to her future artistic development (never again at the Kitty Junction). But before I have time to remark on the vast changes in store for us, Blondie and I arrive at the fourth floor.

We hurry past the Brazilian rain forest like a tornado and burst into 403. To be absolutely safe, I bolt the door. Doing so fills me with an indescribable feeling of relief. No doubt it is something like that experienced by mountain climbers on conquering the very last stretch of Mount Everest. Being alone with Blondie at last, I desperately want to stretch my arms towards the heavens and call: "So farewell to you, bizarre world whose static vision of the universe is insufficient take in the dynamic requirements of our colossal love!" And the echo will return: "God bless your journey together, Blondie and Harley!"

37

Like every romantic and suitably inquisitive being, Blondie rushes straight over to the window. All she can see is the light emanating from a pair of squares and rectangles. They are illuminating the dark outline of the block of flats opposite. It would seem a thousand times worse in Las Vegas—not to mention that everything there would be drowned in a blinding neon glare. I hurry to retrieve the vase of roses from the closet. What I had thought might happen does happen. While looking at this splendor, the enchanting cherry earrings on both sides of Blondie's head begin to tremble.

"That's a very nice gesture by the establishment," she remarks.

"This establishment," I announce, "would not even offer you a free coat hanger. I have selected these roses for you personally. "

"Is it really so important?" she asks with childlike naivite.

"Yes. It really is."

"I am sorry, Harley," she surpresses a yawn. "But when I look back, I'm glad to see today is already behind me."

My darling is no doubt referring to her tiresome journey and subsequent jet lag. And to that frustrating performance later in Kitty Junction. Of course, my day, as I see it, has nothing in common with her day. Mine not only began right now, but is not going to end with tomorrow, nor the day after.

And so instead of telling each other, while almost drowning in a flood of tears, just how much we mean to one another, I just shuffle from foot to foot over by the door and ask, "What about something to eat?"

"Oh no, thank you," she replies. "I had a chicken sandwich in the taxi."

"I prepared a bottle of Champagne on the roof."

"That's all very nice," she says. "But in my state not a thing would entice me to go up on the roof."

Despite all my efforts I can't seem to hit the target. In the end, as if gleaned from some manual for idiotic hotel staff written by McCarthy and Melvin, I repeat, parrotlike, a sentence from page six, paragraph two: "Very well. Your bed has been ready for you ever since this morning, Miss."

"Excellent!" Blondie rejoices. As immediately becomes apparent, the magic charm in this case is the word— bed. My angel puts the vase of roses down onto the small table next to the TV set and starts fluttering to and fro around the room like a butterfly over a meadow in full bloom. Before I know where she is I hear her calling from the bathroom, "Good heavens! What is this, Harley?"

I run straight to the rescue. She is giggling over the wash basin, a soapy figure sliding between her fingers.

"That's Grumpy," I tell her.

"Grumpy from Snow-White?" she asks.

"The very same."

"My dearest," she breathes out. "This is the first time I've felt at home in a hotel!"

My joy is so great I nearly swallow her cherry earrings. Then she asks me to turn round. She will take a shower. In the meantime I am to tell her something about myself. She wants to know everything. Every single bit. Down to the last detail—well, not quite to the last detail. That might be too much to bear.

I turn obligingly to face the door. I am mulling over all the options in my head. For a start, I should try and come out with something amusing. A funny joke perhaps, so that my sweet little Blondie can have a good laugh straight from the heart. According to the latest public-opinion survey, women's principal demand of men is a good sense of humor. And, according to what Amanda tells me, life with me is permanent joy. Therefore this is my strongest point. From the rustling of clothes behind me I am led to understand that Blondie is taking off her white suit.

I am on the point of opening my mouth. But at that very moment Blondie steps into the bath and turns on the shower. She begins to sing "America the Beautiful." I doubt she would be able to hear my hilarious anecdotes even if I shouted my head off.

Blondie. You are taking a shower. I am standing close by and trying to think what to tell you. I have so much to tell you! We were made for each other. But so far fate has not looked favourably on us. We were living our lives in different places, separately, although we should have been living together—as if having one single life. That's our secret's key. The one we've been searching for. At last we've found it. With this key we will open the door and we will see ourselves as though in a mirror. Something ends with this. And something else is beginning. We have so much to catch up with. So much water has gone under the bridge. So many trees have shed their leaves. If we piled them all up, we would have a mountain as high as Finsteraarhorn. Please, Blondie. I don't know how to say this to you. (And maybe someone else has already said it before me.) I am yours. And you are mine. Let us stay this way. Alasta mugli pista. Taspi enigo motulo. This is our new secret language.

"Harley, are you there?" my darling chirps.

"Y...yes. I...I am here."

"Please, please. Would you kindly pass me the towel?"

I find what she is looking for. I race towards the shower curtain with it. Like in the Hitchcock movie, I grope for an opening. As I pass the towel through the gap, Blondie grabs my hand. She growls like a werewolf, "Grrr! I got you... my sweetie! And now I will eat you! Complete with hair!" She giggles as I nearly die of fright. "Well, Harley?" she asks. "Did you say something? I didn't hear anything in the shower."

"I'm getting ready to."

"Out with it... pet," she encourages me.

"Alasta mugli pista. Taspi enigo motulo."

"Good God! What does that mean?"

"The p...past instructs," I stutter. "The f...future inspires."

"And what about the present?"

I get hot flushes. "W...we are j...just going through that."

"My dearest! You are talking directly from the heart!"

Surely the moment of truth has arrived. I clear my throat. "Blondie...I...I..."

I don't get any further. Blondie jumps out from the bath. At the same time a damp towel lands on my head. If I was stuttering previously, now I am completely done for. I cannot utter one single sound. I feel like a coat-stand at a barber's shop. In another sense I am beside myself with joy in the knowledge that the bath towel is soaked with drops of the water that Blondie has literally blotted off the surface of her silken body.

By now my angel is pushing me back into the room. She probably left the comfortable clothes she wanted to slip into after her bath inside her suitcase. Now she is putting matters right. With the towel draped over my head she is ensuring that I don't accidentally see something I am not supposed to see yet. On my way I bump my knee against the corner of the bed. That will be a nasty bruise. From the intense scent of roses I figure that I must have been pushed somewhere near the table with the TV set and vase on it.

For the time being, everything that is unfolding here is the fulfillment of a dream which was well worth living and waiting for!!!

There is the sound of a zipper being pulled. A short while afterwards the towel flies from my head. It's as if a curtain had opened. Blondie, with a smile on her face, curtsies before me. She is clad in a flowery kimono and looks like a gracious Japanese geisha—innocent on the outside but knowledgeable within.

I also bow. But by now Blondie is already waving a box of cigarettes in front of me. "Do you smoke, Harley?" she asks.

"No I don't, but I intend to take it up."

"Excellent. Welcome to the club. I'm a member of the committee of Hollywood Fighters for the Rights of Discriminated Against Smokers."

She's not telling me anything new. This is the fifth-year in a row she has been on the committee. I also know that she only smokes Camels. She licks the white stick. Then she clasps the filter firmly between her teeth, lights the opposite end, drags on the cigarette several times, then rolls it from one corner of her mouth to the other, like a toy. After this captivating procedure she inserts the wet cigarette between my lips. For a while, sitting next to each other on the bed, we swing our legs in the air and blow the smoke into each other's faces.

"Where did you buy those shoes?" Blondie asks suddenly.

"At Sears. Do you like them?"

"Very much. And that jacket—it really makes you look like Duke Ellington."

"Thanks. It took some finding." At this juncture it would be right and proper to bring Amanda onstage so as to mention her fine efforts in purchasing all the clothes I am wearing. "They had a lot of them on sale with more than 30% off," I continue.

"Really? Perhaps I should pop in there tomorrow. What do you think?"

"What are you looking for?"

"A kimono made in Japan."

"Where did they make the one you are wearing?"

"In China, if you can believe that?"

"In China?"

Blondie chuckles. "Isn't this a crazy world?"

"Definitely. But you would even look nice in a kimono made in Paraguay."

"Do you think so?"

I pull on the cigarette and have a coughing fit. "Has Jimmy passed on my message at all?"

"Jimmy?"

"Your brother."

"My brother! I don't have a brother."

"Oh yes, you have. I spoke to him in Buffalo."

"My brother was in Buffalo?"

"Wasn't he? You know, that Jimmy you lent two hundred to in that film."

"Oh that one! He was just an ordinary swindler."

"Hasn't he returned the money to you?"

"Harley. Whether he did so or not, I wouldn't want a brother like that if he was the last person left in the world."

With these words she leans her head on my shoulder. I begin an immediate analysis. There are only two possibilities. Either she is falling asleep or she is, slowly, falling in love with me. I am overcome with a feeling of total bliss. At the very least, we have already become very close friends. We are not like those who go riding on a tandem, sleep in one tent, and yet, other than their lengthy conversations, have nothing between them.

To draw the line where friendship ends and love begins is a darned puzzle. Even so-called experts with degrees in social sciences have a job solving it. Among others Dr. Alex Kinsella had a problem dealing with it. His findings were summarized in a paper entitled—The Kiss. He divides kisses into friendly kisses and kisses of love. The latter sucks lovers into a well of passion (this quotation is from the eleventh and final edition, edited by the author's son Rodney) like a vacuum cleaner. I tell it like it is.

"Aren't you cold, Blondie?" I ask.

"Oh, I'm rather hot and flushed, Harley," my darling whispers.

Ashes from our cigarettes fall onto the carpet. As soon as we finish smoking, I will have to test this theory in practice. I will kiss her and we shall find out how we stand according to Kinsella. I hope Blondie will not turn away. Perhaps my best bet will be to get her into a receptive mood first. I will read a few verses from that collection of poems whose inspiration was her existence. I wonder why I didn't think of it earlier.

Telling her that I have another little surprise for her, I begin a gentle circumnavigation of the bed, heading in the direction of the bedside table. Of course, I will never make it further than the roses and the TV set. From the corridor I hear a sound of whistling. It is wishy-washy improvisation on a theme from *Carmen*.

What follows unfolds according to all the rules of classical horror. The instant Blondie murmurs, "Harley, I am living through what must be a dream, which is changing every little second into a truly amazing reality, and the only thing I don't understand is why I had to wait so long...", someone pulls the door knob of room 403. Since it is locked, that someone begins to knock persistently on the door. "Harley!" I hear a familiar voice. "I know you are in there. Be sensible, don't make any unnecessary scenes and open the door immediately!"

38

I know that if I don't immediately comply with what Melvin asks me to do, he will do it himself. That's why he always lugs that toolbox around with him.

I unlock the door.

"You're smoking, man?" he stares at me. "Does Amanda know that?" He doesn't wait for an answer. His attention is grabbed by Blondie sitting on the bed. He drops the toolbox and whistles, "I see! I get it now!"

The box falls on its side, the lid opens and the tools spill out at Melvin's feet. He pushes me out of the way and is charging straight at my sweetest little angel like a bull at a corrida. "Don't we know each other from somewhere, Miss?" he enquires.

Blondie puffs on her cigarette. "I don't think your face is in any way familiar to me."

Such a response should make any normal person think twice. But Melvin's manners leave much to be desired. Even from these words he is able to extract sufficient encouragement to set his sights on a lengthy conversation with Blondie. "I smoke too, Miss," he says. "But only Havana cigars."

"You're kidding," replies Blondie. "You look like a real non-smoker."

Melvin pulls out a long aluminum box with a picture of a sailing boat on its lid. A few moments later the smoke from his fat Havana hangs in the air like laundry on a washing line.

"Sorry, Harley." Although his attention shifts to my person, his gaze never leaves Blondie. "I have really important news for you. There are three things. First, the young lady here has to flick her ashes onto the carpet. And you know why? Because it never once occurs to you to pass her an ashtray. Secondly: doesn't it seem to you, man, that your manners are appalling? You leave this distinguished dame sitting on the edge of the bed swinging her feet in the air. What if you offered her an armchair? And finally third thing: Yabba-Dabba-Doo!"

"What does that mean?" I ask.

"What does it mean! There I am, sitting in a wine bar with Micky. And suddenly I get this feeling that I, a notorius scatterbrain, have forgotten to turn the light off in the workshop. So I immediately call The Royal Arms. You don't answer. And now I know why. As if nothing else in the world mattered, here you are chatting away with this young lady. Jesus wept! And I thought you'd dropped dead somewhere, man!"

"Dead! I took the luggage belonging to the lady from Las Vegas up to her room. And she had a few queries about our hotel. So I endeavoured to answer them. That's all."

"Okay, sorry. You are excused. I hope you sang Royal Arms's praises highly to her."

"You can rest assured."

I would have expected, if nothing else, that Melvin would now pass Blondie the ashtray or else offer her a seat. But no way. On the contrary, he chucks everything she has hurriedly placed on the armchair (including her white suit) onto the floor. He pulls the armchair towards the bed and, paying absolutely no heed to the our-customer-is-our-master lecture which he had just given me, he sprawls out in it like the Maharajah of Ahmadabad, waiting for us to start cooling him with great fans made from reeds.

It is almost midnight, undoubtedly the most significant midnight in my life, and just as I was on the verge of winning Blondie over with a sample reading from my amorous poetry, Melvin had to come knocking on the door. And now my Angel and I, instead of exchanging pledges of our undying love, are now left with no choice but to listen to endless Walter Mitty-style stories, gushing from this ungaggable loudmouth.

Melvin comfortably puffs away on his Havana cigar and Blondie, on the edge of the bed, keeps swinging her feet in the air. I remain standing in the doorway of room 403 with a disbelieving expression on my face. But one thing is certain. Unless Melvin doesn't come to his senses soon, I doubt he will ever get back to Vicki and that wine bar alive.

"My name is Knedla, Miss," the incredible hulk now introduces himself. "Melvin Jefferson Knedla."

"Ne-dh-la?" Blondie attempts to pronounce it as best she can. "It sounds like a mountain in Iceland."

"Oh no, not in Iceland. I am the pedigree scion of a religious sect known as the Moravian Brethren. Isn't that fascinating? Knedla, by the way, in English means Dumpling. Can you imagine that dumpling and sauerkraut are the side dishes for roast pork, which happens to be the most popular meal in the heart of Europe? In a small country called Moravia in fact. My father used to tell me stories about it. His grandfather's great-grandfather was the first of my Moravian Brethren ancestors who crossed the Atlantic in 1724 landing at New York harbor. Can you see yourself in his shoes? Thirty six foul-smelling days and nights down in steerage living on moldy bread and stinking water!"

"Goodness! It's a miracle he survived!"

"That's it. He did... and here I am. In the pink of health. Native of Pittsburgh. By the way, where did your mother have you, Miss?"

"I was born in Chicago."

"There you are! Brother and sister, so to speak. Just so you know, I am in favor of permanent peace on this planet. But we can talk about it some other time. No worry. Anyhow, what did you say your good name was?"

I'm beginning to feel faint. If Blondie reveals herself now, Melvin will put two and two together, i.e., the title of my poetry collection plus the person in front of him. It would really make him kick out like Tim Tam, the racehorse who won the Kentucky Derby by two lengths.

"Judy Isabel Lawford," my Darling introduces herself.

She must have noticed the way my cheeks changed color. Not to mention the fact she is talking to someone who so obviously has a screw loose. Come what may, she deserves a medal right here and now for wisely choosing anonymity.

Of course, one never knows what Melvin will come out with next. "Didn't you appear in movies?" he barks.

Blondie exhales, blowing the smoke in the direction of the ceiling. Then she answers nonchalantly, "Anything in the world is possible. Do you follow me?"

"With the dog?"

"What dog?"

"You know, the one that nearly drowned in the Mississippi. And you saved it, did you not?"

"You're not mixing me up with Huckleberry Finn by some chance?" Blondie tries to divert his line of enquiry.

"No, wait a minute. This is serious... very much so. What was that dog's name? Astro? There he is, hanging on to a tree trunk by his front paws, desperately yapping for help. And you dive in, just as you were. Fully clothed. Astro climbs onto your back. That's it. Isn't it?"

Blondie must be thinking about all the films she has ever been in. Finally she shakes her pretty little head, causing those cherry earrings to start swinging wildly. "I am sorry," she says. "I don't remember Astro. Once I run over a red squirrel with my Jaguar. I think her name was Natasha."

It looks as if Melvin has decided that Blondie is no movie actress. Or, if she is, she definitely isn't one of the all-time greats—not one of those who leave the imprints of their left hands and right feet for all eternity embedded in a concrete sidewalk in Hollywood.

Just as I am consoling myself with the notion that he may be about to do something sensible, like leave us, Melvin sighs tragically, "What a day it's been, baby."

"You're right," my Angel agrees. "Absolute madness."

Of course they are talking at cross purposes. Blondie throws me a desperate glance—begging me, for God's sake, to tell her what the hell all this means.

Meanwhile, this pushy giant, spruced up to the nines in a chequered tuxedo and a dicky-bow tie, sways at the knees while assuming a vertical position. He then flops down onto Blondie's bed with such savageness that my poor little Darling at the other end of the mattress catapults into the air. She nearly bangs the ceiling with her head.

Melvin, by now spread-eagled across almost the whole bed, promptly retrieves the thread of the interrupted conversation. "Yeah. That figures. Absolute madness. Whenever my boss McCarthy's away, I never know where to start."

To my not inconsiderable surprise Blondie, instead of indicating the exit door to Melvin, asks, "And what exactly do you do here?"

"It depends, baby," Melvin replies. "The biggest hassle is these damned dripping taps."

"I beg your pardon?"

"You know. They drip either because the guests are so sloppy or else because they need new washers. Look, I bet yours don't drip?"

"You mean in LA?"

"Yeah."

"Usually, yes. I have no one to tighten them after me."

"You see, baby? You need someone!"

"I once came back home and water was running down the stairs. A real cascade."

"There you are. I would surely have prevented such a calamity."

I can't believe my ears. Blondie, who a little while ago was sending me visual SOS signals, sits on the bed with Melvin, talking about dripping taps and other trivia. And my Darling goes on to note, "Quite frankly, you don't look at all like a maintenance man to me, Melvin Jefferson."

This, of course, arouses Melvin's interest to no end. He sits up briskly on the bed. "No? And what do I look like, Judy baby?"

"Have you ever tried to appear in a soap opera?"

"Jeeze! Do you think I should?"

"Well, Melvin Jefferson, I'd say why not?"

My hair is standing on end. Blondie's psychomotoric sensors have obviously failed. Without the slightest doubt, she become a victim of so-called Apparent Dependency Syndrome. She is like a hostage who, after a certain time in captivity, will begin to consider the kidnaper to be a do-gooder. She has lost all ability to tell good from bad, positive from negative and a gentleman from an idiot.

In order to bring her back to reality, I call out, "Miss! Wouldn't it be better if you and I took a stroll on the roof to observe the moon?"

The reaction to my essentially pathetic cry appears to be minimal. Melvin behaves as if he hadn't even heard me. Absorbed in his future role as a soap opera seducer, he asks Blondie, "So what are we going to do next, baby?"

"Next, I'm about to go beddy-byes," Blondie replies.

"Really?" Melvin is wondering.

"Really."

For the first time in a long while Blondie lifts her gaze and smiles at me.

"I don't mean to be impertinent," Melvin keeps on pestering, "but I was just about to give you a petunia."

"What petunia?" My Angel doesn't seem too enthusiastic.

"You know, a very rare one. I have one planted over there in the jungle across the hallway."

And Blondie replies, "Harley here has already given me a bouquet of roses. I think that's probably enough."

"Not at all!" Melvin has no desire to be brushed off. "What are Harley's roses compared to my rare petunia? I water it every day and now finally I know for whom."

Blondie yawns for the third time and closes her eyelids.

One thing is sure, however. If I don't do something pretty damned soon, she's going to write me off as a complete wimp. First I clear my throat and take one step forward. "Melvin. Don't you understand? The lady needs to rest. You surely don't mean to sit here till dawn."

But Melvin just keeps on and on, "Harley, listen. Don't spoil my good mood. All I'm saying is that Miss Judy would sleep so much better with the magnificent fragrance of my petunia emanating from her bedside. Understand?"

"I'm trying, but I'm afraid I can't."

"No wonder!" Before Blondie and I realize what is happening, Melvin is at the door. Breathlessly he announces, "I'm off to the jungle to fetch that petunia. I won't be more than a second or two. Harley! Look after Miss Lawford in the meantime!"

The instant he disappears into the hallway, Blondie's eyes turn upwards, "Oh, my dearest," she sighs. "Can't you do something, Harley, about that dreadful person? Something that would shut his mouth. *Forever!*"

She needn't ask twice. Turning on my heel, I'm off on my fatal mission. As I tread on the things from Melvin's tool box strewn across the hallway, I pause briefly. I pick up a screwdriver from the floor. Judging by its weight it must be the longest one. It also has a rubber handle, to keep it from slipping out of the user's grasp when he is screwing something and needs to apply considerable pressure.

39

Everything happens much quicker than I had anticipated. I am standing at the edge of the jungle. It's pitch black. When I sniff the air I recognize that earthy smell of rotting vegetation. The only thing I can hear is the hulk squelching through the mud.

"Are you there, Melvin?" I ask.

"I'm here, brother, right here," he replies. "Why aren't you looking after Miss Lawford?"

"Don't worry. She can take care of herself."

"That's what you think. Her head was lolling, poor thing."

"Are you watering the plants?"

"No. I did that this morning."

"Have you lost something?"

"Harley. Please! Have you forgotten?"

"What?"

"You know! I'm looking for that petunia for Miss Judy. Can't you see?"

"And you can't find it?"

"That's correct. You know what it's like in the jungle. Damn job! Whatever you touch you think it's the thing you're looking for. But far from it."

"You mean to say that you cannot unequivocally identify it?"

"Exactly. Quite clearly you must have *assumed* it was a palm tree you were shoving your bayonet into. Remember that? And in the end it turned out to be a man. Isn't that so?"

This little war episode of mine is obviously keeping him awake at night. "So you reckon this petunia grows somewhere near here?" I ask.

"Jeeze. You're not kidding. Pity it's not a banana."

"Bananas you would find straight away?"

"Sure. Bananas hang on a banana tree in an organized way. Just pick one. Peel it. Eat it. That's all. *A rivederci Roma!*"

Now, that's what I call beating around the bush.
Instead of shutting Melvin up, here I am, talking to him about
bananas. Should he find that petunia, he will storm out of the
jungle like a rhinoceros and hot-foot it back to Blondie's
room. He will drive her up the wall (apparently he now wants
to discuss his role in the peace movement over the last fifteen
years)—but far more importantly, I will miss this unique
opportunity of ridding myself of him for ever.

"Do you need any help?" I volunteer.

"Oh no. You might get dirty, man."

"So what," I say. "A bit of mud!"

He's right. As soon as I step in there, I lose a shoe.
When I find it, the other one slips off. What a farce! But all's
well that ends well. The mud in the shoe makes it stick to my
foot like superglue. Strictly speaking, I have even less
knowledge of the Brazilian jungle than of the Vietnamese
one. In all, I've only ever peered in there once or twice.
However, it's also true that while Vietnam is already in the
dim and distant past, this is the red-hot present. I must
remember that. Carefully I make my way forward, fumbling
in front of me with one hand and holding the screwdriver in
the other. "You're so unselfish," I hear Melvin's voice
somewhere in the dark.

"It takes two to tango. Don't you think?"

At that very moment I hit a rubber tree head on,
making a thumping sound.

Melvin asks hurriedly, "You didn't crash into the
rubber tree, Harley?"

"Oh, no, Melvin."

"If you ever do, let me know."

"Sure."

"Micky once fell off her bicycle. You wouldn't believe
it. She had a bump on her head as big as a tennis ball. And do
you know what I did? I pushed it back with my knee. And
that was that. So if anything happens, let me know. You're in
good hands."

"Thanks in advance."

This is how we will scratch one another's backs, as it were. I will help him to look for the petunia, and he, in turn, will tend to my injury, should the need arise. He's kindness itself. He'd do anything for me. I can even hear him singing praises that we are both employees at the same establishment. How he couldn't wish for a better colleague. He appreciates *my* sympathetic approach to *his* problems. And just wait till next Thursday when we go out together for that cocktail. As ever, I take all this with a pinch of salt. He has many times promised milk and honey. And it always worked out so-so in the end.

"Would you believe that?" he asks.

"What?"

"What! The petunia. Only this morning I was sniffing it."

"Did it smell good?"

"Great! It nearly knocked my socks off."

"Don't worry. It's bound to be here somewhere."

"Oh, yeah. But where? I'm beginning to have my doubts."

"Fear nothing."

"Listen. I hope no one has picked it."

"Who would do that?"

"Bélanger?"

"Jacques would not step into this mud even if you paid him."

"Because he's a fag?"

"More likely out of principle."

"You're probably right. Our Frenchman is full of principles. I like him. And I like you even better. But I don't tell him so. On the other hand, I show my feelings ostentatiously to you. Understand?"

Clearly, he is soft in the head. He's declaring his love for me. In all probability, my intuition tells me, his end is nigh. All the childish sweet-talking in the world can but delay the final moment a short while. He is babbling on and on like a baby. At one moment, as we squelch around in the mud, we nearly stumble over one another. Though I can't see him, his tobacco-tainted breath has found its way through the lianas to me. This foils my plans considerably. The uncertainty of what might happen should we *really* bump into each other is bothering me. He might even start kissing me or something, out of gratitude for my helping him find that flower. That's no use at all. I might need to provoke him somehow—to excite him in such a manner that murder will inevitably follow.

"Look, Melvin," I begin to nag him. "What does it matter? If you don't find that petunia, the world will go on turning."

"It does matter, brother. Although Judy does look as if she can live without it, you'll see how *happy* she will be when she inhales its sweet bouquet. Believe me. I know best."

"What do you know? You don't even know the lady properly."

"Don't I! Excuse me. Suffice for her to say a few words for me to be able to read her mind like a book."

"What do you mean?"

"You know. She came here to have a good time. Don't you agree?"

"What makes you think that?"

But I am not about to get an answer to my question. "There it is!" he exclaims. "I think I've got it."

His sudden discovery scarcely fills me with a rush of enthusiasm. "The petunia?" I ask.

"I think so, man. Wait a minute. Let me smell it."

To this day I don't know what really happened. Probably as he bent forward to inhale the aroma, he lost his balance. The cracking of the bamboo growth resounds. Suddenly my arms are full of Melvin.

"Melvin! Is that you?" I ask incredulously.

First there is nothing and then a gurgling sound. "My friend, did you really stab me in the belly with my own screwdriver?"

"What makes you think that?"

"Jesus Christ. What makes me think that! Feel here. This is my belly, isn't it? There is a hole like a chimney shaft. And out of the hole sticks something that someone is holding in his hand. So don't go denying it. I can recognize you and I can also tell my screwdriver by its rubber handle. Oh, Harley, what have I done to deserve this?"

That "Oh, Harley, what have I done to deserve this!" is almost inaudible. His voice is weakening. In my arms Melvin becomes incredibly heavy. His weight increases like a sack of cement in pouring rain. I'm trying to hold on to him. But in the end we both topple into the mud. During our fall the screwdriver drops out of the hole in his belly. Where to, I don't know. I have other worries. There is a hissing sound, ssss...sss....sss... as if someone is letting the air out of a full tire. I know that hissing sound only too well. But I never thought that I would live through something like this again—and what's more here in the Royal Arms.

"Jesus, Melvin," I cry out painfully.

I kneel over him. When it stops hissing, he whispers, "Can you tell Miss Lawford... no, can you tell Micky... Micky, that... no... tell McCarthy..."

He doesn't get any further. The simple fact crosses my mind that if he had kept to the message to Miss Lawford and not exhausted himself with the other names, he would have been able, –through me, to tell the world what he had in his heart with those final breaths. But he has paid for his indecision. Oh well. He who refuses to be advised cannot be helped.

I shake him once more. All is in vain. Melvin has breathed his last. Such is life. I have mixed feelings. On the one hand, something quite inevitable has just happened. His destiny was written in the stars. On the other hand, no death (at least in a civilized society) is a reason for rejoicing. Fate wanted it this way. We both happened to be in the wrong place at the wrong time. What's more, I happened to have the screwdriver in my hand. The whole disaster was *assisted* by me, without any particular engagement on my part. I happened to be there. That's all.

But these are only theories—deliberations that lead nowhere. At the moment what concerns me is what to do with Melvin's body. Under normal circumstances I would call the police. They would ask me for a statement. But of course the present situation is far from normal. My Darling is awaiting me in her room. I rush from the Amazon, to tell Blondie what happened to Melvin. Blondie has fallen asleep. As Melvin predicted, she has also fallen off the bed. It's a hell of a job to pick her up and put her back. I huff and puff like an elephant. Finally I manage to rest her pretty little head against the pillow. I spread her hair out behind her. My God, she's beautiful! She shines like a comet. I kiss her on the forehead. My sweet little Blondie opens her eyes momentarily, as if she wants to be sure that it *really* is me, Harley Davidson. Before she closes her eyes again she murmurs that she loves me too—but that at this particular moment she would prefer it if I kindly went to hell.

40

The explanation is quite simple. It's a reaction due, understandably enough, to general physical and mental exhaustion. Blondie is absolutely beat. I whisper passionately into her ear: *It doesn't matter, Darling. Put your head down a while. The main thing is that you love me. And I love you. We have been waiting for this for so long. Sleep thight, my Angel. Meanwhile I am going home for a toothbrush. And we can share together one toothpaste. Something with mint flavor. One hour or two will not make any difference. When you wake up, I'll be sitting here, watching you. The ardor of our love will rise to even greater heights...*

Before I close the door behind me, I blow a longing kiss in the direction of the bed. I put the scattered tools back into the box. Then I throw the whole damn caboodle into the jungle where Melvin lies. I take the elevator down to the ground floor. Deep down inside I feel immense relief. Despite my current difficulties, I have no doubt whatsoever about the end result.

The clock in reception shows five minutes past two. I head out into the street. I have a strange feeling. It borders on absurdity. With every step I am walking further and further away from the building where my little miracle Blondie is resting and where, at the same time, the body of Melvin is getting colder and the unsuspecting guests are indulging in their sweetest dreams. Solving such a mysterious mishmash as this would probably even entice Agatha Christie.

I'm in no hurry. On the contrary, I pause here and there, taking deep breaths. Nothing is more refreshing that a breath of fresh air. In the middle of all this I recall leaving the Escort parked outside the hotel. In such delicious moments as this I am even capable of forgetting what my name is.

The next thing I remember is that I'm not out walking anymore but taking a shower, washing off the stinking mud. I want to dry myself (on top of this my teeth are chattering in the early morning chill), and to slip unnoticed into bed next to Amanda. But it's a wasted effort.

"Has she arrived?" she asks.

"She has."

"I still can't believe it."

"Nor can I."

"Did she fulfill your expectations?"

"Absolutely."

"I'm so glad."

"She is fantastic."

"One has to believe in miracles."

"Without faith we could not even survive until tomorrow."

"As you know, I won't stand in your way."

"Nothing could ever stand in our way."

"Far from it. I wish you both every happiness."

"I will pass it on to Blondie. You can be sure of that."

"What are your plans for the immediate future?"

"She is as exhausted as a little kitten. So I told myself to pop home to fetch a few things for the journey before she wakes up."

"Like what?"

"Like for example... a toothbrush."

"You mustn't forget that."

"Can you imagine? In a few hours Blondie and I will be on our way to Europe."

"Really? And what are you going to do there?"

"I could get a job as a ski instructor in Austria."

"You're kidding. As far as I know you don't ski."

"Ski instructors don't ski very much, Amanda. They more or less only stand on their skis and give instructions."

"As you like, Harley. I've known you for six years. And I do know you don't like winter. You don't know much about skiing. All this will wear away your nerves. And to escape the pressure, you might head off somewhere into the unknown. Mountains are dangerous. Wherever you look, there's only snow. Snowdrifts. Something will urge you to take a rest. Once you sit down, that something will ask you to drift off to sleep. Do you understand? I'm worried about it.

Do you hear? If you ever *again* have the feeling that you must commit suicide... please come back to me. I will talk you out of it."

"Alright. If you are so afraid for me, I can operate the ski lift."

"That sounds a lot better."

"And in the evenings I could play the drums," I add.

She says nothing. Obviously she's in complete agreement. On the ceiling above us the shadow of a branch from our catalpa tree moves. The street light has created this effect as if by magic. Just as I am about bring up the subject of Melvin's dead body, my partner begins to play hide and seek. That's her idea of a war strategy. Something like the wooden horse of Troy, Amanda Beiderbeck-style. If I am ever beset by some obsession, like now, she tries to divert my thoughts elsewhere. She thinks that by beginning to search, I will return to reality.

The simple fact is that she has the most unusual ability to be able to disappear inside the bed—in the one place where normal people can never totally lose themselves. Many times I have assumed that she was hiding underneath the bed, but in the end it always transpired that this was simply not the case. She was right there inside it all along. The game is based on her ability to become completely invisible. The harder I try, the more my efforts are in vain. It makes me very angry.

This time I can feel Amanda immediately. She is hiding under the sheet. As soon as I've dragged her out by her leg, she calmly begins to massage me. She kneads me with her fingers into a more *acceptable* shape. Obviously more like a real man should look—in all his glory—according to her way of thinking.

It is true that every Sunday upon waking we do massage each other. But I can't understand what has gotten into her now. It's not Sunday but early morning Friday. All of a sudden I get the message. From the way her wayward fingers are wandering it's patently obvious that Amanda wants to make love. It's as clear as the sun in the sky.

I don't know what to do. I feel as though I am being torn apart. You see, all I did was hop off home to collect a few personal belongings. And, in so doing, I had planned to ask Amanda's advice on what she, in my place, would do with Melvin's body. But since I'm here, I cannot deny Amanda something to which she has, up till now, had an exclusive right. The logic of her claim is indisputable. In brief, whilst I have to remain with Blondie in my thoughts, Amanda at least has my mortal frame at her disposal. I cannot deny her that. I am there for the touching. No wonder she is now reaching out to take advantage of her last opportunity. I solve the problem by pretending not to notice anything. I am lying back, allowing Amanda to take the initiative. Seemingly she is keeping very busy. From time to time she turns the bedside lamp on and makes a mark in her notepad.

The smell of coffee wakes me up. At first I am quite startled, thinking it is midday already. But it's only five minutes to five. Crack of dawn. I'm alone in bed. Amanda is talking to Tiger in the kitchen. She's telling him just how glad she is he came back. At least that way she won't feel so lonely. I can't figure out what he says to that. He's probably glad too.

In a little while Amanda appears in the bedroom with a tray. She has even made a blueberry pie. That's what I like more than anything. We picked those blueberries together last summer at a farm near Richmond. We had so many that Amanda had to freeze half of them. I assisted her by holding the freezer bags as she filled them up with the little blue balls. And how we laughed doing it! One usually doesn't forget such sunny days.

Oh well. Amanda puts the tray between us in the centre of the bed. We tuck in. I calculate that if I push off from here in half an hour, I could make it to the Royal Arms before six. Blondie will be well rested by then. We'll be out of the hotel before Jacques Bélanger gets in to change over with me. He would be dying to know what's going on. And God forbid, we might even be delayed chatting. As I see it in retrospect, Austria is a sure thing. No point in discussing anything with Blondie. If it should all blow up, we could always try somewhere else. Egypt is another possibility.

"At what time do you have to leave?" Amanda asks. She has blueberry stains all over her. It suits her.

"As soon as I finish eating," I reply with my mouth full.

"You're as hungry as a wolf, aren't you? Admit it."

"What do you mean by that?"

"What! What a night!"

"What night?"

"You know, exhausting? Don't you think?"

She hands me the notepad from her bedside table. I can count a total of sixteen marks. "What do they mean?" I ask.

"Sixteen marks, sixteen orgasms."

"I had sixteen orgasms?" I nearly choke on the morsel before me.

"You had nine and I seven."

"I would have to know something about that," I defend myself.

"Believe Amanda." She leaps from the bed straight to the record-player. Immediately the space between the four walls of our bedroom is filled with the exotic voice of Raúl Ibanesios. "Did I tell you that he has a performance at the Congress Centre in two weeks' time?"

"I hope he loses his voice there."

"Would you kindly speak about him with more respect? Raúl has a beautiful face. It's an almost Grecian profile. Even though he is Spanish. And he owns a large ranch near Barcelona with more than one hundred head of cattle. I already have a ticket. Can you imagine? I have a seat in the middle of the second row. Isn't that sensational? Those were the days, when I wanted to go after him... and you always objected. I have peace at last. Raúl is coming to me. And I'm free as a bird!"

I take a sip of my coffee. "Does Dr. Hugo know about all this?" I enquire.

She pretends not to hear. She leans against her pillow. "Do you remember how angry you were that I didn't recognize you at that bus stop?"

"So what?"

"I was only pretending that you were getting on my nerves."

"Nothing new under the sun."

"What's new is that I was already in love with you. Terribly much in love. You idiot. From the very first sight!"

It's hard to say how it happened. I attempted to lean over towards Amanda, or she towards me, so she might get the seventeenth. In any case, we coincide somewhere in the centre of the bed and the coffee cup is spilled. Throughout our lovemaking that ridiculous Spaniard is howling into our ears. As it begins, it ends. Raúl finishes singing, Amanda sighs and I drop off to sleep without knowing when, why or how.

I wake up to the sound of the telephone ringing. I'm in the middle of dreaming about Benny, that hairy beast, running off into Mini Brazil to have a pee. Of course he sniffs out Melvin straight away and drags the body to his master, Matt Jackson, in room 402. I'm so scared I don't even have the strength to reach for the screaming telephone on my bedside table. When I fail to act, Amanda begins to clamber over me, deliberately digging her pointed knees into my ribs. Then she starts having an endless conversation with someone. But apart for some monosyllabic sounds of agreement, she herself doesn't say much. All the while she kneels on top of my belly. As she wriggles, it feels as though a giant corkscrew is screwing through the cork of a bottle, namely my belly.

When she hangs up, she remains immobilized in anticipation of my last deathly twitch, like a lioness biting into her still-living prey.

"You fucking liar!" she shrieks into my ear. "Cheat! I won't forgive you."

"W...what's going on?" I stutter.

She starts hitting me with a pillow. "What's going on! You should ask! That was Jacques Bélanger on the phone. What apparently was the matter with you? Why did you cause him so much worry? He came at six as usual and you were nowhere to be seen. He saw the car parked outside the hotel. Colin apparently called there a while ago. He apologized for Blondie not taking up her reservation. It was his fault basically, because he talked her into checking into another hotel."

"Phew... Colin! What a load of crap!"

"How come?"

"I have clear proof."

"What proof?"

"Blondie is asleep in her room, and Melvin..."

"What's the matter with him?"

"Tell Jacques to take a look in Mini Brazil."

"And what is he going to find there?"

"His stone-cold corpse!"

41

I have never seen such pandemonium. At around eight I call Jacques over at the Royal Arms. I ask if Melvin turned up that morning. When he informs me in a perfectly naturaltone that there is no sign of him, I send him upstairs to see with his own eyes, for God's sake, whether or not Blondie is awake yet. And if she is still asleep, I stress that he should walk on tiptoe. In any case, he should behave in a most gentlemanly manner towards her. Treat her like a VIP. Jacques shows signs of fright. He asks me if I have a fever.

He repeats that stuff Colin told him. Namely, that he (Colin) and Blondie went to sleep in another hotel. According to his (Jacques') judgment, my request falls, *par excellence*, into the category of world's great absurdities. He considers that the whole affair symbolizes the exploitation and therefore molestation of the fundamental formula of existentialism— what we are not, what could we become and why it hasn't happened yet. Only when I beg him, practically on bended knee, to do what I ask in the spirit of sheer comradeship, does this good-natured *Monsieur* finally relent, pack it in and depart for the upper stories to investigate.

In practice this means that he has left the receiver next to the made-in-Hong Kong transistor radio that he keeps on the reception counter. I have no choice, therefore, but to listen to some French station while he is away. As far as I gather, they're talking about love. I can only make out *l'amour*, *Aznavour* and also—*une bouteille de vin.*

My benefactor is back within a minute. Breathlessly he reports that he found the door of room 403 ajar and the bed made up. On top of the bed covers, snoring and spread out, was that horrible dog Benny. Apparently he's lying there on his back like some anthropoid, the man-ape who, according to Darwin, is only one step away on the development ladder from becoming a rightful member of the club founded by the creatures known as *homo sapiens*. From what he could see he concluded that if Blondie wasn't eaten by Benny (which he does not consider very probable), there is no option but to believe that Colin has been telling the truth.

I feel like asking him to go to hell along with Colin. But he might be mortally offended. He might accuse me of not holding his moral sense in sufficient esteem. I have it on the tip of my tongue to ask whether, by any chance, he spotted the roses next to the TV set. But I swallow the idea. He might think I'm about to force him up those stairs for the second time. The same applies to the story of Melvin. I bet that when I describe in glorious technicolor the events preceding the unfortunate occurrence in Mini Brazil, he will drop the receiver. He can be almost pathologically sensitive.

Oh well. I shall have to sort this out myself. Just like that Pythagoras. After all, did he not manage to put all those elements, which were accessible to nobody other than himself, together into one law? According to that law, the area of a hypotenuse equals the total areas of both the legs of a right-angle triangle. And that's exactly my case. I insist that if Blondie woke up in the middle of the night, it could only be because she was desperately searching for me. That much goes without saying. Say she opens the door to the hallway. There is someone or something behind it. It's all hairy. It starts licking her. My poor little darling, all frightened out of her wits, is convinced that it must be Beelzebub himself. She takes to her heels. And because she doesn't know where to go, she makes for the Amazon. Naturally she stumbles across Melvin's dead body and faints. She comes to and faints again. This is how I see it. On the whole, geometrically. A myriad of triangles, squares and, what's more, stars in front of her eyes.

I am just about to map the whole thing out for Jacques. But it doesn't come to that. I can hear him talking to someone on another line. That was McCarthy, he informs me. He's had a message from Melvin. At this, I nearly have a heart attack. He says he is very sorry but he will not be able to make it to work before eleven o'clock. Apparently Micky's wedding ring fell down the john during her morning toilette. Naturally she had a hysterical fit. Now that poor devil Melvin has the job of dismantling the downpipes on the six-story building where he lives.

Someone might as well have hit me over the head with a stick. I fall asleep with the receiver in my hand. At around mid-day Amanda wakes me. She is just about to leave for work at Steinbergs' supermarket. As my shift at the Royal Arms starts at 6 pm, we won't see each other until tomorrow. She calls me her treasure.

She hasn't called me that for at least two weeks. I try to figure out what she is getting at. After all, I cannot expect anything positive. More likely it will be negative. I doubt that once I've found out I will not exactly be jumping for joy. I am to expect a call from her at the hotel this evening. Same as usual. But I should be expecting it tonight more than ever. *Treasure.* And I should prepare myself for a big surprise. *Something beautiful.* For quite some time she has wanted to tell me, always deciding it would be wiser to wait until all this palaver with Blondie's arrival is over.

That's very nice of her, even rather touching in fact. But I'm already writhing in uncertainty, like a child who suspects that it is just about to find out that it was adopted. I keep pressing her to come clean. Right now. Without delay. She knows full well that I can't stand the tension caused by doubt. But it's all in vain. She smiles more enigmatically than the Mona Lisa deep down in the Louvre. Then she kisses me on the head and leaves me in bed, a complete mental wreck.

I'm having another nightmare. This time my mother and father are making their escape after that German bank hold-up in Bayreuth on the Harley-Davidson. But they don't get very far. In this horror show, members of the SS wearing black shirts are catching up with them by a mile a second on far more powerful Harley-Davidsons. By the time the pursuers are breathing down my parents' necks, my mother reaches into the shaking sidecar, grabs me by one leg and swings me around her head, hurling me like some unreturnable boomerang towards the nearest farm building. It just happens to spring out of the mist on our left. I land in a nearby pile of manure, scaring the life out of a flock of hens and a cockerel digging there for food. From then on I observe events through baby's eyes and see how the Harley-Davidson belonging to my parents sputters and dies out completely. Before too long I see two gallows appear on the brow of the hill. Surprisingly, I don't even cry out. That's because, from the distance, my mother keeps on smiling encouragement at me. Even my father steals a wave at me with his hand whenever he can. And if he can't use his whole hand, he just waves with his finger behind his back. But, to cut a long story short, I am about to witness the noose as it cuts into my parents' necks. When, in complete unison, they breathe their last, it sounds as if someone had just blown the oboe and the flute at the same time. Then two white doves fly out from their dead bodies. As they rise towards the sky, the words *"Jüdische Schweine!"* go with them.

I find a message in the kitchen saying that there are two veggieburgers in the fridge waiting for me. Lately Amanda is overseeing (you know, fifty years of age, that's no joke, honey, I must look after you) my cholesterol intake. According to her instructions, I should cook them for six minutes in the microwave oven. I can help myself to mashed potatoes and a knob of margarine to accompany them.

At around five pm Jacques Bélanger telephones. Hercules has finally made it to work. So far he has been unable to fish the wedding ring out of the pipework. Also the boss would appreciate it if I could come to work a little earlier. That's because he is bursting at the seams with yesterday's lecture in Montreal and would like to share his great experiences with us before he forgets them.

I walk to the hotel on my own two feet. Feeling rather tired, I have to drag myself along. It doesn't help that I've been resting practically the whole day long. Everyone is patiently waiting for me, gathered in that minivestibule. Even the chambermaid Ella. She's thanking me profusely in front of everybody for so kindly filling in for her yesterday. That's when she had that terrible stomach upset. She is winking at me, as if only the two of us knew what it meant.

"Harley, man," Melvin greets me from the distance. He's sitting on that box of his covered in stickers. "Don't forget our date next Thursday in the Banana Split for cocktails!"

All signs point to Melvin being the liveliest corpse the sun ever shone on. But that doesn't have to mean that what took place last night is some kind of dubious illusion. What matters is that this giant has played a rather unpleasant trick on me. No doubt about that. He impales himself on purpose on his own screwdriver. He pretended that I murdered him, even making a hissing sound like a tire going flat. *Oh, well, Melvin. Carry on! Keep on smiling spitefully! This, that you cannot hear (and what you can only guess at—ha ha ha) in literature (ask Micky, if she's so clever, who, for example, is Marcel Proust) is called interior monologue. Understand? So firstly, put those old tricks of yours back in the hat. I have formed my own opinion of your roguish pranks. I know very well what you're getting at with your disgusting dying comedy. You're faking your own death, Melvin, just because you want me to admire you more. And here you are, fit as a fiddle. But you know what? You can go to hell, Melvin. Next time I'll be more careful. You can be sure of that. You will never pull the wool over my eyes again. You'll see! End of interior monologue. (P.S. And those cocktails on Thursday are postponed indefinitely. Mark my words!)*

If he guessed all that, his expression doesn't show it. By now, however, the boss holds our attention with his pompous address, "Ladies and gentlemen! What a pity you could not be with me in Montreal yesterday to attend the excellent lecture delivered by Professor Adam Berkowitz. Will the World Survive 2013?"

As it transpires, McCarthy's only concern is to cram into us in a couple of minutes what he and his dearest wife had to listen to for three and a half hours and what cost him sixty five dollars. From what we hear we gather that our future looks pretty grim. The globe is warming up, overpopulating, getting polluted and, where it is not drying out, it's sinking into the bog. In other words, our Earth is slowly but surely becoming uninhabitable.

On top of all this, Professor Adam Berkowitz has received (and that was the main focus of the lecture) a signal from the distant universe, from a source at least two million light years away. It happened when another professor, looking like a cross between a cactus and a newt, appeared in bright colors one day just before midnight on the ceiling of Berkowitz' stale-aired bedroom. He introduced himself as Erik XIX and his message to all of us is that we will survive the year 2013 but in a completely different form.

Melvin immediately wants to know what kind of *different* form he means. He's in no hurry to say good-bye to his extremely fine looks. It comes as no surprise to me when he states that with a face like his he could make it in soap opera! Only you and I know that this gem does not come from his own brain. He heard this from Miss Judy Isabel Lawford (aka my Darling) who flattered him in order to be rid of him. The boss reassures him at once. According to Professor Berkowitz, it will doubtless be a gradual change, which Melvin (he does not mean this personally, he adds) would not be aware of until it was too late.

McCarthy now yawns. It's a clear sign that the boss only has one set of nerves and therefore has to preserve them. He makes the point that tomorrow Radio Shack will be delivering his first personal computer. That's something else. It will enable him to remain in constant contact with all his hotel colleagues, even when in Brazil. When Melvin offers his expert services to install his computer, the boss yawns for the second time. It is obviously clear to all of us that Melvin couldn't even install the ribbon on a manual typewriter.

Then it's time to say good-night to one another (Melvin naturally slaps me on the back in a brotherly fashion) and I am finally alone in reception. About bloody time. First of all I rush to the fourth floor. At the edge of our little Amazon I call out Blondie's sweet name. Of course I don't expect to hear her calling back—"Harley, my dearest, where have you been all this time!"

For the sake of my peace of mind I keep on calling. I don't doubt for one second that Blondie waited and waited for me to come back but in the end she threw her few things into the suitcases and—good-bye Royal Arms! Although love moves mountains, enough is surely enough.

I can only blame myself for all this. For thirty-three years I've been preparing myself for this meeting with Blondie—only to end up the way that marathon runner Ulrich Mendtke did in Zurich in 1929. The whole stadium held its breath when, a hundred yards from the finish, the elastic in his shorts snapped and he fell to the ground. And not only did he not finish first, with knees badly grazed, he ended up in forty-seventh place. He spent the rest of the day crying his eyes out in the lavatory of the Berlin Express on his way back to his home town.

What a stroke of bad luck. An ordinary elastic in a pair of shorts. And what damage it can cause. In my case it's the toothbrush, or socks, two yards before the finish line. Instead of waiting for Blondie to wake up and then buying all the necessary items at the airport (including the latest paperback bestseller—*I Love You, I Love You, I Love You* by Bobbi-Jean Brunett), I end up in bed with Amanda and her freshly baked blueberry pie.

I find the vase on the bedside table next to the TV set in Blondie's room full of roses. I count one rose fewer. Without doubt my Angel has taken the most beautiful one with her as a memento. I'm grateful for that much at least. It could have been that damned petunia of Melvin's. I inspect the room. What if Blondie has forgotten something in her rush? I can't even find a hairpin of hers. Even the half-shrunk Grumpy has disappeared from the bathroom.

I open the shower curtain and—at last! I nearly faint. Luck is smiling down on me, in the shape of two pairs of red cherries with green stalks hanging from a plastic hook. I know what happened. At some time between midnight and morning Blondie took another bath. And she has forgotten to take her avant-garde earrings with her.

No one in the entire world can imagine what this means to me. It's a miracle. I clutch them in my hands. For a little while I caress them gently. I breathe on them. I speak to them with fondness and tender words. In the end I press them against the spot where my heart beats. Thank you, God! A thousand thanks. Only you know how to cheer up your sad little wayward sheep.

42

If Jesus happened to be resurrected at that exact moment, he would have seen me sitting behind the reception counter of the Royal Arms. My legs would be resting against the desk. Blondie's cherries swing from my ear lobes. A broad smile straddles my face. My good mood does not escape Jesus' attention. He's asking me the reason for my jolly frame of mind. Briefly I describe to him the sequence of events of the preceding night. With just a few choice phrases I hint at what is really up between me and Blondie. As far as those earrings are concerned, I will never take them off. No one can talk me into that. I will insist on it—even if McCarthy threatens to throw me out into the street the following day.

And when I tell Christ that in most cases true love lasts until death us do part, he adds that if two people really love each other, love does not end in the grave but continues (in far greater measure) up there where he is. He means Heaven, of course. Apparently everything is basically the same there as it is on Earth, only much more opulent—including the accommodation, food and culture. His sincere interest pleases me to no end. Before saying good bye he gives me his blessing. I am to pass his blessing on to Blondie, when I see her again. Whether it's there or here. It doesn't really matter.

From the guest register I discover that Matt Jackson and Benny have checked out during the day. And so did Arnie Hornsby. Blondie's room is reserved starting tomorrow for a couple from Tokyo. Next I leaf through the newspapers. No mention at all of my Darling's performance at Kitty Junction. On the other hand, Elvis Presley has yet again risen from the dead and made an appearance at the Zanzibar in Hull. It's the third time this month.

This false mix of values does not surprise me at all. We are living in a world which is upside down. All that is exceptional, all that attempts to step out of line, is soon crumpled by the ballast of overwhelming averageness. A stunt man who hangs from an airplane by his leg above Manhattan has a bigger chance of drawing attention to himself than the beaver-like diligence of the talented individual. Blondie should definitely be deserving of a few words of praise—if for no other reason than for endeavoring to show people the true identityof Albert Einstein.

At nine-thirty Colin calls from Kitty Junction. "She was an incredible sorceress," he announces as soon as I lift the receiver. "She performed such magic she left me gasping for breath."

"Who are you talking about?"

"You know who! Blondie! She squeezed the life out of me. Geddit?" He expertly manages to outshout all of the hellish noise emanating from his bar. I have to hold the receiver two feet away from my ear. He sounds as if he was leaning with his elbow on my reception counter. "I must admit, Harley, I haven't experienced anything like that before! This time it was a case of complete mutual fusion, you know, when two bodies and two souls first explode and then flow into one another. Yeah. That's exactly it. Merge and vibrate like a steel cable stretched to breaking point between two steel poles. I mean if you hit it with a steel baseball bat. Something to that effect, Harley. I apologize for not being able to express myself better. You know, I'm not a *master of the pen* like you. It's just the kind of *perfect* harmony—you know what I mean—that makes even a *specialist* of my calibre go weak at the knees. It's not like *being at sixes and sevens*. On the contrary. It's sheer *harmony*! Like Niagara Falls in one dramatic flow! Or, if you prefer, like two violins, then one violin and finally the clarinet solo. Just like in that Gershwin score of yours. That should strike a chord with you, don't you think? Better than the stretched cable analogy. You should know. Aren't you the *great maestro?* As I said, man, I have never been so exhausted in all my life. And nor has she. Can you imagine, she lost twelve pounds during the night. Isn't it great? Better than sweating it out at the Rio carnival. What do you say? Or anything you ever heard from me. Including those steel cables or baseball bats. You know what I'm talking about, Harley, for God's sake. Or am I talking to a brick wall? Or to the wind? Do you hear me?"

"Look, Colin," I reply icily. "Keep the crap to yourself. Honestly. I have enough worries of my own. If you want to get rid of that chip on your shoulder, buy an airplane ticket to China. They have the Great Wall. You can talk to that until you have nothing more to gabble on about. And if that doesn't help, you can climb on that wall, spread your arms and jump down. Like a bird or something. Don't tell me you'd be afraid. Or do you suffer from vertigo? Tell me."

"As you wish," he replies, as if to suggest it was I who would benefit from going to China. "I only thought you would be interested, that's all. Like in *what happened last night*. You know? That's why I called you. She has cut off a little lock of her platinum hair as a memento for me to keep. If you want, I'll bring it with me the next time I come to the Royal Arms. It's up to you. One can only ask. Okay?"

He's talking about it as if it was a half pound of headcheese.

"Listen, *Colin*," I underline his name by raising my voice. "Don't bother. I'm not interested in your old *relics*. Honestly." The *relics* I mean literally. I could have easily said "garbage." Or "hare droppings." It boils down to the same thing. He sleeps with a different woman every week. He must have a box full of similar locks. I can imagine. If Blondie was a brunette like Elizabeth Taylor, he would no doubt be offering me a black curl á la Elizabeth Taylor from his booty. Why should I even bother talking to him? I hang up the moment I finish speaking, so he doesn't get the wrong idea that the longer our discussion lasts, the more chance I'll have of falling for his tale like some brainless idiot.

When I arrive home the same morning, Amanda is waiting for me. First she notices the cherry earrings attached to my ear lobs. When I explain to her that Blondie left them in the bathroom, she nods. No doubt she understands what am I talking about. Then she tells me straight away that she would have called Royal Arms last night, but on Channel 19 there was a Barbara Walters special—an interview with Raúl Ibanesios. She simply *had to* see it. It was amazing. She was so excited that she all but forgot about me. We sit on the balcony. Then she says, "Harley... *honey*." And pauses.

The *honey* and the long pause don't sound too promising. "Yes, Amanda," I say.

"Listen, honey," she repeats. "Here, then, is your *big* surprise... I'm pregnant. I would have told you before. But I didn't want to spoil your preparations for Blondie's arrival."

"H...how is that p...possible?" I manage to stutter.

"H...how is what p...possible?" she mocks my stutter.

"As far as I know, you're on the p...pill."

"Sorry, h...honey. It failed for the first time in six years."

"We have to catch and punish the culprits."

"How do you mean?"

"A good lawyer would know what to do."

"Of course! And we shall keep the baby as solid proof."

"Amanda, I can hardly think straight and n...n...ow t...his."

"Honey... please. Just this *one* baby. You can bring home a set of drums. Okay?"

"Drums! Harley would be creeping about the place on tiptoe."

"I swear on everything beautiful that keeps us together that I will take our child out for a walk every day. You can beat the drums like... what was his name?"

"Ge...Gene K...Krupa."

"Yeah. That one. You'll be able to go wild like him."

"Go wild. And where!"

"You know... in Blondie's room. There is enough room for the cot too, plus the teddy bear and even the rattle."

I say, "Fathers over fifty usually conceive i...imbeciles."

"Don't forget that I'm thirty-six."

"So what?"

"According to Dr. Hugo Wasserman, the next Amadeus is on his way."

"Don't believe everything Dr. Hugo says."

"Apparently we are a most extraordinary couple. Physically and spiritually. An unparalleled conglomerate. Our mutual brain, Dr. Hugo said to me, is by a single circulatory system. We are one complex, mutually complementary unison... and out of such intertwining love only a perfect and unique individual can possibly be created. Like the one... what was her name?"

"Golda Meir," I quickly recall that famous Jewish name.

"Golda! Correct! Except that our girl will be called... yes... can you guess?..."

"B...Blondie?"

"H...honey! Nothing surprises even you!"

Blondie! She thinks she can outwit me. Blondie Davidson-Beiderbeck! I'd rather not ask (just in case her prognosis about having a little girl doesn't work out) what the name of our boy would be. No doubt Raúl Ibanesios-Beiderbeck. Oh well. Before I go to sleep and Amanda to work, I promise that we will hold our debate over until tomorrow. First thing. It will already be Saturday. And if that isn't enough, we will dedicate the whole of Sunday to it. Might as well take the phone off the hook. She agrees, but on one condition—that during all that time we will hold hands and gaze into each other's eyes.

Before parting Amanda assures me that I am her *everything*. She waits to hear what I will say to that. In a spur of a moment I kiss her hand. She accepts it with a great sigh of relief. Nothing in the world encourages an expectant mother more than the feeling that she has someone with whom to share her immense joy. I should know. This is not the first time in my life I found myself in the role of expectant father.

Jiří Klobouk

*   *   *

ABOUT THE AUTHOR

Jiří Klobouk writes fiction, radio plays, poetry and essays. He discovered jazz when he was twelve and later began to visualize the world around him through a camera lens – he worked for 20 years in television. These experiences are reflected in his writing. He created a body of work in which as one critique noted: "We could feel the rhythm and see things from unexpected angles." Many short stories have appeared in literary periodicals: *Partisan Review*, *Chicago Review*, *Stories* and *Artful Dodge*. For *Winter Wolves*, a story published in *Mid-American Review*, he was named outstanding writer in the 1985-86 The Pushcart Prize edition. His list of books includes: *My Life with Blondie*, *Winfield*, *Radio Plays I*, *Radio Plays II*, *Music After Midnight*, *The Stair Climber*, *Anti-Communist Manifesto* (1975), *The Homecoming*, *JAZZ II: Parents* and *Third Wife*. The author lives in New York City.

www.ingramcontent.com/pod-product-compliance
Lightning Source LLC
Chambersburg PA
CBHW031213020726
47499CB00002B/567